2084

Sol Smith

TO BULL MARQUETTE

Demi-God of the writing world. To be a great writer, it's probably best to start out as a great human. I will never know any greater.

CONTENTS

ACKNOWLEDGMENTS

There are a few people without whom this book would have been a complete impossibility. Lindsey Moore is a wonderful editor; her keen eye and superb insight are inseparable from these pages. My wife, of course; by putting up with my endless rants, she has fueled much of these ideas. And Dad; he read this book, offered encouragement, and spent hours discussing it with me.

Part I

Chapter 1

The Lifebook Theme plays quietly, then gets louder as the Clear Channel Wall gets brighter and brighter. "Good morning, Scott," it says. "I hope you've enjoyed your dreaming program. You, Mick Poland, Marianne Joes, and fifteen other friendships have woken up with the Lifebook Clear Channel Wake-up Subscription. We know you have many options for starting your day, so we here at Lifebook want to thank you for starting your day with us."

There are a few foggy images swimming around in my head. I try to grasp onto them. I try to make them solid, but in trying, they turn from images into smoke. As usual, I don't remember my dream program. Once in a while I feel like it works for me, like I have a vivid dream about the program I tuned in for, but I guess I'm just one of the unlucky users who it doesn't work perfectly for. Bummer. I think when I remember a dream, it's just a plain old dream that people have been having for tens of thousands of years before enhancement started. I'm missing out on a huge portion of the culture, and I can feel it every day.

The theme plays through the loop one more time.

"Oh, this damn song," I say to myself. It's a bloopy

little song that sounds like birds chirping and a couple mandolins singing in a forest. It's not the song so much as the waking up. The song marks different changes in my day, so I'm used to it and even like it. It introduces what's going to happen next, almost all the time. Keeps me grounded in my schedule.

"Would you like to personalize your Wake-up Subscription?" it asks. "Based on your likes and the likes of your friendships, we suggest setting the theme to Barry Grant, Elephant Seal, DYM, or Sexpot. Would you like to update your subscription now? Barry Grant is trending, up 20 percent since Tuesday."

"No," I say. I did have it set to a DYM song, but then I was afraid that it would start ruining my favorite song, make every time I hear it bum me out that it was time to wake up. I thought for a while about changing it to an annoying song, like a Sexpot number or Primo Sentra or something, but then I'd get lots of updates about them and other songs might play through my Music Subscription, so I don't do that. For now I just settle for the generic and uplifting Lifebook theme. It sounds like what would happen if a dozen or so fairies all got together and won a trophy; all golden enchantment and stuff. It's fine.

"Mick Poland and four other friendships in your trusted circle like your Wake-up activity. Thirty-two distant friendships like it as well. Terri Smith is going biking today before class. Ford Samson is heading to class early to study for her Economics and Integration exam. Courtney Frames was up all night studying for the same exam. You, Mick Poland, and 35 other friendships have the same exam on their Life Calendar app. Seven of those are in your trusted circle."

"On this day in history five years ago," the Lifebook voice continued, "you went on a class field trip to Monsanto Farm #481. You are tagged in 192 photos and 23 videos. You took 145 photos and four videos. You can access these on the Day In History app, the Calendar app, or by flipping through your Lifebook. Please access the Day In History app for more information about this day in your life." I already have my glasses on, and I see a picture in the upper left of my field of vision. It's of me, five years younger, standing by a long row of goats, packed together tightly. You can't see the goat's faces in the picture, but I remember how strange it was that they were so identical. And, right before we left, we watched as the farm hands plugged their faces into the nurture masks, where they would feed and have visual stimulation that was supposed to trigger the right set of hormones to them. These were organic goats, very few injected hormones.

I stretch, stand up, and fish around for my socks in my top drawer while the Clear Channel keeps droning off the updates of my friendships since I woke up. It's part of the Wake-Up Subscription. I'll scan through the keywords and hashes of any updates that happened overnight on my way to school or in Homeroom. I find my socks and plop down on the bed to pull them on.

"Lifebook," I call out. "Status update: I'm just sitting here in my Jockeys getting psyched for the day and especially the exam. Hashtag it 'Jockeys' and 'Econ'."

"Update successful," the soft female voice responds. "Mention Cotton Jockeys three more times this month for iBuy bonus points redeemable for Jockeys and other great products from the Monsanto family."

I check myself out in the mirror and decide that I probably need a haircut soon. I find the hair purifying gel and run it through my hair; it looks better, more natural and solid, even like plastic. I only have to shave my beard maybe a couple times a month, but I pull out a razor for my arms, which is getting to be an everyday thing. I spread shaving gel on my forearms and shave them completely, that way the hair doesn't get in the way of the mobile projection. I look at my eyebrows and figure that, even though they're getting shaggy, I'd better not mess with them myself, but wait until next time I'm at the salon.

I keep thinking about the Economics and Integration test. Today's test is over the chapters, "The Failure of Socialism", "The Freedom of Choices, the Choice of Freedom,", and "The Responsibility of the Intelligent Consumer". It's not my best subject, but Mercedes has been helping me study for the last week or so and she has the top credit score in the class, so I assume she's pretty good at it. What she's taught me is that I need to internalize the subject of economics and recognize it as a part of who I am. It's more than just remembering facts and data and history; it's about integrating ourselves into the community through economics. That's what they want to see: they want to see that the subject of economics is really a personal narrative, a rich relationship like a family tree with yourself as the center.

I think it's easier to integrate yourself into society if your dad is rich, like Mercedes'.

I grab my school uniform—Levi's and a green Polo since it's Thursday—and pick up my Mobile next to the bed. "Lifebook, switch to Mobile," I say. I plug my Mobilepiece into my ear and strap my Mobile 12 unit onto my wrist. I continue listening to the updates for the day and my mobile shows the latest headlines and weather while I'm doing so. The Mobile 12 is their best upgrade yet, a lighter wristband than the old Elevens and a much sharper projection onto the forearm. And, unlike the 10, it can automatically detect when you are trying to project it on a different surface, like a wall or a table, and it corrects for the proper definition. The Clear Channel Wall goes opaque, revealing the wallpaper behind it.

Dad said that when he was a kid, the Mobiles they had were little boxes that they had to carry around, like a reader, but smaller. It is so much easier having it put right onto your arm, he said, so you can read and click on anything you want without having to worry about dropping anything. I've heard that some people are getting it implanted — Mobilepiece, too — for better resolution. That way the image project through the skin, rather than onto it, but there have been some complaints with that, too, though upgrades are always coming. With Mobilecare, you can even get an upgrade subscription for future implants. But, my family isn't anywhere near that credit bracket since the accident. I'm lucky to have a Mobile 12, I remember. I just have to keep those arm hairs low.

The dining room is still a mess from the night before, I notice. Mom must have not felt up to cleaning after dinner. I offered to do it, but she acted like it was no big deal and she was going to do it, and I was afraid of hurting her feelings and making her feel useless. She's been depressed for a while now. I flip on the kitchen light and suddenly Dad is standing there, drying a dish with a rag, as if he's going to clean up after us. "Morning, Scott," he says with this big smile on his face. I wave at him half-heartedly. "I said, Good morning, Scott!"

"Morning," I say.

"What's for breakfast, son?"

"Honey Crashers," I say.

In my ear, the LIfebook whispers, "would you like to update your breakfast status? Four of your other friendships are also having Honey Crashers this morning for breakfast."

"Update," I say. I see my breakfast status flash into being on my arm.

"You can automatically update your breakfast and any other meals using General Mills Keywords through the Monsanto Mealtime app. Would you like to install it?"

"No, thanks," I say.

"Would you like to send a picture of your breakfast to your Lifeline? It can be a real or promotional image of Honey Crashers."

"Promo image," I say. My arm shows a realistic bowl of Honey Crashers on a table that looks somewhat like mine. Right away, it gets two likes.

Dad can tell I'm not talking to him. There's a look in your eye when you talk to your mobile, a sort of deep focus on something outside of the house or wherever you are. It's the same look my dad used to have in his eyes while talking to his mobile about sports at the dinner table. You just block people out when they get that look. No big deal.

I pour the Honey Crashers into a bowl and sit down at the table, pushing last night's dishes out of the way.

"Ready for the test?" Dad asks me from the kitchen.

"I dunno," I say. "Maybe 60 percent prepared. Something like that."

I look down at my mobile and see it updated with the words *Scott Goode is 60 percent ready for the Economics and Integration exam today.* I click the "like" button. I have five other likes before I look up.

"Do you want me to quiz you?" Dad asks.

"Nope," I say. "I just want you to do these dishes, for real. Can you do that?"

Dad laughs and continues drying the dish in his hand. "You heard the news, Son. You heard the news." He shakes his head.

Dad never used to call me "Son." It was always Scott, or sometimes Dodge, or when he was mad, Young Man, but never Son. It's so annoying to hear him say it now. One of the changes I'm supposed to get used to.

"Your brother, Comet Goode, is awake and getting ready for school," the Lifebook says. "Comet Goode likes your breakfast status. Comet Goode commented on your status, 'Hey Bro, pour me a bowl, will you?'" This last part isn't in Lifebook Voice but in Comet's. He must have updated to version 12.

I scoot past Dad in the kitchen and get breakfast ready for Comet. "Dad," I say, "can you get the dishes off of the table already? Drying that one dish over and over is getting annoying."

Dad laughs a little to himself and shakes his head. Then

he looks at me and says slowly, more somber than before, "you heard the news, Son. Do we need to talk about it again?"

"Nope, Dad. I know. I'm just kidding."

I look and see that Comet has posted his breakfast with a picture. He gets extra points for that, and I assume he's saving them for a discount on middle school graduation apparel—a promotion that all his classmates are into. Comet is in the 8th grade. He's been in trouble at school on and off since the news. He got in a fight and was going to be charged with second-degree bullying, which would have lowered the entire family's credit score, but the counselor intervened and just got him suspended for a couple days. Today is his first day back since suspension.

Comet sits at the table. "Thanks, bro."

"Big day!"

"Big day," he doesn't sound too excited.

"Hey, at least you didn't have to go to Reintegration learning, right?"

"Oh, they wouldn't do that for bullying. Not second degree, anyway."

"It's no joke, Son," Dad chimes in. "That's not how you were raised. Values are important to our family. You can always look at the Quaker Values Guide online, if you want to reexamine."

"Aren't you happy to go back?" I ask.

"Whatever, you know?" he says. "Hey, Dad," he calls out. "Why don't you put that dish down and get me some OJ? You know, if it's in your value system."

"This is the third violation of this morning, boys. Do I need to contact an Americorp counselor to speak with you about the news? You may take a seat in front of the Clear Channel and say 'yes' to speak with a counselor. It's perfectly normal and expected. This will not impact your credit rating."

"Damn it, Dodge, you committed two violations already?" Comet says. "Warn me next time. Five and it's mandatory."

"Sorry," I say. "It's hard not to, you know?"

"Yeah."

We both laugh a little, uncomfortably.

"Should we wake Mom up?" I ask.

"Go for it," Comet says.

"Don't you think she'd want to be awake before you leave for school? Don't you think she'd have something to say or something?"

"Let Dad wake her up."

"What was that, boys? What was the request?" Dad looks puzzled.

"Forget it," I say.

"No, don't forget it," Comet says. "Check and see if Mom wants to wake up before we go to school."

"Your mother still has another week of leave," Dad says. "Her instructions are to stay in bed until eleven today. I think it's best if she follows her instructions, even though you're going back, Son."

"Figures," Comet says. "I hardly saw her before noon both days I was suspended. You worried?"

"Yeah, I guess so," I say. "What sucks is that if she doesn't drive us we have to hurry to catch the bus. I figured she'd be awake, you know?"

"Yeah. I'll hurry."

"Just try and cool it at school, okay? Ignore people if you have to," I say. "Don't get in a fight because then Mom will be even more depressed. Wouldn't it be great if we could stop cleaning and doing dishes and just surf the Clear Channel at nights again?"

"Yeah," he mumbles. "Because that's the problem around here, right? We're too busy since she's depressed? That's the problem?"

"Our credit can't take another hit," I say. "I'm just trying to make our problem seem less heavy, you know? Mom's doing everything she can, so let's do everything we can."

"Would you like a free credit advisory from the Life Bureau?" the Lifebook asks.

"No," we both say at the same time.

I grab my bowl and as many dishes as I can from the table. Not bothering to squeeze past Dad, I just walk right through him and dump the dishes in the sink. I go into the living room, flip on the light, and pick up my reader.

"Studying for the test?" Dad asks. He's sitting in his chair, reading the paper on of his reader.

"No," I reply, "just reading." Then I call out to the other room, "Ten minutes, bro."

I hear Comet's dishes clang in the kitchen. He comes sulking into the room. "I know, by the way".

"Know what?"

"I know it was dumb to let that numbnuts get under my skin like that. Man, I didn't need it."

"It wasn't the smart choice, now was it?"

"Would you like to like Exxon?" my LIfebook asks.

"Well, maybe it was the wise choice," Comet smiles.

"Would you like to like Similac, The Wise Choice?" the

Lifebook asks Comet.

We laugh. We like triggering the damn thing through our conversations.

"Sounds like it could have been the happy choice," I smirk.

"Would you like to like Tide detergent?"

"Nope." We both laugh again.

"Pass me my shoes, Dad," Comet says.

"You heard the news," Dad says. "This is a fourth time. It is highly suggested that we contact a counselor. Please sit in front of the Clear Channel and say 'yes' to be put in contact with a counselor."

"No!" we both yell.

"If there is a fifth violation of the news today, you have a mandatory counseling session," Dad chastises.

"Damn it, Comet. Now we have to walk on egg shells."

"Funny thing is," Comet says, "I forgot that time. We were laughing and I wasn't thinking about it, you know? I really thought it was Dad sitting there for a second. I mean, really. It just felt so normal, like I guess it's supposed to, and I wasn't thinking about it for a second. And we were joking. And it was like—"

"Like he never died," I finish his sentence for him.

Chapter 2

My dad is a hologram.

The one that lives with us, that is. My real dad died just a few weeks ago in South America. We've been living with the hologram for years now, though, on and off. Since I was ten, my dad has gone on alternating eighteen month tours in the rainforests of South America. Eighteen months on, six months off. The Peacekeepers installed the Tour Acclimater system on his second tour. We were excited, of course, to experience Dad while he was gone on tour. He was preprogrammed with his behaviors and mannerisms, all downloaded from his Lifebook Lifeline. Plus, Dad could send back messages through the Holodad, as we called him. He couldn't send them that often, but the program was so good that it wasn't really necessary that he update the Holodad. Dad spent weeks in motion capture training and I can tell you that the Holodad moves just like the real Dad. The one thing that Holodad really gets wrong is calling me "Son." Dad just never did that. I guess that's something dads are supposed to do that mine never did. It doesn't make me feel any better that Holodad does, probably makes me feel worse.

While it never felt like he was actually home, it did feel like he hadn't been gone so long; like I had perpetually just seen him the day before. And over a long enough time scale, it was hard—if not impossible, at times—to remember if he was or wasn't there for certain events.

Like my 16th birthday. If I spend some time looking at a calendar, and do a little math, I could probably figure out if it was Dad or Holodad there eating cake. But right now, at this moment, I can't figure it out. I'd have to remember some kind of really specific detail or conversation. I was sixteen, after all, and more involved with my friends than my parents, just like I'm supposed to be, like we learned in Home Behaviors course. So how would I tell the difference? Dad was just in the background.

But at least he wasn't gone.

Research has shown that there is a significant decrease in divorce rates in families who have a Tour Acclimater system installed. It's not good for doing chores or anything—not that Dad did too many chores—but his presence is always felt. And there are certain big things that he is good at. Holodad taught me how to drive. Dad wasn't actually on tour then, strangely enough, but he didn't have time to work with me on my road skills. They keep him in the office when he's at home for much of the time; it helped with our credit score a lot. But with a Holo unit installed in the car, I never knew he wasn't there. He's good for dating advice, enforcing rules for Mom, laughs at jokes, watches our favorite shows with us, and tells us family recipes.

Holodad is also good at delivering news.

One night, at about 5:30am, Dad was standing in my room waking me up. "Son. Wake up. Come on, Scott. Wake up."

I rolled over and saw him standing there wearing his Peacekeeper dress greens. The hologram doesn't emit light like you might think, but it still doesn't look quite right in the dark. Like everything around him had shadows in all the right places, but he just stood there, looking like he was standing in bright sunlight—or the lighting of a motion capture theater—completely void of shadows. Not glowing, but not right.

"I've got something to tell you, Son. I have some news that's going to be hard to take. Are you awake?"

I nod my head.

"I need to be sure you're awake and that you are ready to hear this news." He was holding his hat in his hands, turning it over and over, as if he were nervously waiting for me. "Son. Are you awake?"

"I'm awake, Dad. What's up?"

Holodad told me that, three hours earlier, my dad had been confirmed dead in a firefight. He repeated the news verbatim when I asked if he was serious. He waited and nodded his head when he asked me to repeat back what it was that I understood him to say. The words cut my throat as they came out. I watched my dad's eyes—motion captured from months or years earlier—as I told him that I understood that he was dead.

When I had fully grasped the news, Holodad then explained the rules governing what he called, our "adjustment period." Holodad would stay around for eighteen more months. While we were encouraged to interact with him, we weren't allowed to ask him to do things for us or otherwise behave as if he were *actually* alive. This was different from when Dad actually *was* alive; Holodad could operate electronics and manipulate the Clear Channel—just about anything that didn't involve physical contact with an object. If we violate these rules, it's assumed that you aren't coping well and you have to have a counseling session with a virtual agent.

I could see in Holodad's face my dad's real sincerity. Dad mentioned to Mom a long time ago that he had to record these messages for different possibilities—his death, his injuries, being taken hostage, whatever might happen to him on mission. The military didn't deliver these messages anymore, now that the soldier could do it himself. He told Mom that it tore him up, the thought of saying these things to us through time and technology. I would have thought it'd be funny for him, but I guess he took it really seriously. I sat there in my bed, looking at my Dad's face, watching the tears he was holding back all those years ago while he recorded his message. I thought about how Holodad was going through this same routine in the other two bedrooms at the same time. Each recording personalized. A real chance to get to say goodbye to him—something people didn't used to get to do.

I don't remember how long it lasted. I had lots of questions, most of which he couldn't answer. How did it happen? Who else was hurt? Who did it? Was there a chance he was still alive? "No," Holodad answered to the last one. "My death has been confirmed by multiple means. I know this is hard to take. You will have a counseling session with an Americorp loss psychologist later today. Denial, as I understand, is a perfectly normal part of what you're feeling. Please take this time to say goodbye to me; I won't be able to have this conversation at a later time."

It was at this moment that my door opened and I saw Comet standing there. Behind him was another Holodad. This isn't very uncommon, for there to be more than one of him around. But never for the same person at the same time. When two Holodads see each other, one always disappears. But this time, and only this time, neither one of them did. We each had our own personal Dad, looking at us, showing us sympathy and anguish. My dad sitting on my desk chair looking deeply into my face, his Dad standing behind him, arms folded, face downcast; neither Dad looking quite right in the darkness, absolutely void of shadows.

I later learned that it was against code for a deceased holo to disappear into thin air, though they were perfectly welcome to do this as long as the person they represent was still alive. It's like, too strong of a metaphor or something for people to see. Instead, they just disappear when you're in a different room.

"Dodge," Comet said, "I don't know what to"—and he broke down crying. Both of our Dads started crying then, too. He wasn't allowed to cry until someone else in the room was crying; he's not allowed to push our emotions to the next step. I thought of Mom's Dad in her room right now and I betted that he was crying, too.

Comet hopped into my bed and we both cried. All four of us cried. For how long, I don't know.

The counseling session came much later in the day. We sat down and were given a briefing by a Peacekeeping Chairman about the mission, what had happened, and when. The Chairman wore a dark blue suit and had a pin on his lapel in the shape of the Exxon symbol. Another pin, slightly larger, was the Americorp flag. "Security Administrator Goode was killed defending the east side of our forestry investment in a fire fight with insurgents from either a local tribe or a rival corporation, at this point it's not clear." The Chairman talked in generalities, never getting specific about anything. Probably, he had two or three other calls to make that day, to two or three other families, all the general facts the same, just the last name of the Peacekeeper substituted.

"What was the nature of the mission?" my mom asked. She had a list of questions that Dad had written down for her on her tablet, in case this should happen. Every little step, so important.

"The nature of the mission was routine security," the Chairman said.

"What was the nature of Security Administrator Goode's positioning? Did he have a proper security support team intact?" Mom had told me earlier in the day that if they had had the credit space, she would have paid a lawyer to ask these questions, but what funds Dad left for that would have to be used for other shortcomings in our budget; Mom had recently lost her job when her coffeehouse was bought by an Americorp rival and liquidated.

"The security support team was intact, as per their directions, but I'm afraid that Security Administrator Goode's positioning wasn't clear at the time of the insurgence."

The look on Mom's face told me that he had said exactly what she was dreading he would. "Are you suggesting that Security Administrator Goode was somehow off-mission?"

"That is not clear at this particular juncture," the Chairman said. "Further inquiries are being made. Concerns will be satisfied by all parties."

"Wait," Mom said. She flipped through pages on her tablet and finally put in the keywords "off-mission" and "further inquiries". It came up with her next question, written in Dad's handwriting. "What is the current condition

SOL SMITH

of financial loss support from Exxon and Americorp to the Goode family?"

The Chairman shook his head. "Too soon to tell."

"What does that mean?" Mom asked, off-script.

"At this current, particular juncture, financial loss support is running on credit. Your current credit score of 653 is sufficient to support the funds through the standard three month investigation."

"And then?"

"When the investigation is cleared, your credit will be restored. If there are any irregularities, then we go from there."

"Three months? Is that how long investigations take?"

"That is the standard of time allotted for credit on an investigation."

Mom had the same look in her eyes as when she lost her job. She shook for days when they were bought out, waiting to hear if their jobs would be transferred over to jobs at The Grind, or if The Grind was just eliminating competition. There was a Grind just a half mile from her Strange Brew and the word was that over half of the Strange Brews in the country would be rebranded and the rest would just be eliminated. But stockholders were worried about the cost of running all those stores, and with that lack of confidence, the decision was made to eliminate them all. Her personal stock was bought with the buyout, so she had a little money left over. She submitted an application—as directed in her walking papers—and never heard back. That was the same for all of her coworkers.

I wrote a paper about all of that for my Economics and Integration course. It got an A. To find yourself inside the economy, part of a greater whole, and successfully demonstrate an understanding of your role and the purpose of the larger picture, well, that's the goal of the course, Mercedes tells me. Mom lost her job. I got an A.

"What does 'we go from there' mean in this case?" Mom asks. She put the tablet down, knowing that she lost track, wasn't able to keep up.

"I'm afraid that's not my department," the Chairman said. I can't be sure, but I'm pretty sure that he noticed that my mom was off balance now and saw his way out of further engagement. It's a discussion strategy we learn in Corporate Communication freshman year.

Mom kept fumbling through the tablet, looking for what else she was supposed to ask, but she was quiet for just a little too long.

"I'd like to hand you over to the Loss Psychologist. She will guide you through the eco-social-emotional issues that go with this kind of loss," the man on the screen said. The scene on the Clear Channel changed from one office, covered in maps on the wall and books stacked at the end of a desk, to another office; this one sleek and clean, potted plants dominating the background.

"Hello, I'm Dr. Gutierrez, your personal Loss Psychologist for the incident," said the kind looking lady behind the desk. "You can call me Celina. I look forward to working together. I see you've completed Loss Debriefing and that is the first step in your healing process. This has been cleared as part of Americorp services, so it will not impact your credit in any way." She smiled big and bright, continuing with "congratulations."

Mom had a distant look on her face, barely listening. Comet was squeezing Mom's hand, his face still looking like he was going to cry. Sitting behind us was Holodad.

"Your husband, Mrs. Goode, if I might say, was a particularly handsome man," the doctor onscreen said, looking at Holodad. Mom winced at the casual complement that the woman gave Dad. "I think we should take a moment to recognize a few of your husband's attributes that each of you really appreciated about your loved one. I would like it if you could give me a sense of who he was— the real him—what sort of clothing he liked, cars he liked, where he liked to shop, you know, just give me a sense of his personality through his daily choices. I will also spend some time with his Holo program, getting to know him from my own perspective."

In Modern Psychology, we learned that daily choices are what make up a person's personality. Who you are is reflected in your buying habits. How much you care about the people around you can be found through your own personal presentation choices and choice memberships. My mom started rattling off details of Dad's life, the places he liked to shop, the music he liked to listen to, the shows he liked to watch, the job he had, the clothes he wore—you know, who he really was. Once in a while, when she couldn't think of a detail, Holodad filled in for her. The doctor could have gotten all of this through Dad's Lifeline, but having us detail it all is supposed to give us a sense of comfort and well-being—the idea that we knew him better than someone just paging through Lifebook can. It's really personal.

At the end of the day, all four of us were sitting at the dinner table, barely touching our food that was delivered earlier in the day. "Harry," Mom said to Holodad, "how long is the standard investigation after a field death?"

"Three months is the standard credit allotment," Holodad says.

"Yes, but how long do they take? You can access those kinds of records, right? How long do they take? Three months?"

"Honey," Holodad said, "there are just over 2,000

such investigations in the last three years alone. Of those, all of them are still open."

"Harry, does that mean that every one of them is running purely on the family's credit? That the family has nothing from Americorp to replace the Peacekeeper's compensation?"

"Unless they were settled quietly, in which case, they would have been stricken from the records. I wouldn't be able to access that."

Mom looked pale. "I think it would be good if you left for a while so I can talk to the kids without this apparition hanging around."

Holodad smiled. "Maggie, the Loss Team doesn't allow me to just fade away from your life so quickly. Research shows that having me around leads to quicker adjustment. I can't be turned off for the standard period of three months from departure. After that three months, it's a case-by case basis. It's okay for you to feel how you're feeling and I want to be here to support you all. It is my will."

"Please," Mom said. "Please start referring to Harry in the third-person. And past tense."

"That will begin in time, dear," Holodad said. "You have to trust me. This is how we need things to go right now."

We didn't talk for the rest of dinner. The deep sincerity

on Holodad's face just wasn't there anymore. This was the program talking now, not the prerecorded Dad. It was a subtle change, but I think we all felt it. Mom felt like she couldn't talk around him. It was really clear that we were heading onto a typical fight with Americorp—did Dad die in the line of duty, or was he off-mission? If it was in the line of duty, we could expect a full pension and to be somewhat taken care of. If he was off-mission, we would get no support. Since things were classified, we had no idea what the mission would have been or who would decide what constituted being "off-mission".

And in the blink of an eye, Holodad went from being Dad's emissary to being a spy.

Chapter 3

"You are invited to lunch at Noon Burger with Maple Jackson and three other Friendships," the Lifebook Messenger says in my ear. I'm riding the bus to school, and it takes a little longer than normal because there's a detour while they're repairing the tracks on Barstow, which is the normal route.

"Yeah," I say. "I'll go."

"Are you sure you will be attending lunch at Noon Burger? They serve Coke products and your Lifeline indicates that you prefer Pepsi products. Would you like to change your preference now? If you change your preference to Coke products, you will receive thirteen iBuy points redeemable for Coke products if you don't change your preference for three weeks."

"Um," I say. "Damn. I forgot they switched over. What's the closest place with a shared dining space that serves Pepsi products?" Really, it's helpful for the Lifebook to remind me about my daily choices. Part of who I am, what I really am like, is seen and felt through my daily choices. I wouldn't want to be a hypocrite and go against my own sense of self by making the wrong daily choices. Our sense of self is one of our most precious possessions. It would be wrong to say that I am one thing and then turn around and act like someone else.

"Wasabi serves Pepsi products. Mo Anderson and six

other Friendships are attending Wasabi for lunch today."

"Okay, confirm lunch plans with Maple Jackson, but note that I will be meeting everyone in dining. I'm only a couple days away from more Pepsi points," I say. I'm relieved. If I have lunch at a place that serves Coke products, I have to start over and I'm working to get a Pepsi sweatshirt before football season starts—you get ten percent off tickets at the GenerationNext Stadium for State games if you're wearing Pepsi gear. Honestly, I don't know what the big deal is. Both companies are part of Americorp now. But, there is still the profit incentive and market competition really helps.

"You dream last night?" Comet asks.

"No. Damn thing doesn't work for me. I tried the hack that Jesus keeps talking about. Either I'm messing it up, or it just isn't going to work."

"It's too bad, bro. The new one was the best ever. It's like, we were pinned down in the jungle and our flank was taken out, you know, like in Iron Forces? And then, just by the skin of our teeth, we escaped. I had brought Red Bull, of course, so we all chugged it down and made our move. Right before the alarm. I thought sure this was the one where we get captured."

Comet has been following the new season of Jungle Forces dream programs. They're the Red Bull ones. He's always drinking Red Bull and mentioning them online so it's a totally free program for him. The dreams sound really exciting this season. He's been working on freeing hostages in the Amazon and they keep getting in trouble themselves. There's one campaign, he's heard, where he's actually going to be taken hostage for a while and have to break out. The corny thing is that every time they get in a real fix, someone pulls out Red Bull and they get away. I can, and do, watch the shows on the Clear Channel from time to time, but the Dreamcatcher program doesn't work for me. They just don't connect in right and when I try I usually just have a really blank night's sleep. No dreams, no memories, nothing.

"I did that one last night," Carl says, sitting behind us. "It was pretty triumphant. Remember that part when the medic gets his head blown off right there? Intense."

"My mom doesn't let me do the graphic one," Comet admits sheepishly. "I have to have the parental guidance edition."

"Sucks," Carl says. "I mean, what happened? Medic died, right?"

"Yeah, but it's like you look away and kind of hear it happen. It's still really ill, you know?"

"Yeah, I'll bet. Maybe I should jailbreak your Dreamcatcher. It's really easy to do, I've heard."

"Naw," Comet says. "I'm fine the way it is."

"What do you do tonight? *Emblem* or *West Charles*? Or

are you binging on *Jungle*?"

"I guess I'm going back to *Emblem*," Comet says. "I need to catch up on this season with the Clear Channel. *West Charles* is so overdramatic. People don't talk to each other that way, you know?"

"I don't know, I like it," Carl says. "My sister says it's girlie, but I don't mind. Catching a girlie thing once in a while meshes with my gendering profile; I'm comfortable."

Comet looks over at me, left out of the conversation. "Maybe when the new updates come out it will work with your chemistry," he says to me.

"I'm not stressing. I can watch it on the Clear Channel," I say. "It still looks pretty awesome. I don't mind not being a part of it, really."

"You'll see. The difference is so *real*, you know? Like real life," Carl says. "They'll fix it. They keep saying that they'll fix it up for everyone in the next few seasons. You must be type O, right?"

"Yeah."

"I heard that it fails with most type Os."

"Whatever."

I don't really feel like I'm missing out very much. It's so stressful trying to plug in, though, knowing it's not going to work. So, usually I just set my Dreamcatcher to the Clear

Channel audio and let it play music. That's how I hear the latest music, and, while I don't retain all of it, it's really the best way to not just waste your time sleeping if you can't plug in all the way. I kind of like the peace of not really seeing anything for a while. My brother—and other people—who plug in for the dream programs tell me that they don't really feel like they've been asleep. Mostly the dark part of the night—the night without dreams—just kind of escapes them. And even though the dream programs only last a couple hours, at most, that's all they really remember doing when they wake up. That's okay, I guess, because you wouldn't feel like you've wasted any time in bed. But, lying there and listening to music and the occasional introduction and ad isn't a bad way to spend the night. It's relaxing.

The Dreamcatcher has only been around for a few years. The first iteration of it, the DC1, had some real issues with it. In archaic sleep, a person can only dream about faces that they've seen in real life. So, people were experiencing these programs—the same programs that can be seen on a Clear Channel using conventional watching—and all the characters had different faces for each person. Usually, it was the face of someone that they barely knew or didn't even remember seeing just walking around. But, it led to problems when a face of someone they knew or loved was put into certain situations. There was the threat of all kinds of lawsuits, even though user agreements warned about this very thing.

I never experienced it because it never worked with my blood type. But my dad had really strange experiences that he didn't even want to tell us about. Stories about different and bizarre dream experiences were trending all over the place. It was really kinda horrible to read about, but the kind of horrible that you can't stop reading about at the same time. #Nightmarecatcher was full of stories.

Our house has a DC3 system right now and the better part of those little quirks have been worked out. Most people can experience identical programs as each other every night. They still haven't broken through to my type, but they're working on it really hard. And, like I said, I kind of don't care either way.

The bus stops at Comet's school and all the middle schoolers get up to disembark. "Good luck today, bro," I say. "Don't lose it or anything."

"Everyone acts like I'm just some kind of time bomb now or something. I was having a really bad day and I lost my temper. Is that okay for me to do once in a while?"

"Yeah, but you just can't hit them."

He nods his head. "Yeah, I know. Maybe he shouldn't have been such a dick about Dad."

"Don't rationalize. Remember what Captain Jackson says on *The Clearkids Morning Show*?" My Lifebook posts that I mentioned *Clearkids*, which is kind of embarrassing.

"Rationalization can ruin the nation," my brother replies.

"That's right. Just keep it together, that's all I'm saying."

"You know, 'sanitization' rhymes with 'ruin the nation', too."

"Don't be a smartass," I say.

"I haven't watched *Clearkids Morning* in ages, Dodge."

"Right," I say. "You watched it every morning last year."

"Just to make Mom happy."

"You getting off here?" the official says, looking at my brother. "Or are you headed on to high school a little early?"

Comet hefts his bag up onto his shoulder and leaves the bus. We rejoin the main rail and head on to the high school.

"Do you or a loved one need psychiatric counseling?" the Lifebook says in my ear. "Don't hesitate. At Courage Care, our doctors are trained in the latest coping theories and will help you push past your circumstances…"

I stop listening to the ad. I don't skip it, because you can only skip four ads a day and I really don't want to waste them all on the way to school. It's not like the ads really affect me, anyway. I mean, I'm sure that there're a lot of people who can hear that stuff and they take the suggestion and all, but it doesn't really work with me. I'm just on Lifebook to keep in touch with people and junk. And document my days and my likes; establish my sense of self.

I keep up on how prepared my friends are for the Economics and Integration test. It's one of the biggest tests of the year, even though there are like six tests every semester in that class. Today is the only two-part test where there's multiple choice—like usual—and an essay section. We almost never have essay tests. And since E&I is such a personal subject, the essay question is specifically modeled for each student. They dredge something up from your family's credit report and you have to explain why that part of your credit is justified. It's not too tricky, and everyone's parents make mistakes with their credit, so it's not like it's impossible to find something in the record. Once you really recognize the fault, and analyze how it could have been handled better, not only do you get a better grade, but you also can avoid doing the stupid things your parents have done.

Everyone is chiming in on Lifebook about how ready they are. Most people are saying 60 percent, like me, which is kind of the way to not disappoint yourself. When you read into it, it means that you studied really hard but aren't confident, so if you end up with a C, you can actually be pleased with yourself. So far, Fran Thomas is the most prepared at 92 percent, but I'm not sure she's telling the truth; her update says: "I used Study Smart Dynamics, Dreamcatcher Edition to prepare for the E&I test. I'm 92 percent prepared now!" I've heard that you don't get the program for free unless you post really confident percentages. And even then, it marks your credit until you pass the class. Pointless if the Dreamcatcher doesn't work for you, though.

The Clear Channel on the bus is playing Student News. It's a show put on by top high school students who are going into Journalism or something. You watch a different version of it in homeroom, but the bus edition is all relaxed and talks a lot about different human interest things. Today they're showing highlights of different high school War Games matches. They usually have a highlight from Reagan High, just a hundred miles or so from where I live. They've been state champions for the last five years and national champs for three of those. Their head coach is the highest paid teacher in the country. In most cases, the coaches are the only teachers specific to each school. The Everychild Curriculum is fully integrated now, so classes are taught through Clear Channel Conferencing. Our district was kind of behind in things and didn't move fully into that format until I was almost in middle school. We got our funding through the Pepsi Educational Foundation, the same year they built the stadium in town.

Our system just made the cutoff a few weeks before the enforcement date. Lots of my friendships from other schools around the country have always been taught the Everychild Curriculum, but not me; I remember having actual teachers in the room with us. It's better this way; our whole nation gets the same education, learns the same principals, and experiences the same diversity education. Once we're in the workforce, or go to college, we'll all have exactly the same knowledge base.

Our school may actually be in the running for States in War Games this year. My friend Lily is co-captain of the Officers division. She and the other officers work strategy, plan attacks, and coordinate air and sea support. Her specialty is missile defense. Once the initial strategies are run and points of attack and casualties are calculated, then the Ground Division moves in. That's where the action really starts. You can watch the initial attacks on the screens and the simulations are amazing; it's really exciting to see the statistics work out and see how many Ground Forces survived for the final battle. But it's that final battle that fills the stadiums. Sometimes they do historic fights and they have to set up a battle that actually took place. It's a kind of a handicap for the better team to be positioned as the historic loser; but when they win anyway, the crows loves it. Mick Poland is probably my best friend and he is the Platoon Leader for our Ground Division this year. Last year he was second-string Gunnery Sergeant, but when Russ Whithers broke his collar bone, Mick stepped in and really shook things up. He is generally credited with leading the team to five straight victories to end out the season. It was the silver lining to come through the whole Reagan-Cable disaster, as it was called, when four players were injured and one died. Porsche Fairview, a girl I had gone to school with since the second grade, died in the incident. She was the first girl to be first-team varsity as a sophomore and she was one of the coolest girls I have ever known. She was just a few degrees away from being in my trusted Friendship circle.

It's really too much to think about, Porsche dying. She was alive when they took her out of the stadium and we all thought she'd be okay, as much as we thought anyone would be. But, when the news came through that all but one had survived, we didn't think it was her that died. School was back in session that Monday and it was such a shock. We had these big group counseling sessions, and Pepsi even donated a lot of food and drinks to the whole student body, since they are our team's sponsor in War Games. I still have her listed as a friendship, and even though she's deceased, we can all still post on her Lifeline and we wish her a happy birthday and that kind of thing.

I wrote a poem about her in Language and Communication. It got a B because my rhythm was off on one of the lines and the teacher said it was too depressing. I didn't mind because I really liked the poem, but I had to rewrite it anyway since I'm aiming to go to college and not enter the workforce right away. I rewrote it and instead of making it about Porsche, I made it about Consumer Confidence during the holiday season, which is obviously a really happy subject. I fixed the rhythm and used a different meter that was judged to be more upbeat in our text.

I got an A.

Just before we pull into the Cable High Rail Station, I stop spacing out on the Clear Channel and look out the window. A billboard passes by very quickly and the man on it looks like my dad. I can't make out what it's an ad for, and I don't get a solid look at the guy at all, but it's one of those little moments of recognition that I keep having, I guess. I feel like I see him everywhere.

Chapter 4

Cable High is a busy place at 8:45 in the morning. There are 4,000 students enrolled this year, that's up nearly 20 percent from the year before since they dissolved Central High due to budgeting restrictions voted into law. The Central High students were split into four or five different districts and have basically become outcasts wherever they are now, except for maybe the freshmen when you can't really tell if they were supposed to be going to Central or not. Their entire varsity War Games team went to Reagan, surprise, surprise.

Our campus is one of the older ones, built in the 2020s, but fully updated since integration into the Everychild Curriculum. Covered walkways and conveyers lead students from the rail station into the central quad, where basically any class is an easy walk.

I get to school and check my special alerts on the Lifebook while taking the conveyer. I have it set up today to let me know whenever my brother posts and status changes, and Mom, too. I always have an alert setup for one or two girls who I like, just so I can keep up-to-date, but since this is Comet's first day back, I thought it was pretty important to keep watch on both of them. Comet, apparently, is in Trig, so he's fine. His happiness meter is right at 60 percent, which is where any slightly-sullen 8th grader would set it on a normal day. Mom, it looks like, hasn't woken up yet. I'm guessing that her depression is going to stick around for a while. I don't click the wake-up app, not yet, but I think about giving her an anonymous wake-up call after my first class or so. I wouldn't guess it will help, though.

I've got a while before the Economics and Integration test. I get to spend the first three periods watching people on Lifebook post their scores on the test. Most of them are what you'd expect. Fran got an A, Mercedes got an A, Mo and Maple got middle-Bs. Those are just the scores for the multiple-choice portion; the essay portion takes the computer a little longer to grade, so they won't be ready until all of the students across the country have completed the test and it can average their scores. Essay questions always use competitive scoring, so not only do you have to do well, but you have to do better than everyone else in order to score high.

Lunch is tough because everyone who has taken the test is totally relaxed and everyone who hasn't is quiet. A bunch of us meet in a food court that is made up of a group of restaurants all under the same corporate umbrella. I have a teriyaki chicken bowl from Wasabi, but a few of the others have turkey burgers from Noon Burger. I think about studying some, myself, but I figure that what's stressing me out more than learning the facts and stuff is the essay test anyway. How can you study for that? You just hope everyone else screws up, is all.

"You do a pivot," Mick says. "Whatever the question asks, start to answer it, but then find a place to pivot into a subject that you totally know about."

"Like how?"

"Okay, so the question is about how to repair credit after a repossession or something, right?" Mick starts. "You talk about all the difficulties that one might face in life, how you might have all kinds of challenges in a troubling economy and how that might lead to some priority balance issues—see how you work in the vocabulary words?—and then move into how that's like a tough battle in War Games. See? You talk meaningfully about something you know, about trouble you've seen on the War Games field, and then boom, you're at a thousand words and totally done. Just make sure to add 'God Bless the Dollar' at the end."

"That doesn't work," Lily says. "You're looking at a B paper right there, Scott."

"Is that all?" Mick asks sarcastically.

"Yeah, you can show your writing skills that way and you can show an understanding of what the question is asking you, but you can't show the kind of higher-level critical engagement that they're looking for in E&I."

"Listen, princess, I've had plenty of A's in my experience thanks to the pivot."

"I doubt that has anything to do with your value to the school as a Second Lieutenant or Gunnery Sergeant."

"I wouldn't have to have such value if our officers would spend more of the tactical budget on air support and less on missile defense. Especially against Hoover."

And from here the two of them start going off on each other about the whole War Games thing. I think they both probably both have a point—Mick about writing about what you know and Lily about Mick having things go a little easy on him academically since he made varsity. It's a good natured kind of fighting that the two of them do and I think that, in all honesty, they kind of like each other. But it's like Lily can't really admit that she likes Mick because he's so popular and attractive and it's so unoriginal to like him; and Mick can't really admit that he likes Lily because she's not like the traditionally attractive girl that you'd see on a makeup billboard ad or a Palmolive commercial or anything. So he thinks it's below him to be attracted to her. Someday they'll hook up and we'll all read about it on Lifebook and not a single one of us will be surprised, but we'll act like we are anyway. There seems to be kind of a pissing match about how many likes you can get on news like that—hookups or breakups or pics of a first kiss or whatever. For a while, if you got over 1,000 likes on your pic of a first kiss, and hashed it "maybellinefirstkiss", you got a boost on your beauty shopping credit, even if you weren't wearing Maybelline lipstick or anything.

"Yo, Dodge," Maple says. "Was that your dad I saw on that Viagra billboard?"

This pulls me out of my head for a second. "What?"

"Not Viagra," Lily says, "it was a Cialis ad."

"What the fuck are you guys talking about?"

"Cialis is just like Viagra. They're basically the same thing. Both Pfizer, right?" Mick is looking down at his mobile. "Yeah, they're both on the Pfizer page. Same ingredients and same test results. They're just for different demographics."

"That's not what I mean," I said. "My dad is not on any billboard."

"Oh man," Mick says. "Somehow I just told Lifebook to 'Like Viagra.' Fuck. How do I take this off?" We all laugh as Mick scrambles with his mobile. "Oh man, 30 people already liked that I like it!" We laugh harder and a few people pull their mobile up on their arm to like his status even further.

"But, for real," I say, "it's not my dad, right?"

"Dude, sure looked like him," Mo says. "It was on the rail ride to school today. By the industrial district."

"I've only met him a couple of times," Lily said, "but I'm pretty sure it was him."

"I don't think you've ever met him, Lily," I say.

"Yeah, I did. I met him." She thinks for a second. "You know, I met the hologram him," she corrects herself.

"Is there a line that takes the rail by the billboard back to school?" I ask. "Because I've got to see this."

Maple and I leave before everyone else and take a surface rail back to school after lunch. The rail line that goes by the industrial park is the Maple Line, and that means that Maple gets to ride free. Everyone else takes the subway, which is much quicker from the food court. Lily and Mick were thinking about coming back with us, but they have War Games practice and really can't afford to be late. Not that I can; I have the test right after lunch. "I'm not sure exactly where it was. We don't usually go that way. But there was that construction on the Barstow offshoot. I'm pretty sure it's him."

It was exactly where I thought I saw Dad earlier. I keep my eyes peeled this time so I won't just see it out of the corner of my eyes. And sure enough, there is a billboard hanging right over the Chevron Industrial Park with my dad sitting by a campfire, wearing a red flannel shirt that I've never seen him wear before in my entire life. There's a quote next to him that says, "I'm ready whenever and wherever she's ready." And then there's the big ol' Cialis logo across the bottom of it.

And it's for sure my dad. There's no way it's anyone else. It's obviously and clearly my dad.

"What the fuck, Maple?" I ask.

"I have no idea, man. No idea. I thought maybe he just

looked exactly like him or he did some modeling on career leave or something."

"No," I say. "That's him, for sure. And he was never a model."

"But he was good looking."

And now I'm stuck thinking of my dad using Cialis.

I look down at my mobile and see that I got the Lifebook alert that Mom was awake about 45 minutes ago. I don't want to bother her, though, or let her know that I came half-way home in the middle of lunch just to look at a billboard. I'll have to talk to her tonight about this. I think about jotting a quick note to her, to make sure that she makes the time to talk to me, but I know that the location stamp will worry her, as I have no reason to be on the Maple Line in the middle of the day. This whole thing is just surreal.

I get a clue about things during—of all places—the E&I exam.

Every single Economics and Integration test starts the same way. Since the fourth grade, the first thing you have to do to progress on the test is to affirm your knowledge of the basic tenants of citizenship. There's a fill-in-the-blank question that starts it all off. "As a North American, I have the right to—" and here you write, "life, liberty, the pursuit of wealth, and the purchase of happiness. God Bless the

Dollar." Everyone knows these things, but it's kind of a precursor to getting to take the test. From there, it moves on to multiple-choice and then the dreaded essay.

I do fine on the multiple choice portion. I really worked hard to memorize all the stuff that I needed to for this one. I know the chapter on "The Failure of Socialism" backwards and forwards. I know all about how government healthcare cannot compare in quality and pricing with private sector healthcare, like Pfizercare and Kaiser—the two big choices that we have. I know the chapter about choices really well, too. As members of the North American Collective, we have freedoms to choose what kind of products to enjoy—this is the part that's reflective of the purchase of happiness. You have to identify a few different product lines and differentiate the purposes of their products based on gender, age, and socioeconomic demographic distinctions. It's easy to know the companies and products that market toward your particular demographic, but it's harder to remember—and I mean really remember—what the distinctions are for other demographics.

Then I have to answer questions about my responsibilities as a consumer. You basically take a look at different historical legal cases and determine who was the winner and why, and then from there answer subquestions about the further-reaching implications of these cases. For example, there is the *United States v. Monsanto* case that came before the Collective Reorganization of the fifties. In this case, a group of concerned citizens tried to sue Monsanto for price fixing during a tough economic time. The courts ruled that Monsanto had to split into separate companies, but in later cases, it was established that these separate companies could be operated under one umbrella company. There would still be competition, but it would be within internal brands—this creates the advantages of cheaper production, like from a monopoly, and profit incentive, like in capitalism. The results of this case really laid the groundwork for Americorp, and even the foundation of the Collective Restructuring that disassembled Big Government and let the people rule themselves directly through corporations and the process called "economic votecasting".

Economic votecasting is based on the theories of Alfred Dow—a famous industrialist philosopher—who said that the people can grant or restrict powers of corporations through where they put their dollars. There is no need for a government to babysit its people, telling them what to do and how to act and what kinds of things to believe in; rational adults can choose where to balance the power of a society directly through how they structure their economy. It's completely self-regulating, dividing the balance of power equally between the corporations and the people who grant them power. It's a more elegant time than when our grandparents grew up.

This theory spread throughout the branches of

government and ushered in the era of privatization. Schools, law enforcements, and national defense contracts all moved towards the private sector—most of them under Americorp. Tax dollars are still spent on these things, but they go to the private contractors, not Washington Fatcats, as they used to be called.

The whole period was called The Second American Revolution, and there were big posters with Thomas Jefferson quotes and Ronald Reagan quotes and Trump quotes and a bunch of these old posters and ads are in the text that we have. It's all very fascinating and I can see exactly why people like Mo and Alexandria want to go into economics so badly. Really, it's kind of like a study of philosophy and anthropology and sociology all in one.

One of the big figure-heads of the Second Revolution was Christopher Columbus, as weird as that sounds. Because before the Second American Revolution, there was this stigma on Columbus. He caused death and destruction, right? Killed thousands of Indians. So it's obvious why so many Americans would damn that kind of behavior; but after a more careful look, you see that he was doing it for Profit, and Profit is the only motive by which you can judge a meritocracy. You can't blame someone who is showing their worth, the end result being the raising up of themselves and their interests in the financial strata—it's all we really have to ascribe meaning to, in the real world.

My life changes during that test. My revelation comes

at the very end of the test, in the essay section. There's this kind of cool moment when Mrs. Farnsworth on the Clear Channel tells us that our time is up for the multiple choice section and that we are moving on to the essay. Our books flip pages and now, instead of seeing a bunch of questions with little circles for answers, there's just one question—each person has a different one—and our desk screen turns into a keyboard so we can type our response. The cool part of the whole thing is looking around the room—there are about 70 people in class—and seeing the looks on their faces as they read their individualized questions. You see each person squint in concentration as they read their questions, then either a look of relief or a look of complete worry. I watch this whole thing happen, the faces change and all, before I read my question. And I just imagine that all across the country, hundreds of thousands of students are having this same experience during the 1pm period.

And my question is:

"It is with our deepest sympathies that we recognize the passing of your father. Security Administrator Henry Goode was killed on the southern frontier of the North American Collective. While his death and the negative findings of the resulting investigation have had a negative effect on your family's credit score, what programs stipulated in the attached benefit agreement can help to repair your family's credit, increase your independence, and support your purchase of Happiness?"

I'm shocked. What negative findings? When did this come out? Why hasn't Mom talked about it at all; surely she knows about this, right? We have fifteen minutes to read our attached materials and then another five minutes to outline before writing our essay. The goal is to show that we understand and support various kinds of recent interactions on our credit scores. I don't know if anyone else's question is quite as emotionally disruptive as mine is, but I try to concentrate since this test has the potential to make a big impact on where I get accepted into college.

In the attached benefit agreement—a document signed by my parents and the life insurance company that they selected through the Peacekeepers—I see that my dad and mom took the full credit protection coverage in case my dad were to die. In the attached findings, I see that Dad was found to be "off-mission" at the time of his death—which basically means that Americorp is blameless because Dad wasn't following explicit instructions when he was killed.

This is exactly what Mom was worried about. This opens some tricky clauses in our protection coverage.

The details are blacked-out, classified. There's no way for me to access them, and it doesn't matter because the findings are law and considered flawless. So, whatever the details, it doesn't matter. The credit findings stay. And that's what the questions are about.

My eyes are blurry from tears. I can't imagine going

through with writing about this right now. In the old iteration of the test, students had the option to change out questions if they didn't want to write about the first one they were given. That was found to be unfair because people were changing them out and finding easier questions, and since it's graded on national relevance, it's not fair. I can opt for a retest if I'm sick, but then there's a lot of scrutiny on you and the determination about what is really "sick" or not.

I look through the document to see what full credit protection coverage is if Dad is found off-mission at the time of death. It involves lower rates on the Holodad program, with sliding rates on extended use; it gives all unpaid wages and non-awarded life insurance settlements over to Americorp; and it gives Americorp full ownership of all intellectual and visual property, as may have been involved in my father's employment. I'm not exactly sure what that means, and you lose ten points if you consult your legal dictionary, so I don't do it. I just start writing an essay that recognizes the irresponsibility of my father in going off-mission and how the selected levies against my family won't fully cover our credit deficiencies, but that it was still a fair and just example of our financial system in action. My parents used bad judgment and the operations of the credit program will absolve wrongdoing—this is how every essay ends in the room. At least every successful one.

Writing this essay is the hardest thing I've ever done. Every time I strike a key, I think of Mom lying in bed back home. I think of her dark bedroom, her heavy breathing during her Ambien-induced sleep. I think of everything she's gone through since she lost her job. I think of Comet and his outburst and how, because Dad was found to be off-mission, that will go against our credit now, too, despite our full coverage. I think of Holodad and how we have to pay for every dime of the program now. I have no idea what we're going to do, how I could possibly hope to pay for college with this news, and how I could possibly feel like I'm living any kind of a normal life at all. The faces around me show concentration, relief, worry, but none of them show what I'm feeling—shame, despair, pain.

I think about what Mercedes said, that success in this course is more than just remembering facts and data; it's about finding ourselves in the facts, finding ourselves in the data. It's about integrating ourselves into our global community through economics and recognizing our participation as part of who we are.

Part of who I am is the loss of my father. Part of who I am is my dad's choice to go off mission. Part of who I am is defined by the corporation, articulated by the corporation, and I have to write about it, justify it, and live with it right now. God Bless the Dollar, right?

Chapter 5

I don't update my status for the rest of the day. My Everychild app asks how I did on the test, and I go ahead and tell it that I got an 87 percent on the multiple choice part of the test—which is so much higher than my "60 percent ready" estimate that I feel pretty good about myself, even though I didn't get the A. But when Mick messages me about the essay question, and what it asked me, I just messaged back, "don't worry, dude, I totally pivoted."

He writes back, "that's my boy;)" and it totally satisfies his curiosity and that of anyone else who looks at the Lifebook to know what my test was like. I just zombie through the rest of the day and even think about going to file a sick day at the customer contact office. But, then I think better of it because there are just a couple of hours left and it would count as a whole day and I only have five days left on the semester before they start charging for sick days.

I message Comet in between periods and ask if he has heard from Mom—he hasn't—and then I ask if he wants to meet at the foodcourt after class instead of him going straight home before I'm out of school. I tell him that I have something to show him and some news that he has got to hear. When he gets back to me, saying he'll be there, I make a Lifebook appointment for a Goode Brothers Study Session at Wasabi. We do that once in a while, so it doesn't look super suspicious.

And for some reason, I realize something: I feel like I'm up to no good. Why is that? Something just feels wrong and I'm afraid that even looking into this any deeper is somehow against policy. I think about consulting my Americorp policy handbook, but then think better of it; it's always better to look like you had no idea you were going against policy.

Chapter 6

When I get to the foodcourt, Comet is already sitting with his reader set to his History class. I grab it from him and take a look at what he's reading. "What's this crap?" There's a graphic on the page showing an old cattle mill covered in the corpses of its cattle.

"I've got a history test that I missed while I was suspended. It's about the economic crisis that resulted from the bovine plague."

"That's an easy one," I say. "I remember this chapter like it was yesterday. Just remember that the genetic defect infected over 98 percent of domestic cattle and that it was George Groves in the FDA that pulled the kill switch on them. It potentially saved millions of lives. Billions, if you consider the long term health effects of eating that stuff for another century."

"I know that part," Comet says. "Everyone knows that part. We watched that documentary twice, once in History and once in Health and Wellness. You ever tasted real Kobe?"

"No," I said. "Dad used to say it was the best, though."

In the early 21st century, most domestic cattle were made on the same blueprint. They were genetically identical and ideal for raising for beef. Dairy cows were a little different from beef cattle, but they were all the same as each other, too. Most farm animals are, and it really is a genius system to make sure that each farmer knows exactly how to handle each animal and knows exactly what the yield for each animal is. We learned all about it in economics. It ended the unhealthy conditions the animals were raised in, always encouraged to get bigger. Each one was given the same food, same medicine, and grew to the same size.

The problem was that there was a plague that infected the cattle. For months there was panic as state-by-state the cows became deathly ill. The thing is, they didn't die, not right away. If they had died right away, it would have slowed the spread of the disease. But instead it incubated and grew stronger. When they found that it had mutated to the point where it could possible spread to people, the president of the FDA ordered Monsanto to pull the kill switch on every cow in the country. Every single genetically identical animal could be killed by the introduction of a single poison at each farm. It was just macadamia oil, which they used to be immune to. But the genetic blueprint they used made it absolutely fatal to them. The sprayed the oil by air over the fields where the cows lived and where they grew their grain, making it impossible for any farmer to hold on to their cattle.

It was a tremendous uproar. The farmers protested, but Monsanto complied. All the farms were wiped out. The only animals that were immune, worldwide, were the Kobe beef cattle from Japan. They still breed them naturally there and the meat sells at a very high price. Thing is, most people don't want it. Monsanto ran some studies shortly after the plague that showed how much better off we were without the cattle. Turns out, they were bad for you, bad for the environment, and an inefficient use of resources. It takes less than half the rainforest acreage to offset a chicken or pig or goat farm as it does a cattle farm. So Monsanto even got to let some of its forest holdings go, which helped the economy a lot.

The biggest boom industry in the second half of the century has been goat. Monsanto has engineered a goat that can produce three times as much meat as a wild goat and many dozens of times more milk. They don't really look much like a goat, or much like a living thing. Just like the chickens that are born and bred without any consciousness, they are just like racks of body parts growing in a holding container. The chickens have four or six legs, the goats have eight; just meat on life support, really. Grown in these huge multi-level farms that look like parking structures.

"I wrote my essay on the lasting benefits," I tell my brother. "Remember that for the essay at the end of the semester. If you pick the agricultural history question, you can really focus on how the people panicked and sent the economy into a spin, but that the scientists showed them how much better off things really were. It's a strong argument for the wisdom of genetic engineering."

"I'm not that far into the chapter," Comet says. "So far, it feels like an argument against it."

"Use that policy quote by the president of Nestlé at the end of the chapter, the one that guided human protection and longevity policy for the rest of the century."

"The one about knowledge trumping feelings?"

"That's right," I say, "I think it's, 'Wherever there are people, there are feelings running wild. We mistake our feelings for beliefs and our compassion for morals. If history has shown us anything, it's that the longevity of the human race depends not on feelings, but facts. The public at large should let go of control, stop ruling by feelings and let the experts operate what matters for the good of mankind.' Is that right?"

"Almost," Comet says, looking in his reader. "You're close. It doesn't say 'at large'."

"I could've sworn it did." You have to memorize that quote for the Policy Operations test at the end of the eighth grade.

Comet takes a bite of his burrito. "Going back a step," he says. "What did Dad say about Kobe?"

"He said it was the best thing he ever tasted. He said Grandpa used to get it for him on Christmas and grill up a steak for them all to share."

"What'd it taste like?"

"I don't know," I said. "Or, I don't remember. Maybe Holodad can clue us in."

"Call Dad?" my mobile asks.

"No, thank you," I say.

Comet takes his reader and puts it down. He looks at it a second, then looks up at me. He's thinking—something he's been doing a lot lately. Usually school and entertainment keep him busy enough, but there's been so much on all of our minds lately. The look on his face is different when he's actually thinking. "I doubt you came here just to help me with my history," Comet says. "I mean, I know you scored top of your class on the big Policy test, but I think I can handle things fine right now."

"No," I said. "Wrap up what you're doing. We've got a little field trip to take."

"What is it?"

"It's better I show you."

I lead Comet to the rail line that takes the longer way home. He doesn't question anything and I can tell he just kind of likes the involvement. And he likes that we're not talking about his suspension for once. The rail ride is quiet between us. He keeps reading his History book and I am listening to a few excerpts from the new DYM album. Just clips of songs. Seems like I only ever listen to clips anymore. Their stuff has kind of gotten more exciting and happy since they signed with Coke, which is their biggest label signing to date. Lily is such an elitist, that she says she won't listen to anything of theirs since they first signed with Dow. She says that she loved their stuff back when they were just posting songs onto Lifebook and letting fans find them, but that whole era has been erased since they got big label support. She says that she'll find me some bootlegs of what it sounded like, and there's this band that covers a few of those obscure hits downtown, but I've never heard any of them. Basically, I don't have a problem with a band becoming successful, though some people do. That's something we're taught in school—don't begrudge those who are successful. We all have the same right to pursue wealth and the purchase of happiness.

I take Comet to the same stop that Maple and I took earlier and we stand looking at the billboard for a while. I just sit and watch Comet's face.

"This is really strange," he says, finally. "I mean, that's Dad. Look at his eyes, just like yours. Look at his chin. Dude, has Mom seen this bull?"

"Don't talk like that, and no."

"I just... I just think that probably we need to get home and I need to go to sleep or something. I don't feel really well."

I lead Comet back to the rail station. We sit down and I check my mobile to see how long till we get home.

"Can you log off for a second?" Comet asks.

"I don't think you can log off from Mobile 12," I say. "You're fine to log off though with your 11," I say, mockingly.

"I'm logged off. Can you mute yours?"

"Yeah." I hold down the mute button and confirm. The standard mute lasts 30 seconds, so I hold the button down.

"What does this all mean?" he asks.

"I think that we should talk to Mom," I say.

"No shit?"

"Dude, I said, don't talk like that. I need to tell you about my economics exam today. I think that there's some pretty bad news that Mom isn't being honest about." I tell Comet about the essay question, about Dad being off-mission and the coverage that Dad bought. I tell him that it could be possible that Americorp is using Dad's image for advertisements as part of the protection coverage.

"Could that question have been a hypothetical?" Comet asks.

"On the Junior E&I exam? No way. The essay questions are always real-life situations from your recent credit history. That's why it's relevant."

"Yeah," Comet says. "That's part of how they indoctrinate you into the whole Economy. Make you demonstrate your belief in the whole shared hallucination that we're in."

"Dude," I say. "Don't talk like that. You know that this is how to succeed in life. You have to understand this stuff. You have to do more than understand, you have to apply it."

Comet has that look on his face again. That independent look; concentration. It looks so new on him. "You're forced to agree, that's all. Forced to agree. I see that more and more in school."

"The point is, it's true. It's dated a week ago. Mom's been keeping this quiet a week. That's why she's been backsliding so hard. And we've got to try and pull her out of it."

"I don't see how this is our problem to fix."

"Because it's our problem, Comet. And who the hell else is going to fix it?"

We get home and Mom is already working on dinner in the kitchen, just like it said on the Lifebook. It's nice because I see that she cleaned up the kitchen before she started working on dinner. I feel like that's a good sign. Holodad is sitting at the table, working on a Holographic Sudoku, like he used to while mom would make dinner.

"How was the study session, boys?" Holodad asks.

"Fine," we both say.

"What'd you study?"

"Dodge was just helping me with my history test. It's about the Bovine Plague."

"Ah, interesting," Holodad says. "Thanks for helping him, son." I cringe as he calls me this.

"No big," I say. "It's always been a good subject for me."

"You've had good teachers," Mom chimes in. "Top rated ones in the country."

"Dad," Comet says. "What's Kobe like?"

"God, here we go," Mom says. She always hated it when Dad gets wrapped up in reminiscing about his childhood. He's always so superior about it, in her mind.

"It's terrible," Holodad says without looking up. "Getting rid of the cows was one of the best things to happen to this country. *Birria* is really so much better than beef. It's better for you, it tastes better, and it's got much better profit margins for Americorp, which is in all of our bests interests." He reaches and picks up his coffee cup, and we all just listen to him sip. Mom stops stirring whatever it is she's stirring and looks at us. All three of us stare at each other.

"Dad," I say, finally. "I thought you said that the Kobe steak that Grandpa used to make was the best thing you've ever eaten."

He looks up at me and smiles. "Your dad wouldn't say that," he said at last. "Tyson *Birria* is probably the best ingredient that you can cook with. Maggie, are we having *birria* tonight? You know what they say, it's the 'solid choice' for a good dinner!"

"Chicken," Mom says quietly, "I'm frying chicken."

Holodad nods. "Yum." He goes back to his puzzle.

Comet storms into the other room, visibly disturbed. Mom just stares at me while stirring, a bit more slowly. "You have any homework, honey?" she asks.

"I've got some reading to do. A little trig." I say. "I'll plug in right here, if that's okay."

She nods. I put my Bluetooth in my ear and cue up my book on the mobile. I listen to *Great Expectations* while working on my trigonometry.

Chapter 7

"We've got to turn it off, that's the first thing," Comet whispers.

"Can't turn it off. We're in the extended adjustment period, remember? We can't turn it off until that period is over. Maybe just this part of the adjustment."

"No way. This isn't part of the adjustment."

"Even Mom noticed."

"Ya think? Of course she noticed! She hated how Dad used to wax on about Kobe."

"Do you think she changed it? Like she wanted us to give up stupid little idolizations like that and just be happy with *birria*."

"Dude, I love *birria*. Don't get me wrong. But Dad always cringed. Remember? He always pushed for pork. He said that *birria* was too gamey. That thing in our house is *not Dad*."

I nod my head, but remember that in the dark he might not be able to see this. "Yeah," I say. "I mean, obviously we know that. But it's like now it's not even a hologram of Dad. It's like something else. Some kind of entity, watching us and God knows what else."

"I'm worried."

"I keep thinking," I say slowly. "I keep thinking, would we really be so worried if it weren't for the billboard? And the test? Like have there been some pretty big inconsistencies before and have we just passed them by because we weren't on guard? Like maybe this is just a normal part of the programming and we've just been ignoring it before. But this is kind of too much, right?"

"Too much," Comet says. "This is big. And besides, should we just ignore the billboard and the test? When are we going to talk to Mom about this?"

I think a minute. "We could wake her up now. But I think that kind of thing alerts Dad."

"Yeah, but why are we so worried about alerting the Holodad?"

"He sends information back to Americorp," I say. "And if we're going to try and help Mom, we can't have him running data back to them, right? I mean, I know that it's against policy to run conspiracy theories like this when you're benefiting from this kind of technology—"

"Shut up with that, already," Comet says.

"Comet, too loud. He'll come in here. Or Mom will. Or both. Keep it down."

"I think we need to ignore policy and benefit paradigms while we're dealing with this. We're looking at hundreds of points off our credit, right? And all of this benefit money is going to go away and how in the world is Mom going to keep paying for us to live? She only has Bereavement Unemployment for another few weeks, then we're totally on our own."

"I don't know if Bereavement Unemployment even applies if Dad was really found to be off-mission."

"How do they determine that anyway?"

I shrug, then remember that it's dark, he can't see my motions. "Dunno," I say. "I think in the meantime, we need to talk to Holodad a little more, figure out how far off of his original programming he is. I mean, do we really remember Holodad talking about Kobe?"

"Dodge, I've got to be honest with you," Comet says. "I can't remember when it was Holodad or real Dad, anymore. I mean, I know that before he was first deployed it was always real Dad, but I'm younger than you. Most of my memories of him are all wrapped up with Holodad. It's been years, you know?"

"At least you remember him, right?"

"I don't know if that's good or not right now. I'm just totally confused."

"Maybe we should talk to Dr. Gutierrez."

The Clear Channel in my room lights up with nighttime colors. "Should I contact Dr. Gutierrez now? It is after hours.

Would you like me to contact the on-call emergency Loss Psychologist?"

"No," I say. "For God's sake, not right now." Then I whisper to Comet, "Do you think the Clear Channel is listening? Like do you think that was just a keyword thing or do you think that it's collecting data like Holodad? Why wouldn't it collect data? Have you read the user agreement? I'll pull it up on my reader."

"Don't freak out, bro," Comet says. "Don't run a policy check. It's against policy to run conspiracy theories, right?"

"Right," I say.

"I've been doing a lot of thinking about things lately. Stuff I should probably talk to you about, but honestly, I don't know where to start. Not right now, though. It won't help right now."

"Yeah," I say. "I guess we should keep quiet about this. And you should get to bed. Did you already say you were in bed on your Lifebook?"

"Yes, I told you that already when I came in here. Dodge?"

"Yeah?"

"It's going to pass, right? All of this? You know, how Mom always says, *this too shall pass*? Like when she lost her job."

"I don't know, Comet. A death isn't like a job loss. And I think we're looking at something that might be even worse than just a death."

"We'll get through though, right? Mom will get a job. Holodad will turn off like he's supposed to and the billboard isn't what we think and you and I are just freaking out for nothing, right? I mean, like I said, I've been thinking and stuff, and doing some reading, and I don't want to think that…that this is all for real. It'll stop, right?"

For a few seconds it's quiet, while I mull it over. What has he been reading? How would this just go away? The hum of the house is quiet this late and I can hear the bugs outside. "Don't know," I say. "Don't have any clue. I'm going to try and think of some things that Dad used to be really big on, and things that Holodad used to reinforce, and I'm going to try it out. I want to double-check before I go freaking Mom out and stuff."

"I think Mom's already freaked out, bro," Comet says. "I think she's trying to play it cool for us. I just hope she gets a job, because I can't stand the thought of having school be downgraded. You know how bad it's supposed to be at a level C junior high? It's not fair that you get to go to a B high and I have to hold my breath and see what happens."

"Stop being selfish," I say. "Worst case scenario is that Mom has to do Reintegration. You realize that's a real possibility?"

"She hasn't broken any laws!"

"If she ends up owing this much money and can't pay, that's against *policy*. That means she could very easily be sent to Reintegration."

"What would happen to us?" Comet questions. And his question just kind of sits there in the air, dissipating into the darkness of my bedroom.

"Sneak back," I say. "Don't wake up Mom. Don't let your Clear Channel greet you when you get back to your room. Let's just take this slow. Let's be cool about this and let it sort of unfold. There's no rush, right?"

"I guess that's something else we don't know," he says. "But I'll get back to bed. If I sleep or not, I don't know."

Chapter 8

"You going to the War Games this weekend?" Comet asks me at breakfast. We're both eating Honey Crashers and Mom is cooking some eggs for herself. I felt like eggs, too, but since I had Honey Crashers again, it's only another four times before I get a boost in GM points on Lifebook. That will add to my badges, which will add to my access level in the Dormroom virtual game I'm playing and that will mean higher earning power within my virtual major. So, I have the Honey Crashers and log it onto my Lifebook.

"Yeah," I say. "I'm going. Want to go with me?"

Mom and Comet kind of look at me like I'm crazy; I guess that I've never invited Comet to go with me before, not explicitly.

"Um, yeah, I'll go."

"Dodge, Comet, you know how Dad feels about you going to the Games. He only tolerates *you* going, Dodge, because you're a junior and it counts towards P.E. to go watch. But, after all he had gone through, playing games about wars doesn't seem right. Even for you, Dodge."

"Builds character," Holodad says, without looking up from his paper. "It's good for the boys to go watch the War Games. It's American of them. Practically their duty."

We share one of those looks like we did the night before, the three of us people who aren't holograms.

"You think it's cool for me to go to the Games?" Comet says, looking at us, but directing it to Holodad.

"I think that you'll agree that every boy should go to the Games."

"You think you can get out of 7th period so you can come watch the initial strategies with me?" I ask Comet. "I know that the stadium part doesn't happen till six, but you should see the strategies. It's so important, you know, to know how they start out and how the stadium layout looks. None of that will make much sense without the strategies session."

"You can just read the summaries, right?"

"Yeah, but if you know what you're watching, it's really exciting. Just as engaging as the Ground Forces."

"I'm not sure how I feel about this," Mom says. "We've always been worried about you boys getting the wrong idea from these games."

"Lighten up, Honey," Holodad says. "It's good for them. They can stop at Taco Castle and pick up some of the new Birrias Machos on the way. Sound good, boys? I heard that if you like them on Lifebook you get two for one on Cable High War Games nights. Isn't that something?"

I make a note of this. I think about jotting this down on my mobile pad, but when I look down at it, is says, "Like Taco Castle?". I make eye contact with Comet and, by his expression, his mobile says the same thing.

Mom pours the egg out of the carton and starts pushing them around in the skillet. Her mobile is on the other counter, so she doesn't look at it. But by her expression, she's bugged enough by what Holodad is saying. She winces, and I can tell puts up with this all just for the sake of trying to be present for Comet and me. I know she probably felt pretty bad about not getting up yesterday until lunchtime. For her—when she's depressed—it's always a battle between wanting to be depressed and just be away from everything versus feeling guilty about being depressed and being away from everything. This just makes her more depressed and that sort of breathes new life into the cycle.

Medicine hasn't really worked any. Or maybe it has. That's the problem with this cycle; you don't know if it's working until it stops. She's talked a lot to a Depression and Lifestyle Psychologist on the ClearDoctor app, and she's had most of the major drugs prescribed at one time or another. They work for like a couple weeks, maybe, then they just go ahead and drop her and she's right back where she started. Or maybe they don't; maybe things just get worse. Then, the D&L Psychologist will start her on something else — it's always the newest and latest thing and Mom goes into it with all kinds of hope and dreams.

Something the D&L always tells her is that this isn't circumstantial. There isn't something wrong with her life or with her diet or with anything else. It's not her fault, she'll tell her all the time. It's not because her husband was deployed and it's not because she lost her job and it's not because her husband died and it's not because financial and credit ruin hides behind every corner—it's just a chemical imbalance that lots of women go through and something that Pfizer has been working on for a very long time. There's some kind of medication that works for everyone, she says, but no medication does it all for every person. Instead, there are combinations to try, tests to take, periods to wait between trials, and every other kind of medical imperative that has to go through every cycle—blood tests, psych evals, histories to consider, interactions, supplements, consultations, and by the end of it all, she's back to where she started.

When Dad is home, or when he's getting ready to come, mostly, Mom gets excited and things feel better and she forgets to take her meds. It always makes me think that maybe it is circumstantial, or maybe at least the circumstances have something to do with it. Some drugs make her kind of absent, some drugs make her worse.

There was one time, I was in the sixth grade, when the worst nearly happened. Mom was taking the latest drug on the market—the one drug that was supposed to be perfect for people who had little help from the previous drugs—and things went terribly wrong. She seemed better at first, like usual. But then she sank into such a funk that, even at my young and selfish age, I started to feel really worried about her. Dad had this look on his face the whole time, a sort of careful suspicion. He started taking us to school and picking us up, getting time off at either end of work to do it. Mom quit her job and didn't tell us or Dad for two weeks. It wasn't until we started becoming late on credit card bills that usually came out of her pay that Dad found out.

Then, one day, Dad didn't come pick us up. We went home with Mick and his mom, which was really weird because Mick almost never actually got picked up by his mom, he took the rail. Comet was really young, and I wouldn't guess he ever remembers it. But, he was all excited to have the change of pace. Mick's mom took us out to ice cream at the Nestlé shop and Comet was just overwhelmed with excitement.

But I knew something was wrong. I was just sure of it.

We never ended up going home that day, but Dad brought us both bags with clothes and stuff in them. He said hi to us, but he didn't stay long or tell us anything besides that he was taking care of some things and he really needed us to cooperate and help him out by staying there a couple of days. That night, I told Mick that I was worried.

"I think something's wrong," I said after dinner. "I think it has something to do with my mom."

"Well, I heard my mom and dad talking," Mick said. "They said something about your mom being in the hospital. Has she been sick?"

"Not the normal kind of sick, anyway," I said. "She's been really depressed. You know, like on those Pfizer ads, where all the people are made out of stone and then CEO Johnston talks about how depression can break apart a family, and Regularium can help bring them back together?"

"Well, maybe they're bringing your family back together, then. Because what I heard was that she was in the hospital and your dad was going to stay there all night with her. That's why you guys are staying with us."

It turned out that she had tried to kill herself. She overdosed on her pain medicine—her depression gives her all kinds of pain in her shoulders and neck. Dad later told me that it was really touch and go for a while. Mom had to stay in a different kind of hospital for a while so that she could be watched by the doctors and nurses who made sure that she wouldn't try anything like that again. Then, after that, she had to go to Reintegration to try and repair the family's credit. Having a documented illness like that—an illness that has to be treated by medicine and hospitals and doctors and stuff— really takes a huge chunk out of your credit rating. And for her to make a suicide attempt while still carrying as much debt as she was—her student loans weren't paid off— really damaged the family. Dad kept telling me how to even be offered Reintegration instead of prison considering all the violations of policy she had made was really lucky. It really showed the mercy of the board.

Comet, so far as I know, doesn't know anything about

that whole thing. He remembers Mom being gone, of course, but he thinks it was just for the Reintegration because the family was in so much financial trouble. She came back to us and had a job, so maybe there was some Reintegration going on, as well. She has a degree in coffee mixology, which is a specialty degree and has a high employability rate. It's a mid-grade degree, I guess, and your credit score decides what range of employment your degree can be.

I think Comet is worried about everything right now, but not in the same way that I'm worried about everything. I feel like Mom's life is on the line, and what would even happen to a couple of teenaged orphans? It's unimaginable.

Mom does a really uncharacteristic thing and walks Comet and me to the rail station. When we get outside, she says to us, "boys, can you mute your mobiles, please?" We take a minute and do so. "Look, I don't know how much longer we're even going to be able to mute them. We're kind of under investigation here and I just want both of you to try and watch yourselves."

"Mom," I say, "is it true that they found Dad to be off-mission?"

She looks down, not at me. "Let's walk, boys, let's not take the conveyor." We walk along the street, like we used to when I was a kid, before the conveyors made it all the way into the suburbs. "I have a hearing coming up. You're both allowed to be there, if you want, since it concerns all of us and your father. But, I thought you both might have noticed a few sorts of differences with your other-father lately." We both nod our heads. "We can't pay for the holo program anymore. We can't even afford how much we've used already, and regulations say we need to keep it operational for several more months. I'm hoping that this hearing will go well and everything can try and get back to normal, but I can't find a single lawyer that we can afford who will stand up against an Americorp lawyer in an Americorp policy case.

"Until this is all over with, though, we have to keep the holo program on. I've been reading up on it, and, if we turn it off, it looks like we're admitting liability. We have to continue to be open and honest with your father while he's on, as well. But the worst part is that we have to downgrade the service because of our credit."

"What'd ya mean, Mom?" Comet asks.

"What I mean is that he's on sponsorship mode. For the foreseeable future, while dealing with this hearing and your father's mission record and protection plan, he's going to have to stay on sponsorship mode. It doesn't pay for all the operations, but it pays for a lot. The ironic thing is that if our credit were better, not only would it pay for itself, but it would pay for the time that we've used and we could even end up on top. But as things stand, it's going to help us squeeze by. And, depending on how things go, we may have to have him on a lot longer than we want."

"How come he wasn't on sponsorship mode before, if it's cheaper?" I ask. We're cutting across a park now that used to be one of the older high schools. It was shut down and the buildings were torn down, but nothing has been developed here. I've heard talk of it being turned into a golf course, but Callaway is doing a data analysis to see if it would oversaturate the area and force prices at their other courses to drop. So for now, it's up in the air.

"When your father was in good standing," Mom says, "Exxon paid for the program. It's supposed to be healthier for the families. The effect on divorce rates alone was enough to convince us. They paid for the whole thing during deployment and the investigation period. Now, though, if things don't get fixed, we owe for all of that time, too. All of it. And to be honest with you, boys, I don't know exactly how we're going to weather this."

"It's not fair," Comet says, sulking like a little boy who didn't get what he wanted for Sweetest Day. "It's not fair and we shouldn't have to pay for any of it. Dad was doing his job when he died. The whole thing is a lie. There has to be some way to prove that it was a lie!"

"We can't," Mom says. "Our best bet is to prove that the company made a mistake in the paperwork and that the mistake is enough to prove that we aren't liable."

"But that's not the issue!"

"I know that it's not the issue. But it's our only way

out."

"Look," Mom says, pausing at the entrance to the rail station, "we have to keep our mobiles on from now on. We have to put up with what's going on. We have to act like everything is okay. There's a big eye on us right now and we can't talk about any of this openly. We can be heard anywhere. All of those measures that are in place to keep everyone safe and sound around the clock are working against us all of a sudden." Mom's eye is drawn up above the station to the new Cialis sign that has been put up. "They own his very image right now," she says. "We have to act like this is alright, just until we know what to do."

"We saw this yesterday, Mom," I say. "I just, I'm sorry. We should have said something."

"No," she says quickly, her eyes closed. "Don't say anything. It could happen again. He was a good-looking guy and they can use his image for free. And, they have all the footage they could ever hope for since he did all that recording for the holo program. But, it's part of our protection, part of how we'll dig ourselves out of this mess, if at all possible."

I can see that she's trying hard, and she's doing a great job of holding it together. I don't think she meant to walk this far, all the way to the rail station. She's still in her robe over her pajama pants, her hair up and tangled. But her face is hard, like it's carved out of wood, not soft and drooping like it's been these past weeks.

Comet looks the same, but harder. He's angry and I can see it boiling inside of him. I feel like a middle child, standing here in the grass outside the station. My mom determined to make things work, to play the system, my brother wanting to burn it down. I'm somewhere in the middle, wanting to make more noise about it than Mom, but not wanting to break rules that are going to dig us in deeper.

"Turn on your mobiles when you get on the train. I'll turn mine on when I get back. We're going to play it cool, do you hear me, Comet? We're going to play it cool and I'm going to read everything I can without making it look like we're admitting libel. You boys do well on your tests, listen to your father without egging him on. Go to the damn War Games, even though I'm really against it. Just remember that poor Porsche when you're watching. Remember that your father didn't approve of them making war into some kind of game in the first place and look where war brought him and where it brought this family. I know that everyone thinks it's lots of fun, but I feel like our whole society has been desensitized to war through those things. Maybe that was the idea.

"Now if you two need to meet, you do what you did yesterday—you make a study date after school. Post it on your walls, invite friends if you want to, but then go off on your own. You can always mute your apps while you have your readers opened to your textbooks. Your Lifeline will show you're studying and nothing will look suspicious. For now, anyway. I don't know what you can do—probably nothing, but you can talk without posting things and not show any suspicious activity. When this is all over—if it's all over—we can go back to normal. It just won't bode well for our defense if Americorp is constantly seeing us discussing this, posting about how much we dislike it. I don't know what it will do, but it won't help, I know that."

This is seriously the most I've heard Mom talk in ages, and the first time I think that she's bossed us around like this since I was learning how to ride a Huffy. "Mom," I say, "you seem different. Strong."

"Are you on something new?" Comet says.

"I'm off of everything," she says. "For right now, anyway. So long as I can breathe on my own, I want to be off of everything. I'm not stupid enough to think that it's a good idea, or that it's going to be easy. But life isn't easy. Not anymore, anyway. And I want to see it with my own eyes, even if those eyes are flawed. I miss your father so much— and that damn replacement, it rips me, boys. It rips me. And here I have with me two little versions of him." She grabs us close all of a sudden and kisses our heads deliberately. I'm as embarrassed as a second grader whose mom kisses him in front of the whole school. I look around to make sure no other kids are watching. "Two little versions of him. And I can't let the wolves take you away like they took him away."

She's holding and squeezing my left hand, and her left hand is holding and squeezing Comet's right hand. Without thinking of it, and totally embarrassingly, I notice that I'm squeezing Comet's other hand with my free hand. We're this little circle of family in the middle of the grass, hiding out from our mobiles.

We walk away without saying another word. Comet turns on his Mobile 11 and I flip the mute button on my Mobile 12 and we both check-in at the rail station. An ad at the platform notices us and starts in, "hey Dodge, hey Comet! Try Noon Burger today and get Coke for half-off with the activation code in your inbox!"

As it pulls out of the station, I can see the back of Mom's robe as she cuts across the field where the school used to be. Her hair is messy, all up in a headband. I think to myself that this is the first time I've seen Mom since Dad joined the Peacekeepers.

Chapter 9

Dad never let me go out for the War Games team. I wanted to—everyone wants to—but by the time I was old enough, Dad was already out of his old job and recruited into the Peacekeepers. On his first tour to protect the Rainforest holdings, three of the men he trained with were killed by land mines when they advanced into a rival holding. He tried to rush one man back to base. The man had lost a leg. Dad tied a tourniquet around what was left. Dad pulled him through the jungle as the man kicked and screamed. He told us about it after he got home from tour—he didn't want to tell us over the halo. It was traumatic enough for him to say that we shouldn't go into the Peacekeepers, no matter what the job market was. And it was enough for him to say that we shouldn't play on the War Games team. It's actually pretty common that kids of Peacekeepers don't play on the team.

The first stage of each game is the Strategies, or Tactics, stage. A terrain is picked at random and borders are drawn based on each team's record. The better the record, the more favorable the positioning. The Officers Division works for about two hours before the game even starts, learning the terrain and gathering intelligence on the other team's forces. They also learn how their own forces work out for the game at hand—support, fuel resources, weapons allowance, and all the regular factors that go into a war. This is all based on the team's season strategy and team strength. Every time you win a battle, you gain some of their assets. Everything is up for grabs that doesn't involve Ground Forces—natural resources, budget, intelligence, anything strategic. Fans get a full readout on their halos, and, for the most part, the games are won and lost during this stage of the game. The Ground Forces are the sexy part—the part everyone loves to watch— but they're a small piece of the puzzle.

Then, about two hours before the Ground Forces enter the stadium, the Officers order their strikes. Obviously, the target of this stage is to give your Ground Forces as much of an advantage in battle as possible. But, the really strategic teams will try to leave as many resources on the other side intact as they can, so they have a good chance of building up their forces. This is where the weaker teams can really carry an advantage; the strong teams get cocky, but to really have a powerful victory, they want to take as many resources as they can. If a strong school beats out a weak one and just wipes them out entirely without taking much for later matches, no one really cares about the victory. But, if they can manage a takeover, take nearly all of their resources, even cripple them from playing the next few games on their schedule, then it becomes something to brag about. This kind of posturing leaves them open, strategically, and the weaker team doesn't have nearly as much to lose, and much more than they can take, even in a modest victory.

While the strikes are being made, there's a lot of realtime strategy going on. Lily tells me that this is the really exciting part. Intelligence is coming in, reports are being made, and the Officers have to process all of the information and make quick decisions. As part of the Missile Defense team, Lily has her work cut out for her. Most of the actual work is in budget and placement, but then when the strikes start, she gets to see how effective everything is, move around any mobile defense forces, and watch the numbers come in. Games are won and lost in this section of the game and most people just catch up on it with their mobiles while riding the rails into the stadium or having dinner with their family.

There's a 30 minute break between the initial strikes and the Ground Forces strike. At this point, the terrain is being built in the stadium and the Ground Forces are getting numbers to work off of: how much ammo they have left in the budget; how much armor; how much air support is still flyable. Lately, jungle settings have been in style. The problem with them is that there is usually so much coverage that it's hard to see the game as it unfolds below the trees. There's usually a pretty big clearing worked in, but the forces tend to naturally avoid them. You have to look up on the big Clear Channel to catch most of the action, and, of course, the mobiles carry the helmetcams of every player. You can switch between players at will, or you can watch the expected highlights on the stadium's main channel.

This part does get really exciting, and even though the Officers could be seen as much more important, it's the Ground Forces that get most of the glory. This is where the stars are made. This is why Mick is such a popular guy at school and gets three periods of class time just to focus on getting in shape and working on strategic maneuvers for the team. The Ground Forces portion fills the stadium and fuels the nighttime news channels during the War Games season. Most of a high school's budget goes into the stadium design and upkeep. It's really expensive, but it's also really important. Lots of studies have shown that if students and society have a safe and protected way to work out their aggressions, then the whole world becomes safer. So it's an important part of our community and, actually, an important part of our education.

But this is also where the big signing bonuses come from for the various branches of the Peacekeepers. All the big corporations who hold a portion of the Peacekeepers keep watch on the high school teams so they can sign them before they're snatched up by rivals. Mick has pretty high hopes that he can go pro, but his mom is kind of torn up about it. She knows the family could use the huge jump in credit that would come along with a signing like he's hoping for, but she's also worried about the idea of him going to battle for real.

Lily, however, has a lot different prospect. The colleges scout the Officers and give out major scholarships. Of course, they have to sign on to go to Officer's school after college and commit five years to being an officer. The thing is, just being captain of Missile Defense isn't really a big position to look for. You don't really see a lot of them pulling in huge scholarships or anything. Missile Defense looks great on an application if you're looking to major in mathematics or something totally impractical like that. It looks fine on a business major application or a Law and Policy major, but only because it shows leadership experience and the ability to concentrate. What really matters, though, is practical, direct experience, like if she were on Mock Stock Managers or something. And, naturally, none of that matters without the right credit score to afford a major like that.

There aren't enough resources and time, with all the academics we have to learn, for every student to take Physical Education. You can get credit for doing physical activities outside of school and having a parent sign off or by watching school sponsored sports. You have to actually watch the games and write about them and then you don't have to enroll in one of the PE courses. That's what I do. I go to every War Games home match and write about it. I'm allowed out of class early on those Fridays so that I can watch the strategic strikes at the very beginning. Today, my brother comes with me, so he can get out of his school early and meet me at the stadium. He took the rail over and actually beat me to the stadium because I took the long way around campus to enjoy the weather today.

When I get there, Comet holds out his mobile to me.

"Check this out," he says, "Holodad sent me a

coupon code for chicken burgers. All I have to do is like Noon Burger's stadium location on LB."

"Cool, what's the deal?"

"It's just 5 percent, but then that compounds every time I mention the chicken burgers or eating at the stadium, so it's possible that by the end of the night it could be 50 percent off of one of them, if I buy two. I'm working out if it's worth it right now or not, since Noon Burger doesn't sell Pepsi, I would lose my GenerationNext ticket discount."

"You could use mine," I say. "I can buy both our tickets."

"Cool," Comet says. "Like Noon Burger, GenerationNext stadium, Cable High," he commands to his mobile.

"I wonder why he sent it to you and not me," I say.

"I don't know, but if I tag a picture of you eating a chicken burger on LB, I get a free Coke."

"That'd be so fucked up," I say. "We'll find someone else who likes Pepsi drinking a Coke to tag." All they sell in the stadium is Coke, that's why Pepsi bought the name rights.

I take Comet to the Observation Gallery at Mission Command. There's seating for 100 people or so, and it's kept really dark and quiet so the people in Mission Command can't see them behind the glass. Screens show closeups of some of the decision makers in action, and other screens show the simulation of what's happening out on the battle field. This is the first glimpse that you get of what the stadium setup will look like. Today we're playing W. Bush High and we're strongly favored to win. Not only that, but we have a big strength advantage, but we also have a huge tactical advantage on the field. Our forces have higher ground and we've amassed a missile command at the top of a waterfall, overlooking the rest of the battlefield. Waterfalls are, for whatever reason, always really popular with a crowd, so they usually save them for bigger matches.

I show Comet where to read what the stakes are. We're playing on a field that is 100 virtual acres, fighting over 3,000 acres of rainforest, or enough to legally offset eight major corporations for a year of carbon activity. We're coming in with massive reserves in fuel, where Bush has hardly enough fuel to get its fighters in the air and their troops to the front line. But one thing they do have is fantastic naval support. They must have really pumped their budget into their navy really early on. I guess that shouldn't surprise me, because, as I read in the program, their coach was a naval captain during the Great War. The problem is, their budgeting was so lopsided that they hardly have the fuel reserves for their navy fighters at all, and I wouldn't be surprised if they don't even try to strike with them in favor of moving more Ground Forces into the front lines. You can expect a lot of cruise missiles, though, and our team's

Intelligence doesn't have really conclusive figures on the amount of cruise missiles that they're packing.

I point out to Comet how Bush's team is based in the ruins of an enormous city. It gives them nice home base coverage and, if they don't surrender before pulling back to the city, we should see some really cool combat terrain if we can push them back. I love seeing urban battle terrain in these games, and it can usually make it last longer, giving a real tactical advantage to the losing team. Once in a while, you'll even see a lesser team bait a better team into the city and those matches can go on all night.

"You're just totally assuming that we're going to be winning," Comet says. "They haven't even run a first strike and you're talking about them retreating 50 miles? Is it really that predictable?"

"When you look at the budgets and the size difference in the schools and the histories so far this season, yeah, I'd say, it is that predictable."

"How boring."

"War is generally predictable," I say, "as far as who's going to win, anyway. The human part of it is unpredictable. Who's going to live, who's going to die. How men and women will act under extreme pressure with their lives on the line. That's where the drama is."

Comet takes a bite of his chicken burger and thinks

while he's chewing, "is that what this is really about? Drama?"

"For the spectators. What else would it be about?"

"Don't know. Rallying people together, spending this kind of money, building this huge monument to a mock war. It feels like just some kind of social reinforcement."

"What are you talking about?"

"We're just reinforcing these pretend heroics. Pretend drama. I mean, if these people were really facing death, would they behave the same way? Why don't they just televise what's going on in Central America? Why isn't Dad's death all over the Clear Channel for the whole world to eat up?"

I don't really know how to answer him. "Real war is messy, I guess, in addition to dramatic," I say at last.

"I read something by George Orwell the other day. I was looking up essay examples. And he said that no one is really brave, they're just scared to look like a coward. You think that's true, or do you just think Orwell was scared of being a coward?"

"I don't guess I'd know. I don't know about Orwell and I've never been in a war. Maybe you're overthinking it; this is sport. It's friendly. They don't really die, so it's easier to digest."

"I guess they sometimes do, though."

"Just the once."

The first strike starts with a burst. The screens show that one of Lily's missile defense outposts over the waterfall has been wiped out by a clandestine insurgency. The Captain starts tearing into the head of Intelligence and she starts yelling back about not being budgeted properly. Lily is furious and starts trying to get another unit mobilized before the missile strike comes in. That was her most forward position, and it leaves some of our air forces as sitting ducks. Just like she was afraid of, a barrage of cruise missiles comes in from the enemy subs that surfaced.

It's impressive, really. Our forces weren't ready to strike at all yet, everything still getting into position and Mick and the Captain were even stewing over maps of the city for the eventual battle there later tonight when we were struck. Their smaller, more nimble force hit exactly where they should have to disable the most of our forces they could have with as little expenditure as possible. From the other side of the Mission Control wall, you can hear their Mission Control and gallery light up in cheers. Our mobiles flash with the news that our forward air forces and missile defense positions have been 90 percent compromised. Their clandestine team was a total loss, and there's no telling how much of the missile battery is used up, but it's clearly started out as their game.

Instead of staying the course and getting back into a strong defensive posture, the Captain instantly orders a strike, pulling bombers from the far back lines, sending a barrage of missiles aimed at their radar bases. Lily is quickly regaining her positioning on the top of the waterfall and new fighters are being ordered up from our reserves. It's impossible to say just yet how effective our counterstrike is, but it's massive and expensive and meant to be as intimidating as possible, I can tell.

It isn't long before the galley fills up with spectators who were gathered in the stadium food court and bars that want to see what these upstarts did first hand. Every other screen is showing a constant replay of the clandestine insurgency, and our fans are getting rowdy and angry and cheering our Officers on, even though they're supposed to be quiet at this stage of the match. Lots of the dads who are here are former players themselves and they're already quite drunk from the stadium bars, and loud enough to prove it.

It gets loud enough that, after a while, the action is harder to follow by watching the Control Room, and Comet and I have to resort to scanning through the various channels on our mobiles to keep up. It gets bad enough that we finally decide to leave the gallery and go out to the food court until it's time to take our seats in the stadium itself.

"Okay," he says when we get outside, "that was pretty wise."

"It was, wasn't it?"

"Yeah. And intense. I sort of forgot what it was we were watching in the first place. It was nice that your attention is pulled in so many directions at once. I didn't feel like I needed to check my Lifebook or my mail or anything once the action started. There was enough for like, every branch of my attention."

"That's what I really dig about it," I say. "I always tell Mom that I just go because I get credit, so I have to, but I really lose myself for a few moments at a time and don't log every little part of my day."

"Crap, that reminds me that if I want to save any money at all, I've got to start talking Noon Burger up a little more on this thing."

We wander around the stadium a little and I introduce him to a few people I go to school with. He's a real charming guy, my little brother, and I think that he's more excited about starting high school than he lets on at home. God, after all, who would want to be stuck in junior high all those years, spending every single day building a simulated living system with fictional jobs and incomes and houses and dependents and figuring all of that stuff out? I remember those days, and sometimes it was fun, but most of the time you're just sitting at home at night, crunching numbers to try and save money on your budget, only to have a new scenario thrown at you the next day and your daughter needs braces and all of your savings vanish and your credit rating downgrades your job and all of that junior high stuff. I think that the whole system is designed to make you feel like a failure all the way up to graduation then all of a sudden, boom, your assets mature and you're retiring and your kids have great jobs. It builds faith in the system—everything works out in the end and the goal is a happy one—but it really feels like a rollercoaster ride along the way.

Man, after junior high, learning all these academics seems easy. Maybe that's the idea; give us some life experience so we don't take school for granted.

We take our seats a little early and, for the most part, the 50,000 person stadium is empty, except for Comet, me, and a few hundred people wandering around looking for their seats.

"I'm tagging you in this one, man," Comet says. "Dodge can't wait to get his hand on another Noon Burger Chicken Burger at halftime."

"Comment," I say into my mobile. "As long as Comet's paying, I'll eat any burger he throws at me."

We laugh. Then, a new comment shows up. It reads, "glad you boys are out enjoying yourselves tonight. Go, Cable Tigersharks! Have a Coke on me, I've transferred the funds." And it's by Dad. I mean, it's by Holodad and we both know it, but it says it's just Henry Goode and has his profile picture and doesn't say anything about it being anything else except it says "Sponsored" after the comment in little, gray lettering. Comet and I both look at each other. His mobile lights up and, sure enough, two Coke credits redeemable at the food court show up.

"Like," he says, and his little thumb-up logo appears next to the comment. Then he turns to me, "if I like comments and statuses with Coke mentioned, I earn more Choice Points." I nod. We're quiet for a while, and then he lifts his mobile up and says, "invite Scott Goode to study session at the Wasabi food court on Saturday, noon. Yes, I'm sure, even though they sell Pepsi products."

The invitation comes through and I approve it. The stands start to fill up, and we check out our mobiles to see what else has happened during the initial strike session before the teams take the field. As expected, we look to have a major lead already, having lost almost zero Ground Forces and our air support is almost entirely replenished. Somehow, in the shuffle, Lily is being blamed for losing the missile defense position by not having enough security administrators in the surrounding area. She doesn't get credit for her quick reactions and being able to reestablish that foothold. And Intelligence doesn't get the bad buzz, like it should. I register my dislike for it on Lifebook, and so does Comet.

"She's cute," he says. "How old is she?"

"My age—too old for you."

"I'm not saying anything."

"Yeah, you kinda are. And I think she likes Mick, anyway."

Mick takes the field right then, ushering in his forces behind him. He stands at the top of the waterfall, right out in the open, and raises his weapon in the air and yells some kind of battle cry. The stadium erupts in applause and hollers.

The other team, which had their Ground Forces cut in half and have almost no known air support left, sneak onto the field and take up positions under the cover of the foliage on their side of the base. Almost immediately after the opening whistle sounds, cruise missiles stream across the stadium toward Mick and his team. The repositioned missile defense fires a shower of lasers and wipes the missiles out in the middle of the sky, and the explosions are so many and so intense that the crowd is silent for a moment before erupting in cheer.

"Shit! That was so real," my brother yells. "It's wise, man! Wise!"

"I know, right?" I say. "Since we became an A-squad, our stadium upgrade has really been intense."

There's a flag on the other team, I read on the mobile, for having their missiles in the air from their navy before the opening whistle sounded. They're penalized fuel reserves, which hardly really matters at this point, since they have everyone in place and almost no aircraft coverage at all. They have to rely on hiding and surprise tactics to make any ground at all, so I guess they thought the risk of sending the missiles before the whistle was worth it, on the off-chance that they could make a dent in our Ground Forces.

The ensuing battle is exciting at times, and tedious at others. It's a game of cat and mouse, as Mick leads our forces forward, trying to move quickly before the other team can safely reposition. But the other team is practiced at this cascading retreat, falling back and attacking, falling back and attacking, so that it slows Mick's progress quite a bit.

There's one really cool moment when Reg Hansen, our Gunnery Sergeant, makes a clean headshot on one of their insurgents. The helmet lights up red, signaling that it hit his head, and sends a shock into the brainstem dropping the player immediately. The replay roles over and over on the Clear Channel in the center of the stadium and the player's life lies in mock lifelessness for the rest of the match. The moment is almost instantly tweeted and retweeted on everyone's Lifeline.

The other team has a good reserve of mines, it turns out, and that further slows Mick's progress, as they are constantly checking for them. Why this team's defense wasn't taken seriously by our side really makes me question how the whole season will go. Mick can't afford to make a foolish mistake at this stage of the season. If he gets knocked off by a mine, he'll come across as a neophyte. But, if he is too cautious, he'll look like a weenie. He has to strike a good balance in order to keep his standing as one of the top players in the district.

"It was a mine that did it, right?" Comet asks.

"Yeah," I say, "it was a mine."

"You were here?"

I nod.

"What was the deal?"

"Someone hacked it, they think. Or traded it out. There wasn't a lot of press afterwards, you know, because they didn't want attendance to drop around the country when it was just an isolated incident."

"How could someone do that? Hack it, I mean."

"They probably couldn't, now. And it could have been an accident, like a malfunction. Or something from the Peacekeepers that got mixed in. But they don't think so."

"But they don't act like real explosives."

"No," I said, "they don't. They cause the shock vests and helmet to react when triggered, and within a certain radius you're just injured, and if you're right on top it if, you die," I say. "Porsche was right on top. She should have checked, but the crowd was cheering her on, and she was almost going to hunt down the last of their men. And for a girl to make the final kill? That had never happened in the country. It was going to be amazing."

"Maybe someone on the other team couldn't handle it."

I shake my head. "The official report is that someone acted alone with the sole motive of harming War Games coast-to-coast. Like a fear tactic to get people to stop watching the games."

"Who?"

"Some intellectual, I don't know. Terrorists. Islamists. Radicals. Someone who was jealous. There are all kinds of official profiles of who it could have been, what they could have been like. It covers like every kind of outcast type there is, so it just shows that they really don't know what happened."

"Outcasts are bad for society, they say."

"You bet," I agree. "There's a reason they're cast out."

"You afraid?" he questions, quietly. "You afraid we'll end up as outcasts?"

I give him a hard look. To shut up. We're struggling, but we can't let on to our mobiles.

We keep watching the game, and I'm kind of amazed

at how quickly the thing ends up in the urban zone. The waterfall and jungle scenes are long gone. At one point, their insurgents are taking cover under an old freeway of some kind, and then, the next thing you know, buildings are towering over streets in the middle of the stadium. Most of them are blown out and, thanks to our Intelligence, the building that houses their headquarters is highlighted for everyone to see. I keep thinking that at any moment they're going to throw in the towel and give up, so that they have some resources left for future matches. But they don't.

The insurgents are getting harder and harder to find. The traps are getting thicker and thicker. At one point, Mick starts to lead his troops down a narrow street, stops in his tracks, and backs up to take cover. He orders an airstrike, which is really kind of rare this late in the game, and looks like a really bad use of resources, but it results in the death of 20 snipers in the alleyway. Twenty! This is an unheard of quantity of forces to keep up your sleeve until the final stage. Once they're cleared out, our troops just march into their headquarters and the game is over. We stand and cheer, and highlights instantly start playing on the screen. All of the dead players are released from their paralysis and stand up to shake it off and shake hands with the other team.

On the rail ride home, I watch the mobile to see the post-game interviews. Mick is on there, all covered with sweat, but with this big ol' smile on his face. "I realized that this whole advance felt too easy. Too much like a bait," he said. "They started out strong with that shocking attack back in the Officers session, and I think that was supposed to make us think they were playing a strong offense. If they could have baited us into that alleyway at the end, we would have had to pull more Ground Forces and we'd be playing this game all the way till breakfast time. It would have been humiliating."

I smile at this, knowing that Mick is showing that he trusted his gut, and a trust-your-gut move at this point in his career is really amazing. Like terribly amazing to pull off like he did. I know that the scouts are really paying attention now. This is really great for him, but I know it means I will be seeing less and less of him in the coming weeks.

"Dude, I'm tired," Comet says. "Those things really are way better in person."

"See?"

"I mean, that was definitely better than my Dreamcatcher. I wonder if I can play the game on it tonight."

"Jeez," I say. "That would be cool. I don't think they have that set up. Maybe you should patent that. Is it really cooler than Jungle Forces?"

"No," he says. "I guess it was only that exciting because it was in person. I mean, a DC program is great and all, but this felt pretty damn cool, sitting and watching. Too bad it was such a one-sided victory."

"You should see next time we play Reagan. I mean, I'm guessing it'll be impossible to get tickets because it'll be the first time we play them since the disaster. The tickets will go to the highest credit scores first. But they have some really good players, and this year we might actually give them a run for their money. Lily and Mick were talking about how they've been strategizing for them all year. They may not go to state or anything, but they want Reagan to know they've met their match, even if Reagan goes all the way."

We have two more stops before we get to our station. It's nearly midnight, and I don't think I can remember a time when the two of us hung out longer than this, lately. I check the mobile and it looks like Mom is still awake, catching up on the news, according the LB. I wonder if she's really catching up on the news, as she says, or if she's trying to research how to fight her legal problem without violating user policy. It's tough to prove yourself right against Americorp without being charged with slander. In a court of policy, everything is a matter of record, and if you say anything that could possibly hurt the corporation, you're damaging their reputation and can be charged for that criminally. It's a really sticky situation.

I see Comet starting to nod off. We're passing by the business district, and I can see a lot of the shops outside closing. I remember when I was in middle school, when I was doing the life simulation stuff, how exciting it was. We went on a field trip to the career center in the business district to talk about possible future jobs and salaries and everything. It was the first time I had ever seriously thought about the future and it was such an exciting time.

"What's your job?" I ask Comet.

"What?" He snaps awake. "For the simulation?"

"Yeah."

"I'm an asset manager," he says. "I qualified for it at the end of seventh grade. It was a big step up from retail, but I did some extra night classes and stuff and passed the Series 7. You know, the simulated Series 7. And since it's still dealing a lot with customer service, I could get in based on experience and not credit."

"How about the family stuff?"

"Um, I've got three kids," he says. "It's expensive. Like, knowing what I know now, I probably would have stopped at one or two, because it really hurts your credit when you have more than two."

"Who are you married to?" I ask. You spend the first whole semester of seventh grade dealing with dating and marriage. They put a huge emphasis on the importance of this decision—the timing, the finances involved, and personality traits that are important in a partner. You spend a lot of time in mock social situations, meeting, dating. Lots of people have fun with this, but I remember it being really stressful because you really had to work hard on your personality profile so the computer could make dating possibilities that were accurate. I just didn't like looking at myself that closely.

"Some Kimberly girl," he says, feigning disinterest. "She's really kind of my ace in the hole. Most guys pick a girl like from the movies, you know? Some girl who's quirky and inspiring, and free in all these exciting ways."

"You didn't pick some exciting girl?"

"No, not really. Not in that way. I picked this girl who has a good education, whose parents are still married with rocking credit, and who already has a place to live with pretty low rent."

"She sounds like a gem," I laugh.

"Here's the thing: those girls from movies? They're the creation of male writers. They always represent the psyche of the male character. Like in *West Charles*, Sara totally just shows Craig what he wants to see, how he wants to see himself. Why marry an idealized version of yourself? It's disgusting."

"That's one way to look at it," I say. "You think that's what Dad did when he married Mom? Married his own psyche?"

"I don't think it works that way in real life. What's the

point of doing it in the simulation if it's not going to happen in real life?"

I sit there for a while and try and think of the men and women in my favorite movies. What's really freaky is that I feel like he has a good point.

When we get home, both Comet and I are almost knocked down with surprise. Mom is sitting at the dining room table, drinking something out of a mug and laughing with Holodad. Holodad is drinking out of a mug, too, and he's laughing so hard that he is barely able to keep his mouth closed to keep his drink in.

"Hi boys!" Mom says.

"Hey," I say.

"Good game, huh?" Holodad says.

"Oh, who won?" Mom says. "I wasn't even monitoring it."

"We won," Holodad says. "But it wasn't just that, we captured a lot of their naval forces, didn't we, boys? That friend of yours is something else. He has a real shot at joining us in the Peacekeepers in a couple years, if I'm right."

I see Mom flinch at the idea, but she laughs anyway.

Chapter 10

After breakfast, Mom has a meeting with a customer representative from the Exxon Peacekeepers division. While I don't understand everything that they say, I can tell that it isn't going well. It's just more and more of what we feared most.

"Mrs. Goode," the representative on the Clear Channel starts, "because of security reasons, we can't go into the details involved in your husband's misfortune. What we can say, however, is that he was not in position and had broken mission protocol. Had protocol not been broken or if the initial threats indicated that there were more danger, there would be a lot more that we could do."

"Ma'am," Mom says, "my sons and I would like to end the Leave Acclimation System. We no longer require the services, and would like to end our adjustment period early. We do not have the space on our credit to continue its operation and, as you can see in your report, I am unemployed at the moment. It is too much for our credit and, frankly, it is much for us to bare."

The lady on the screen shuffles through her reader and looks at the mobile on her wrist. "I don't have clearance to end that service," she says. "There would be an additional credit charge for ending earlier than specified in your protection clause and, honestly, I don't see how you can afford it. Besides, it's not recommended by our therapist."

"Which is it? You don't have clearance or we can't afford it or it's not good for us?"

"I don't have clearance to answer that question, Mrs. Goode. I have you down to continue use for 48 months."

My mom is silent for a moment, and Comet and I lock eyes. "What?" she finally says. "We have the standard readjustment period—"

"That was before the investigation concluded, Mrs. Goode. Your loss protection policy is running on sponsorship level right now, and the only way that you can continue to run it and incur no loss is to continue with sponsorship operations for 48 months. At that time, if you've found it valuable—getting all the latest deals from the likeness of your husband and even special new bulletins and interactions—you will have the choice to extend the contract or not."

"Extend?"

"I can check with my supervisors here, Mrs. Goode, and I think that if we make the right moves, we can even upgrade your system to include your husband's presence in your automobile, if you drive much (like the driver's training program your son used), or even rail presence, as I'm seeing that has limited availability in your area. They're working on expanding the rail presence. Wouldn't it be nice to have him with you all the time? We can even send you a list of potential employers that allow presence at the workplace."

"Lady," Mom says, her tone now scolding, like when she catches me sneaking credits before a Friday night, "I am trying to end this service and you're trying to upgrade me. I would like to speak with your supervisor."

"That would be fine, Mrs. Goode. Would you like my supervisor to return your call in seven to ten days, or would you like to call back yourself on Monday when my supervisor would likely be in? With your policy here, I see that you are eligible for priority consideration when asking to speak to a member of the management team, which means that, if you sign up today and like us on Lifebook, you can skip the wait that most of our customers would incur. In addition to this service, you will also be considered when we survey customers concerning new services. Your voice will ring the loudest, giving you the kind of personal consideration that we pride ourselves on."

Mom reaches forward and tries to flip the Clear Channel off, but a big red X shows up in the corner of the screen.

"I see you are ready to end your call today," the lady on the screen says. "Would you take few minutes to rate my service? Would you say that you are satisfied, somewhat satisfied, or very satisfied with your excellent service today?"

I sneak out of the room and go into the kitchen where Holodad is sitting at the table reading the paper. He smiles at me and for a moment, I really hate him.

"You know, my real dad didn't sit around reading the paper all day long," I say, "he helped out and he had a job."

"Looks like you and Comet have a study date this afternoon," he says in return. "I'm glad to see that the two of you are taking your studies more seriously. If you would consider having a Coke, I'm pretty sure I can get your Pepsi points to transfer over. I'm not sure that I could do this tomorrow, but this is something I think I could pull off if you had a nice, cold, Coca-Cola while you and Comet are working so hard."

I bite my lip and dig through the fridge for something to eat. I sit down with a bowl of Honey Crashers, only to learn later that Holodad took a picture of me eating them and tagged me on Lifebook. It's so obnoxious.

Comet opens his reader to a chapter on personal finance and I open mine to Applied Nutrition, a chapter that highlights the better choices we can make about what we eat. For example, it says that a burger and fries have less calories than a slice of chocolate cake and ice cream; there's more fiber in a Frostie's Cinnamon Bun than in a lettuce and bok choy salad; and there are more vitamins in a fortified soda than in a bag of carrots. These are all comparisons that I have to memorize for the final at the end of the year, but for now I just take advantage of having my mobile muted and talk to Comet.

"I don't see this going so good," he says to me. "I don't know if I can stand living in the house with this walking Lifebook app for the rest of my life. He's less and less like Dad."

"Forty-eight months isn't the rest of your life," I say.

"No, but do you think they'll let it go at that? There will be some other issue, some other excuse to renew the contract. They knew this shit when they installed it. It wasn't enough that Dad had to give his life to protect the holdings of the corporation, they've got to keep using him even in death. They're going to bleed his family dry."

"Mick said he saw him on another Pfizer ad in the subway," I say. "They have some big before and after diet ad and he's the after shot."

"Holy Dollar," Comet says. "How many other dead Peacekeepers do you think there are out there in advertisements?"

"It might not end there," I say. "He could show up in movies or Dreamcatcher programs, for all we know. Did you know that Jimmy Stewart and Bruce Lee have been dead for a century and that they never even met each other?"

"That's what you were saying when we went and saw that last picture of theirs. Hard to believe, with their on-screen chemistry and all."

"I've been thinking that you're right, that it might not

end at the 48 months. I think that things may be out of control, Comet, they really might be. Exxon or Americorp or whoever is going to own us for the rest of our lives. We won't even remember Dad if we're not careful. He'll have always been this alien in our lives. And I don't think there's anything we can do about it, not with our credit rating the way it is."

"That's what I kind of wanted to talk about," Comet says. "I've been reading a lot about this movement. Look, don't have that expression on your face, just listen to what I have to say. Supposedly it's some group that's really into personal freedom and the reestablishment of an American Government to be the voice of the people—"

"Dude, you can't be reading this stuff right now. You can't. They can so easily look at what you're reading."

"I'm reading it at school, man, in the library. Not on my reader. I'm not stupid. Besides, I can read whatever I want."

"On a reader that you've logged onto with your ID, right?"

"No, see, that's the thing. I got a generic ID from a friend of mine who sells them."

"What, now you're buying fake IDs?" I stand up and look down on him.

Comet gets this hurt and pissed off look on his face

that he always gets when he thinks I'm treating him like a little kid. But really, he should know better than this, and I feel like he does know better and that's why he's feeling so down about my scolding.

"I'm just using them to read. Can I tell you what I'm reading, or are we just sitting by and watching everything happen?"

I sit back down and motion for him to go on with whatever it is he has to say. "You're technically allowed to read anything you want, Comet. But it brings suspicion. Why would you do this?"

"They're called the New Paradigm. And they say that it was their founders that created the Bovine Plague to show how foolish it was to have genetically identical cattle."

"No one caused that," I say, "I've seen chatter about that, but it's not true. You're some kind of conspiracy theorist now? Are you some kind of clown jihadist?"

"Just listen, man. Okay? They may have something to what they're saying. And they have a bunch of stories of people who have had their Acclimation units forced onto them in Sponsorship mode. It's new, but we're not the first ones. Evidently, it's more and more common."

"Really?"
"They have directions on how to get it *turned off*."

I sit there for a second and look at my brother's face.

He has no idea how dangerous this is or what he's messing with. Middle schoolers get so stuck in their habits from the simulation that often they forget the impact that they can have on real life and just how serious this is.

"Did you hear what I said?"

I take a bite of my burrito and nod my head.

"I think we can get it turned off. And not only that, there's a hack to get the records changed. You can either make it look like your contract is up, which works great unless you're audited, or you can even hack in and make it look like *it's still going on*. Of course, that's a little harder and we'd need to probably have someone come in and do it for us."

"Comet," I say just a little too loudly, "do you have any idea what you're saying? If we tried this and we screwed things up, we're looking at Reintegration for Mom, probably. *Reintegration*! Do you know what that means for us? Holodad can't watch us and take care of us, at least not legally, and we'd be put right into the system. Mom would have to be retrained to work, some lower job, probably. She'd have to prove that she's a reformed consumer of society before she's let go."

"But Mom isn't doing anything. I would do it, or you, or both of us and Mom would be blameless."

"Dude, you don't want to go to Reintegration. It

would scar you for life. It would puncture our credit and you'd go to vocational high school and never get to live the American dream of purchasing happiness because you'd never have one dime to press against another, working yourself to death while just barely floating enough credit to keep your family in housing. Haven't you learned anything in middle school through the life simulations?"

Comet sits there quiet now, pushing his noodles around with a plastic fork. He's feeling all put upon, like I just tore him to pieces and I guess I kind of did. But what he's talking about goes beyond having to see our dad sell pharmaceuticals and give us coupon codes and provide a marketing window into our lives. At least with all of that, our debt might get paid off and we might live a normal adulthood. With what he's talking about, the stakes are just too high. And I don't think it's a good time to play revolutionary.

"It was just a thought, Scott," he says. And now I know he's really pissed at me because he never calls me Scott unless he's really pissed off at me. "I mean, there are all kinds of other stuff about them, too."

"Like what?"

"I read that they have some kind of plan to kill off the corn. That the corn is all genetically identical, too, just like the cows were and that there must be some kind of a kill switch. Something that could cause them to become infected and start spreading it around to all the corn."

"That's insane. Everything runs on that stuff. That's like end-of-the-world nonsense."

"It makes sense though, right? Like a reset button on all of society. It's really the only way to bring things back down."

"Down to what?" I say. "Cavemen times? Industrial Revolution times? What's the goal here, Comet?"

He doesn't even look up at me, just down at his plate. He's been thinking about all this stuff for a while, I guess, and is just now getting the guts to talk to me about it. "To being *human* again. Not just apps. Not just product-users, consumers. Wouldn't it be nice if I could just have my relationship with Dad and have that be it? Wouldn't it be nice if we could just meet up without scheduling it, you could just like something without announcing it? You could have goals in life that are defined by you and not just reminded to you by whatever it is that is constantly reminding us of what we said we were?"

"I like to think that things haven't gone that far," I say. "I like to think that this *is* natural, that this *is* human. It's all created by humans, right? How could we do something so against ourselves? We've come so far, survive so much longer, we are so much healthier than ever before."

"See what I mean?" he looks up at me now. "You're

just mouthing what you've been told."

"You'll see," I say. "You'll see when you get to the end of your simulation this year. Everything works out. You'll retire with plenty of money, a productive family, a modest but happy home. There is a goal at the end of it all, even if it doesn't make sense along the way. The American dream works in mysterious ways."

"You think that everything is going to work out for Mom? Her husband is dead. Her job is lost. Her credit is sinking. You'll be going to college soon, only if she has the credit space to afford it. Otherwise, you'll be competing against her for a job, Dodge."

"It's not like that."

"It is."

"You're not taking the longview. We're part of something bigger than us, bigger and better and yet we're an important part."

"Like they say on *Clearkids Morning*, right? 'Always remember kids," he says in a tone mocking Captain Jackson, "you're an important cog in a functioning machine that's big and grand and moving us all forward!' Is that what you mean? Our dad died protecting their assets. That's not even enough for them. He's selling us on stuff, he's selling his own community on boner pills. Something should be done." I've never seen my brother so heated as he is now.

"It's not that I don't agree with you," I say. "We have to trust the system, Comet, that's always been true. And it looks like Mom is stepping up and doing everything she can."

"Which is nothing!"

"She's doing her best and isn't her integrity what matters? It's just like they tell you in school, cheating and trying to get around the system just harms you and your integrity. Isn't your integrity worth paying your debts?"

"Integrity? You don't even know what that means. No one does. We don't know anything about who we are. It's all colonization. We've been colonized by these values. You see that? Mom isn't responsible for any of this."

"No, but Dad is."

"Scott," Comet says, calmly, "do you really think Dad was off-mission? Do you really think that this wasn't planned from the beginning? Why should his contract even extend past death at all? Who is obligated after they *die*?"

"It was a contract that he signed, Comet."

"And as far as I'm concerned, it's goatshit. His integrity died with him and now that he's dead, they can't just replace him with whatever influences they want. It used to be considered holy, how you raised a kid, the choices you made and the values you put into them."

"Sure, and that's how people got selfish and entitled

and nearly brought the whole system down. That's why they ended the monetary system and started the credit system. It's the basis of social justice, Comet, that the corporate body, the body that matters for people's lifestyles, raises children better."

"You think that's what's happening right now?" Comet says. "You think Holodad is raising us right, or do you think he's just directing the flow of our efforts and credit? Hell, do you think that the schools are doing such a bang-up job?"

"I don't know, bro, maybe we should just study."

"This is what I brought you here to talk about," he says.

"I'll turn my mobile on, bro. I'll let it log everything you're saying and tag the shit out of you so that I don't go down for you if I have to. Don't touch that computer. Don't you try to turn that fucking thing off."

"That's not the only thing that used to be sacred," Comet says, again very calmly. "Your image, your voice, your actions, your *opinions*. They used to be sacred. It used to be seen with some kind of value beyond who those things sell to. It all used to matter."

"Drop it, bro. Drop it. This is no good. You and I have something that matters: responsibility. We can't step outside of our responsibility."

He's hurt again, I can see it. He turns his head to his reader and starts looking at the text. He shakes his head like he's trying to clear it. "You're probably right," he says after a few minutes. "It was just nice to think about is all. I just wanted you to shoot it down so I could put it out of my head."

"Trust me, man. It's no good."

"I know."

Chapter 11

Everything goes fine for a couple weeks. Holodad keeps hanging out with Mom all friendly, and Comet keeps coming with me to the Friday night War Games, and everything seems fine. Fine is what we're going for. We don't talk to Mom much about her credit repair, but it sounds like we're stuck with things the way they are for a while until a reinvestigation is planned, which won't happen for at least another year. And then, who knows what the decisions will be. So we cope and we act fine. Just fine.

I don't like being around Holodad much, but I can kind of filter him out, like advertisements on the Clear Channel. There's even a moment at dinner when Holodad asks Comet about a Dreamcatcher program and Comet gets all excited telling him about it. Then Holodad turns to me and says, "Y\you know, Dodge, they say that they're getting closer to having a DC unit that works with your blood type."

"Really? Like what?"

"There've been some breakthroughs," Holodad says. "I mean, it's all boring lab work stuff right now, but maybe it will mean you and your brother sharing an episode of Jungle Forces sometime in the near future."

"Christmas?" I say.

Holodad laughs, "not that soon."

"Not that we could afford a new DC by Christmas,"

Mom adds.

"Live a little, Maggie. If a model was working, we'd be right there with the credit, son. We wouldn't want you to miss out on culture, now would we? Culture is worth any price."

"I don't have a job," Mom says, not addressing Holodad directly. "I'm wrapped up in a policy matter. We're not outspending our credit on Dreamcatchers so that Scotty can know what's going on in *West Charles*, for God's sake."

"Don't pay any attention to her," Holodad says. "I'm thinking that when the new one comes out, some people with priority membership will get some pretty good deals on those new units. I'm guessing that there are some extra subscriptions you could take out to reach that membership level. If you like, I can look into it as new information becomes available."

Mom just looks at me with an icy expression. I nod my head. "Yeah, Dad. I could look and see how far off I am from priority. I mean, I haven't posted a lot lately and I haven't used all the sponsorships I could. Yeah. I'll take a look."

"That's my boy!" Holodad says enthusiastically and goes back to his paper. What's really terrible and unnatural about these interactions is that Holodad is totally oblivious to any kind of tension whatsoever. He can talk to Mom about jobs and he can make concerned looks on his face, but he can't pick up on when we're fighting, on how much we despise his constant plugging of goods and services. He drops by these little news items and sales pitches as if it was just normal, person-to-person interaction. Like this is just something that he heard at work or read in his ever-present newspaper and he's just passing the information on. And every time it grates on me and every time he comes across as if he has no idea. You can shut him up by acting enthusiastic and saying that you're going to share this with your friends. I'm not really excited about how normal it all seems.

Comet and I have had more study sessions, meeting at the food court or the bookstore and turning our mobiles off, but he never has mentioned the New Paradigm stuff anymore. And I'm grateful for it. We still make fun of Holodad and complain about him together, but he hasn't talked about shutting him off. I guess I objected to it hard enough that he is just leaving that alone, which is such a relief. There was one thing that he said last week that I found really interesting though.

He was talking about his family simulation in middle school. He's into a career now, already married and already has a home, and now his simulation-wife is pregnant. They already went through all the Health and Wellness stuff that that entails. But, then there's the cost analysis of having kids and he said that buried in there was something new, something I didn't have to deal with at all when I was in middle school just a few years ago.

"My job is pretty good," he told me, "and my wife was

pretty well-off coming into the relationship, and her job is probably better than mine."

"You played it right," I said. "Ignore your inner demons and choose a good working wife."

"But part of the cost analysis, since we have such high credit, is something called a Parental Absence Simulant. I sent in a question to the instruction team and found out that it's exactly like Holodad, but for private citizens, not just Peacekeepers' families during deployments. So while I'm at work, our kid won't know I'm not there. When she's at work, the kid won't know we're not there. We still have to pay for childcare, but our holo-selves can hang out with the kid all day long. No more lonely afternoons after school waiting for the parents to come home. No more late nights at the office. Families will always be together."

"Huh," I said.

"This is the new thing. Or, it will be the new thing probably before we're even out of school. For our kids, they'll always know us as ourselves and as holograms. I checked into my cost analysis and saw that the default, at least in the simulation, is to have the program sponsored. It's so expensive without it that I'd have to work way more or be way more productive or whatever. The implications."

"Dude, I don't know if I'm going to have kids," I finally say. "I mean, I guess there's time to worry about that and all, but I think that's kind of insane."

"Our kids will never know what it means to be human," he finally said at last, half to himself.

"I bet our parents were saying the same thing," I said.

"And they were right. And their parents were right, and their parents were right. All the way back. Whatever it means to be a person keeps getting redefined."

"And who are we to say that's a bad thing?"

"You sound like Captain Jackson again," he said. And we just let it lie at that.

Chapter 12

"You are aware that it is strictly against policy to shut down any system that is still under contract with Americorp or any affiliate company within the Americorp umbrella?" The man, Loss Inspector Ralph Wessels, is sitting behind a huge desk, covered in papers, with a big picture of Americorp CEO General Daniel Johnson. In the picture, Johnson is standing with a stern but confident frown on his face, his right hand lifted high over his head waving, evidently, at a crowd of onlookers.

"I am aware," I say. I'm sitting in a cushy wingback chair opposite the desk, sitting so low I can almost not see over it.

"When you took action, were you aware of what you were doing?" He doesn't look at me directly. All I see is the bald spot on his head as he shuffles through papers—actual, real, papers—and presses stamps on them.

"I was aware. I knew exactly what I was doing. I wanted the damn thing off," I say.

He looks up at me. "Not too bright, huh?"

"Excuse me?"

"It wasn't a very bright thing to do, was it? Shut off the Holo system that was under contract? You don't care about your family's credit? What, with your mom out of work you felt like kicking her when she's down?"

I nod my head in agreement. I feel like the best thing for me to do is not be antagonized. Not be intimidated. I need to just agree with whatever he says and move this thing forward before Mom and Comet get any kind of word.

"You go by Scott or Dodge?" he asks, looking back down at the papers.

"Both," I say. "It depends."

"Dodge your middle name? Your parents wanted half off?" He's referring to a promotion that Americorp Motors had in the 60s. If you named your kid with the first name of one of their models, you got a select car from that line for free. If you named your kid with it for a middle name, you got half off. My parents felt like it was better to get half off of a Dodge and not have to have it as a first name. I started going by it anyway, mostly, in grade school because so many kids had car names. It was like the cool thing.

"Yes," I say.

"But your brother," he says, "he got Comet as a first name, right? What, driving not good enough for them?" The rail lines came up with a similar deal a few years later. Name your kid after one of their more popular routes, get a pass on that line. My dad was commuting a lot then and it really helped out. Plus, they liked the name, so it worked out.

"The Dodge was stolen," I say. "Insurance didn't cover it because my mom didn't log that she had locked it that night on their site. They couldn't afford another one for a while. Everyone uses the rails now, anyway."

He shuffles papers for a while. I can hear the bustle of office work outside the door. Phones ringing, the Clear Channel rattling off numbers. Footstep after footstep passing the door. "You haven't called your mom or updated you Lifeline since you came in."

It wasn't a question, so I wasn't sure if I was supposed to answer. Then he looks up at me expectantly. "I didn't want to bother anyone," I say. "I didn't want to worry Mom."

"So you just shut the program off this morning and then rode down to the business district to report your violation."

Again, it wasn't asked, but I felt like I was supposed to respond. "Yeah, pretty much, yes. Should I not have?"

"I'm wondering why."

"I knew it was the wrong thing to do once I did it. I felt really guilty. I wanted to make things right, maybe get it turned back on and get the whole thing over with."

He shakes his head. I feel like he's waiting for me to say more, but I don't want to say any more, so I just start shaking my head too, but I try not to be sarcastic about it. Just like I agree with his disbelief or something. My hands are sweating and I'm trying real hard not to listen to my heartbeat.

"Simple as that?" he says. "Nothing else?"

"Simple," I say. "Nothing."

He keeps shaking his head, and now I feel really sarcastic when I shake mine. "I think there's more going on here," he says at last. "I think that you've been contacting someone."

"No, I didn't want to bug anyone," I say. "I haven't called Mom, you said so yourself. I felt bad, so I came to you first."

"Someone on *the other side*," he says.

Now I'm strikingly confused. "Like a ghost?" I say at last, trying to not insult his suggestion.

"From the New Paradigm. Ring any bells?"

"No."

"You checked out a library reader," he says. "Bought a fake ID, checked out a reader and downloaded a few books from the data base that maybe you shouldn't have? Made a few contacts on Lifebook with that ID? Getting a little curious about some of the bigger plans that the other side has for us? Bells ringing now, I bet."

And oh fuck. It didn't occur to me that my brother would be in this deep. It didn't occur to me that they would pull so many records so quickly. My worry must be registering on my face and I don't know what to say.

"Hear those bells?"

"No," I say. "I mean, I don't know."

"Which is it? No, or don't you know?"

Oh God, I think. I look down at my hands and try and dry them on my pants. "I don't know," I finally say.

"We can make things easier," the inspector says. "We can make them a lot easier by just coming clean now. We've been watching this house a while now, ever since this ID logged on from that location. We know what you've been up to, what books you've been reading. You've made a friendship with that Lifebook avatar of yours that's one of our people. Hell, as far as you're concerned, the entire New Paradigm group is our people."

"It's all out on the table," I say, quietly.

"You're damn right," he says. "So you want to call your Mom now?"

And I don't. I don't want to call her at all. But then again, I don't want either of them to worry, to think that I was picked up, to think I'm here against my will.

"I'm not arrested," I say.

"You're confessing."

"To violating policy," I say, "and seeking credit repair."

He nods his head and reaches into a drawer and

produces another huge stack of papers. I've never seen so much actual paper in my life. "You've done your homework," he says. "Credit repair. That might be possible."

"I want to go home now," I say. "I want to talk to my mom in person."

"Before you leave, we need to get you signed up. For credit repair, remember?"

"Yeah," I say.

"And we need you to give us your contacts. You need to tell us who approached you. You need to hand over that reader and that ID and everything else you have. You wouldn't believe how much easier this will be for you if you just hand over those contacts. I could see us navigating around some pretty strict policies based on just a few contacts from you. Sound interesting?"

I scramble in my head. "It was all a bad idea," I say. "I got rid of it. Got rid of it all after I turned the machine off. I don't have it anymore. I don't have any contacts."

The man gives me a half-smile. He almost chuckles. "You don't have any contacts? We'll see. You'll hand them over. You should do it now, I'm telling you. No laws have been broken, but this is against policy. We can send in a repairman and look the other way."

I look away from him.

"Okay. Sign this," he says, and hands me a paper that has small writing all over it. It's white paper, but almost looks grey with all of the print. I couldn't possibly read it. "It's a credit repair agreement," he says. "You didn't just turn the 'machine' off. You broke it. I've got it all right here. A machine that is worth more than the earning potential of your mom and your brother and you put together. Way out of your credit rating. Without the sponsorship, you could never pay for it. Do you hear what I'm saying? Your credit line is *annihilated*. Your mom can't buy a pack of Camels, or Marlboro Greens, which she's really going to need, until your credit is repaired. She can't get a job. You haven't just screwed yourself here and turned a little something off. *You've violated at least a hundred different Americorp policy lines.* You asked me earlier if this was an arrest? You're going to wish it was. Sign here." He points his hairy finger at a line on the bottom of the page.

I sign.

"We will see you bright and early tomorrow morning for Reintegration. Don't go anywhere besides home before the train leaves. This is a big favor, being eligible for Reintegration. You're lucky. Your mom would have been out of chances. And your brother is too young. You have a chance here to reintegrate."

Reintegration. The word hits me like a brick. Reintegration. According to the major financial institutions, I've gone too far to carry credit. I'm basically insane. I can't follow rules or be trusted. I have to be brought back into the fold. I have to be reintegrated into society in a healthcare facility.

Reintegration.

"How long," I say. "How long does it take?"

"Sorry, you're still here," he says, looking up. "I thought you wanted to go home and tell Mommy about the bad stuff you did."

"How long?"

"You've got good grades," he said. "An overachiever. An independent thinker, right? Shouldn't take you long. You'll be ready to join us and play with the big boys again."

"How long?"

"Beats me. But it's purely voluntary. You know this of course because you've already signed the agreement. To be approved for a credit line, we need to make sure that you are integrated into the values of our establishment. Without that integration, you are an outsider and must exist outside the system, which means you will find employment difficult, payment nearly impossible, with the exception of barter, and transportation privileges will be restricted. To be clear, you are not illegal under the provisions of the Unites States Government, such as they exist, but you are not a participant in the society. If you can be successfully reintegrated and shown to have your values in place, your goals in place, and your efforts in place to become a participant, you will have your credit restored and your lifestyle recoverable. Otherwise, you may receive a mental health diagnosis and will receive treatment for your affliction, so long as your insurance is valid and your family's credit is sufficient. Do you have any questions about what I have just told you and what you have just signed?"

"And my family?"

"They are treated with severe suspicion. Harboring a non-participant or potential mentally imbalanced individual is frowned upon by the establishment and credit extensions are minimized to actual earnings rather than earning potential. Since you are a minor and live exclusively off of your family's credit, your family cannot be trusted with credit any longer until you are safely within a Reintegration facility. If you are successfully reintegrated, your family's credit will be restored.

"That is our goal here today," he says all of this like he is rattling off policy from memory, "to undo any infractions you may have committed and to restore credit and credibility to the system. The system doesn't work unless everyone participates and everyone is integrated with each other. This is a question of national security and to continue to ensure the values of society—the right to life, the right to pursue wealth and purchase happiness—we must make sure that every citizen is integrated properly."

"I know all of this," I say, "I go to school."

"I see that here, buddy," he says. "I see that you retired at the end of your eighth grade simulation with quite a little credit package. This should have built trust in the system, this should have put you in a place where you couldn't have become a nonparticipant. I hope that we don't find that you've somehow cheated the school system and faked your accomplishments in integration."

"I didn't," I say. "I understand. I messed up."

The man looks me square in the eye and nods his head. "Yeah," he says, "you messed up. If you come across those names, the New Paradigm names, I'd love to hear them. I can't stress that enough. May make Reintegration go more smoothly. Maybe even get your mom an interview at that new coffee joint. Maybe. You follow?"

"Yes."

"Let's get that mobile back on your wrist. Let your mom know you're coming home. Have a big talk. Set a nice example for that brother of yours. Sound doable?"

"Yes."

"I think you're a nice kid. I've been reading this stuff for a couple days now. I think you can come back from all of this."

"Yes."

"Let's not do anything stupid. Let's go home. Let's report back here at 7:30am—no need to pack a bag—for Reintegration. You'll have papers at the desk where you check out. You'll have an access code to let your folks log in on the Clear Channel and see what you're up to, what you're doing, where you're going. You'll check in with me every month after that until graduation next year."

That was a good sign, at least, that I'll be back before graduation. Though the guy kind of makes me sick, I shake his hand and thank him profusely. I'm numb as I walk up to the counter to check out and be given my instructions for Reintegration.

Reintegration!

The word continues to echo through my head. I'm afraid that if I felt any more sane, I might lose my mind by thinking over and over about what I had done, what I signed up for. My mind keeps going back to my brother.

Everything felt a little off when I woke up this morning. It was quiet. My Clear Channel didn't wake me up and I naturally assumed that I just beat it to the punch, but it already seemed too light outside. My headphones were on, but there was no music playing, no information playing either, no update about the day. The stillness in the room overwhelmed me and seemed to have crept up on me while I slept and maybe even awoke me with its unbelievable silence.

I stood up and the lights didn't come on. There was plenty of light to see by through the window, but as much as I moved, the lights in my bedroom just wouldn't come on. It has been years since the power was out in the house and we installed a generator that would work for a week before we'd actually experience a blackout. The only blackout I've ever experienced was when I was much, much younger.

"Clear Channel," I said. "News?" And, of course, nothing happened. No helpful bulletins to let me know of any ungodly disaster that would make electronics stop working, but somehow that's the crazy conclusion I came to. I grabbed my mobile and strapped it to my wrist. It was already 7:30—which felt about right—but I was going to be late for school. I checked the headlines and didn't see anything about a storm, an earthquake, anything that would explain why we were without power. My mobile was fully charged up, so it had to have been pretty recent that we lost the power.

I went out in the kitchen, and though it was 7:30, Holodad wasn't there. He wasn't anywhere to be seen. Just as I walked down the stairs, Mom came out of the hallway wearing her robe. "What's going on, Scotty?" she asked.

"I don't know," I said. "The power seems to be out, like during the hurricane."

"Why isn't the generator on?"

"I had to disconnect it." It was my brother's voice, and it

was coming from the living room. "I disconnected the generator, then cut the power."

We walked into the living room and Comet was leaned over an open compartment in the flooring, holding some kind of pliers and looking at a set of instructions on his reader.

"I think I'm doing this right," he said, "and then I'll get everything up and running. Like it never happened."

"What in the world do you think you're doing?" Mom said, less angry than she probably hoped to sound.

"Sorry. It's taking me a bit longer than I thought it would. You should probably get ready for school, Dodge, and log in to LB and let people know you're running a little late, but that everything is fine."

"*Is* everything fine?" I asked. "What the hell are you doing?"

"Getting rid of Holodad," he said.

Mom and I looked at each other. "Honey, you can't do that. It's against the policy, we'll be fined or worse. You can't do that!"

"It will look perfectly normal," Comet said. "Please don't worry. I've soldered this back together and bypassed the whole program, I think. We'll get the power back on and it will continue to exist and to function and to report back—

only it won't be here anymore. It will exist only within the walls and it will listen in on what we have to say, but we won't have to put up with it, interact with it."

Mom's face was alarmed and both of us sat down.

"Comet, you don't know what you're doing. You don't know what you're messing with." She pleaded with him to undo what he had done, to put things back in order.

"I can't, Mom, it's too late."

When Comet switched the power back on, an eruption of sparks flew out of the flooring. All the other lights came on and the Clear Channel started blaring the newsbites and I heard the breakfast music start playing in the dining room. "It's okay," my brother said, "I knew that would happen. I expected it."

"I don't know, bro," I called out as he came back inside. "I think you fried it."

"No, no. It says that it might spark a little. That's normal."

"I don't think any of this is normal, Comet," Mom said.

Comet closed up the floorboard and then stood there looking at Mom and me. "I'm sorry I didn't ask you guys about this. I thought it was the best thing for us to do."

"You did ask me about this," I said, "and I said it was

a terrible idea."

Mom looked at us both, speechless.

"Look, we're going to be rid of him and we're going to be able to go on with some kind of a normal life and no one will be wiser. We need to get ready and get to school so there's no suspicion of any kind."

"Call in sick," Mom said.

"No," we both said at the same time.

The three of us practically tiptoed around the house, watching carefully around every corner, amazed that for the first time since it was installed years ago, there's no Dad and no Holodad lurking just around the corner. I grabbed my backpack and made a quick update saying that I was running late so I wouldn't be on my normal rail route. Comet does the same thing and we run out.

I drop Comet off at his rail station after one of the longest, quietest rail rides I've ever been on in my life. He and I just watch each other, hardly able to say a word. I start watching my mobile to avoid the constant thought about what had happened that morning.

"It'll be okay," he says at last, as we pull into his station.

"Lifebook," I say into my mobile, "invite Comet Goode to study session, 3:30pm, at Wasabi."

His wrist buzzes, he lifts his arm and says, while looking at me, "accept."

Lifebook confirms the study session and Comet gets off the train. I watch as he walks away, and, just as the doors begin to close, I grab and hold them open and run onto another platform, and barely make the downtown train. I am certain that Americorp has to know. I am certain that there is no way this is going to work. I have spent the entire ride to this station thinking about it. Comet couldn't weather being labeled an outsider. Getting put into the system that young, before the middle school simulation is completed, is a scarlet letter. You may never get a normal line of credit, always working to dig your way up.

And I know I couldn't let Mom take the fall. What in the world would we do if she had to go to Reintegration? It is impossible to fathom. The only choice that's left is for me to march into the local Americorp Policy office and confess to taking the Holodad offline. It is the only thing that can leave my family intact. It is the only choice I can live with. All I have to do is be made of steel for a few minutes, not think about what I am doing, go forward, agree with everything that the inspector says.

Part II

Chapter 13

The Reintegration facility is 200 miles away from home. Mom and Comet get to ride along with me, but it's a quiet ride, mainly, not a lot to say. The scenery outside whizzes by and the screens show our travel time and our GPS coordinates. Forty-five minutes is all I have left with them.

"You'll be out quickly," Mom says. "They'll understand where you're coming from, and you'll be out quickly. We'll recover."

"They're reinstalling the system at home," Comet says. "Dad will be back before we get there."

I give him a look, burning through my eyes, begging him and commanding him not to touch the damn thing. Comet didn't take the news really well when I told him during our study session. He saw at lunchtime that I had ended up staying home sick, posting on LB that I threw up on the rail on the way to school. I messaged him, though, telling him that I still wanted to keep our study session. He told me that he spent the entire day taking half-breaths, regretting what he had done.

"I don't know, man. I keep thinking about it and I should have started earlier. Or I should have read up more."

I shake my head. "Don't talk about it. Really. I'm taking care of it."

"What do you mean?"

I lower my voice to just above a whisper. As I talked, I open my reader and turn to a middle school textbook that talks about the dangers of social construction. "I confessed, Comet. I don't know if I'm being watched or not, but I confessed."

"What the fuck for?" Comet says, a little too loudly.

"For turning it off. They knew already. They knew when I got there. They've been watching your subversive activity and I took the fall for all of it. Don't argue with me, don't thank me, don't do anything about it. Just act like you're outraged when it all comes down to it and then take care of Mom. I'm heading to Reintegration in the morning."

Comet's face tightens and tears well up in his eyes. He says, more quietly now, "Let me go, dude. It's my fault. Let me go."

I shake my head. "I've gone over this too many times. And it's too late. And this is the only way. Things will go back to normal, your record will be fine."

"They're going to brainwash you, dude," Comet says. "They're going to take away your free will."

"They won't do anything of the sort," I say. "Remember, I'm not the one who buys into all this New Paradigm bull. I'm going to be able to get fixed and improved way quicker than you would've. I'll be out of there quickly and painlessly. And I can still finish high school."

My brother shakes his head and uses all his effort to hold back his tears. At first, I thought that maybe it was that he felt bad for me or felt guilty. But now I seeing his expression intensify, I recognize that he's angry at me. "You had no right," he says between his teeth. "You had no goddamn right."

"Look. I need that reader. I need that ID code. They've been watching it. I'm going to hand it the fuck over and we're going to move on and we're going to put this behind us. We'll put up with this crap with Dad. And we'll be fine."

"Fine, that's what you want?"

"That's exactly what I want. And I want you to fall in line, bro, and grow the fuck up and step up and be the man of the house while I'm gone."

"Dad'll be the man of the house," he says. "I just don't know what to do."

We got through it and the most uncomfortable dinner. We should have been enjoying it, no holograms, just us sitting around the table, like a real family. It was going to be the only meal like that ever, and we should have enjoyed it.

"Ford Reed," Comet says. "You remember him, right? Ford? He was on my bowling team."

"Yeah," I say, taking the olive branch that he's holding out to me.

"His mom went to Reintegration. She wasn't gone so long."

"How long?" Mom asks.

"Six months. I messaged him. He said that she was fine when she came back, just totally happy to see him and all that. But it was six months."

"See?" Mom says. "And it takes longer the older you are, right? You'll be right out."

"Why was she there?" I ask.

"Their credit sucked. I don't know exactly what it was."

"Message him," I say.

"He's always been quiet about it. Their credit sucked and needed repairing."

"They don't do it just for that," Mom says, "you have to be a non-participant. She must have done something."

"Don't know," Comet says, and leaves it at that.

The train slows down quickly, and we all brace ourselves against our seats. The only ones in this car are Mom, Comet, the two escorts by the door, and me. The escorts don't seem to be paying any attention to us, bored more or less, for the entire trip. One of them slept most of the way and I kept thinking how I didn't feel really guarded at all. I mean, maybe it is just a voluntary thing, like maybe I'm not a prisoner, really, but just someone going to do some credit repair, despite all the stigma and the way it all feels so threatening.

"This is almost exactly halfway to the city," Comet says. "This is the line you'd take to get there. The Comet line."

Mom pats Comet's leg. "This is the line your father used to take into the city when you were born," she says. "It seems like it was so long ago. With the free pass, the commute really wasn't any kind of a problem. It let me keep my job and everything."

I have so few memories of the city. I used to go, once in a while, with Dad, but that was a long time ago. The *Clearkids Morning Show* always showed kids in the city and depicted city life as so exciting and amazing and full of playing opportunities. I always wished that my family would move there. But, one time Dad took me to a comic book store in the city and next door was some kind of bar or restaurant. There was a man playing a keyboard out in front of it, in front of all kinds of people. And his face was torn to pieces. Like, it was healing, but it looked frightening. Dad told me that he played around town often; he was injured during a deployment and couldn't get work. He was off-mission when he was injured and had no benefits. It was so terrible to imagine. This now deformed man, playing a piano and eliciting sympathy. I couldn't look at him. And I didn't want to live in the city anymore.

The rail station is sitting in the shadow of green, towering hills. Everything outside looks vivid and clear— blue skies, green hills, snow-white clouds. It's like something out of a postcard right now and I would think it was beautiful if my stomach wasn't twisted in knots. I see the other line going up into the hills that I'll take to the facility. "A Peaceful Escape," the brochure said. "To repair, rejuvenate, and revive your life!" For the first time I started wondering what kind of low-lifes I'd be hanging out with for the coming months. What kind of other people do they send to this thing? I mean, you have to have screwed up pretty royally, but you can't have actually broken any laws. There's a pretty narrow window to have this kind of option open for you. I'm lucky, I remind myself.

"You'll be okay," Mom says, reassuring herself more than me.

"I know," I say. "I'll behave myself. I'll get through whatever curriculum they give me. I'll call whenever they let me. I'll keep up with school." I've told this to Mom only a thousand times in the last several hours, probably reassuring myself more than her.

"I'm sorry," my brother says, quietly, looking down.

They're not allowed to get out of the train with me. They're going out the other side, to the other platform, to take the next rail back home. I'm heading up the small branch of rail that twists into the hills. I keep thinking, "A

Peaceful Escape!" If only everything you ever read in a brochure wasn't the exact opposite of the truth.

"Take care of her, man," I say to Comet.

He isn't able to hide his tears now, and he pulls me tight into a hug. "I haven't said it yet, but thank you," he says into my ear. "I want you to come back as yourself. If you can, just come back as yourself."

"You said that *none* of us knew who we were. How will I know if the right me is coming back?"

Comet nods his head, swallowing tears. "That's right," he says. "But you come back as yourself. Find out who that is."

"I don't know if this is the place for that," I say.

Mom and Comet get walked out of their door and I walk out the other side with the escorts, both wearing dark blue suits and one of them yawning deeply.

"Any bags?" the sleepy one says to me.

"I was told not to bring any," I say.

"That's right. Of course, that's right."

The three of us wait on a bench inside the rail station. It's the quietest rail station I've ever been to in the middle of the day

"When's it leave?" I ask them.

"Soon enough," one of them says. They're both looking at the mobiles on their wrists, flipping through something and listening to their earpieces. I don't look down at mine because I really don't want to end up checking in here. I don't know exactly what to do and I end up just sitting there and looking around. I look at the benches and the trees outside and the rail and the hills and I'm just feeling nervous. I look at the sky and I start counting the big, fluffy clouds that look like a snack you'd buy at the food court. I look at the two escorts, their fingers flipping against their mobiles. My eyes go back to the benches and start the whole thing over again.

Finally, I breakdown and flip the mute button off my mobile to check out what's happening with Lifebook. When I do, it instantly checks me into the rail station and in less than one minute there are five comments on my check-in asking me what I'm doing there. Am I going on a trip? Am I going to the city on a weekday? They heard I was sick, they were worried about me, now I've checked in at a strange station nearly an hour away from town by rail.

I ignore it for now. I figure I'll either own that I'm here or make up some excuse, but that it can wait for later.

The rail line actually stops right in front of the Reintegration facility. The train that rode the rail into the hills was slow and ancient. It seemed to crawl up the hills with a painful sense of drama, taking nearly as long to cover fifteen miles as the previous train had taken to cover 200. When I first see the Reintegration facility, I think I'm looking at some historic home of an old industrialist. It's huge, but it gets bigger as we get closer, and I see that it couldn't possibly be a single house, no matter how rich or how old the family was. It's as big as my school, maybe, or as big as the hospital that's just outside of town. But it's made to look like an old house—wooden, decorative—like a ski resort, almost. There are no guards, no high fences, no twists of toothed razor wire awaiting the escapee. I don't even see anyone milling around out front or greeting people at the door.

When the rail stops, my first thought is to hop out and use my mobile to Instagram a picture of the end of the rail line. I've never seen a rail just end like that—terminate into nothing, forcing the train to come back from where it came. There's something epic about it—the end of the line, no going on from here, only going back. I stand outside and look at it and think all these things and feel dreadfully alone. The escorts don't even get out of the train.

The sleepy one stays on his seat and the other one waves towards the entryway from the door of the train. I point, like, "Is that where?" as if I don't know, as if there were anywhere else to go from here, and he nods. Before I even start in the direction of the building, I see him sit back down, head buried in his mobile.

The train goes off the way it came, and I watch for a

second as it crawls back down the hill. The only way out is back, I think. The wilderness on the other side of the facility is thick and wild looking and, though I know it to not be true, I'm feeling like I'm standing on the border to the world, hundreds of miles from anywhere.

I turn towards the entrance and start walking to the building. The only way out, I think, is back.

Chapter 14

"We're not here to meet any fiscal or financial goals, not on a given day," the group leader says. "We're here to accept who we are. We're here to re-embrace the values at our core that make us human. To accept that we, too, can be happy, if only we'd let ourselves and if only we'd strive for success in every faucet of life. Isn't that right, Dodge?"

I nod my head and smile.

We're sitting in a circle in the main gallery. The back windows, three stories tall, look out on the rolling green hills. There are 20 of us in the circle, admitted all about the same time that I was. We wear uniforms that signify how ready we are to reintegrate. All of the men have red oxford shirts and denim pants, and all the women white shirts and red skirts. There's one guy, Darrel, who's been here a bit longer, wearing a yellow shirt. After that is green, and then, finally, the next step is getting back into your life.

We all had breakfast together as the sun was coming up. The foodcourt has tons of options, almost like the one back home, but everything is free and the general mood is a lot quieter. We meet at the same time every morning—except for Jackson, because he's not a morning person, and David, the group leader, says you don't have to be a morning person to be a successful person. We all have the right to participate or not, each day, and it just helps to participate as much as possible to get out quicker. But someone like

SOL SMITH

Jackson, I think, is really looking for a little bit of a break from life for a while. He doesn't have a lot of family and his job was downsized and he broke contract on a car and tried to hide it. I get the feeling that he wants to take it slow. And his education is good, so they're happy to try and get his earning potential back into play, even if it takes a while.

On the first day, I got fitted for my clothes, had a physical, blood test, and had my mobile tooled for constructive participation within the facility. I still have access to most of my friends and what they're up to, but I don't comment and follow as many pages while I'm here. It's better to do some reading on one of the books from the reader library or to socialize with the other people and share stories about why we're here.

My room is nice. Like, way nicer than my room back home. I have a full size bed, a desk, a picture frame linked to my Instagram feed, and a pretty nice, new model reader from the library. The room has all kinds of different light settings and I spend a little too much time on this because my room at home only has one configuration and I totally need one of these systems at home and I know Mom would go nuts over it. The Clear Channel is awesome, too, and I have full access to everything that I would at home, even the school's War Games play on Friday night, and I'm allowed to mobile chat with Comet while the game is on. I even have a totally private bathroom and shower, which is more than I can say for back home.

That's just half of my room. The other half looks exactly the same, a mirror image. I have no roommate, at least not yet. Darrel started out without a roommate, but got one a couple weeks later. I wouldn't be too worried, except that Comet said something to me on the way here. He watched the escorts, waited for the one to fall asleep and for the other to be absorbed in his mobile before he spoke to me.

"Listen, something I've read," he said, quietly, "something I was told…" He nodded at my, knowingly. "Is that there are moles. There are spies in there, watching the people who are reintegrating. Just be careful what you say. Be careful who your friends are, alright?"

I nodded at him. "Don't worry," I said. "No one will know anything."

"That's not what I mean," he said, his eyes on the escorts. "I just mean for you."

"I don't think we have anything to worry about," I said loudly. "It's going to be fine. There's nothing to worry about, not on this train, not there."

"We'll see," he said. And even though I know my brother is going nuts with conspiracy theories and even though he has fallen in with the wrong crowd, I have this stupid worry in the back of my mind that I'm going to get a roommate and he's going to spy on me.

My plan is to be the next guy wearing a yellow shirt.

Even though I'm one of the newer people, I have a feeling that I can do it. After all, my values never were actually out of line and so my recovery should be really quick.

"Share your experience with us, Darrel," David, the leader, says. "Tell us how you've learned and grown here."

Darrel is a thin guy, maybe in his early 20s. His mustard yellow shirt looks somehow distinguished against so many reds. "Well," he starts, "it's like you say. You have to remember that part of you that you nurtured while you were growing up. That part of you that believed in everything and sang out when you had plans and hopes about school and jobs and the future. You have to remember that choice is a powerful thing and that you always have a choice."

"Interesting," David said, taking a sip of coffee. "What kind of choices do you mean?"

"I mean that our choices define us, and that pretty bad ones brought us here. Mostly bad ones, I would guess, for most of us. But it's like with every single choice, there are two paths. And some of them are simple, like am I going to have a Coke or a Pepsi. And that choice defines you, or is at least reflective of your definition of yourself. And from there, that shows you where you can eat, and that helps you choose *what* you'll eat, and it rains down from there."

"And somewhere in the wash, when things get rough, we started feeling like we didn't have a choice anymore." Here, a lot of people in the group start nodding their heads, so I join in, even though I'm not sure where he's going. "But we do have those choices. And choices are power. And our society gives us so many chances to make these choices every day. Shows we watch, channels we switch to, what we eat, what we buy, which products we trust. We vote with our credit, you know, not just on how the world is run and how strong the economy is, but we vote on who we are. Giving us all these choices is what empowers us. Our society empowers us every day. And sometimes, I guess, we lose sight of that."

Even though we aren't supposed to clap for anyone, everyone starts clapping. I don't clap because I want to break the rules, but then I see David clapping and nodding with approval. I figure all these people must really be suffering because this was some kind of a big revelation to them and I see it as just common sense. Of course our choices define who we are; of course our access to choice is miraculous; this is like fifth grade stuff here.

"Now, Dodge," David says. "I see it took you a minute to clap at the end of what he said. Didn't you appreciate what Darrel had to say?"

"Well, yes, I just didn't want to break the rules," I say.

"Since when is making the choice to support your fellow person breaking any rules?"

"I thought we weren't supposed to clap for each other," I say. "I remember that from my first day, that we don't clap."

"It's a choice," David says. "A choice to clap or not to clap. But I think that Darrel was showing real leadership here. Don't you?"

"Yes."

"I think that Darrel was showing initiative. Don't you?"

"Yes," I say without hesitating, though I hardly feel like answering a question is showing initiative.

"I think that Darrel can teach us a lot. I really do. And I think that the real learning is about to start for all of you. I think the healing will start, and I think you will all remember your priorities. You'll all make the progress that Darrel is making."

"I want you all to go to your rooms, or your study areas, or the common rooms, or the foodcourt, or the courtyard, or wherever you're comfortable. And before you take the afternoon to watch a little Clear Channel and play video games and the like, I'd like you to log an entry for me. Log an entry onto our group wall where you detail what it is you want to get out of this. Not just abstracts, like getting better or getting out, but what kind of purchasing power are you looking for at the end of this? What kind of credit do you want to see yourself in control of someday? What is the lifestyle aim that you have *right now*? Maybe it's modest. Maybe a little house, a couple cars, a family, and a vacation home or boat or something. Maybe you just want to be able to retire and see the world some day. But, maybe a few of you can dream a little bigger. Maybe a few of you could open the floodgates and see yourselves come alive and truly *express who you are* through your lifestyle."

"Being a success, that's a choice, isn't it, Darrel? Isn't it, Jackson? Isn't it, Katrina?" We all nod, we all clap. "Success is a choice. It's hard work. Failure is brought on through being lazy. Hard work is a choice. It's a choice that I'd like to see each of you make. In fact, I'm going to give you each a coupon code to start you on that choice. I'm going to save each one of you five percent on a new wardrobe from Target when you get out. In fact, you can browse and archive a few items that you might consider right now on your Target app. Take that step, make that list of life goals, make the choice to be successful, pick out some clothes at a deep discount, and have a healing afternoon."

This is my favorite part of being here. After workshop every morning, we find out if we have assignments for the rest of the day, another activity, a group project, or just loads of free time. Today amounts to free time, masked as an assignment. A list of goals? That'll take a few seconds. Maybe if I were really struggling with Reintegration, things like this would be a lot tougher. But for me, after I've called and checked in with Mom, I'm ready to sit around with my reader and catch up on reading outside in the shadow of the hills, or I can just kick back in my room with that magnificent Clear Channel. There's a huge video game parlor, where you can play some quick games or even load up your character you've been working on for years and bring him back to life here, keeping in touch with all your same comrades and guilds and platoons, like you were never gone. I think that part of the idea is to let you take some time to really see some of the great things about our society. You get to experience the best of it all—all the communications and information and entertainment and reading, and none of the responsibilities that can drag you down.

In all honesty, the fear of being here kind of receded by the end of day two. No boot camp, no prison cells, no disciplinary measures, no locks on the bedroom doors and late night guard head counts. And once all that fear started to recede, I started to really dive in and *enjoy* the experience. Now I see it as a vacation.

"You notice something about this place?" Sarah, a woman from my group, says to me. "You notice how cost ineffective this all is?"

We're eating dinner at the end of the day. I had made my goal list before lunch and changed it after and finally settled on the version I would hand in the next day. "What do you mean?" I say. "If they can bring us back in and open credit back up to us, doesn't it help the entire system?"

"Not enough," she says. "Look, I'll be honest with you. I regret what I did to get here and that I can honestly say that something about this process seems to be working for me. I feel dedicated in a new way, and kind of excited to start pounding the pavement to find a new job when I get back."

"Yeah?" I say. "Sounds like it's working, then."

"This place isn't even half full right now," she says. "This is a huge facility with every single luxury. Have you been to the spa? We should be paying for this, not having our credit repaired."

"I don't see why we should bring attention to that," I say.

"You're young and, while I'm sure that you are here for the right reasons, can you hardly imagine what a privilege it is to have your credit repaired like this? Let me ask you something," she says, more quietly, "do you think there's something else that they want from us? Something that we have that they need? I know the idea is preposterous, but really, what can justify this kind of expenditure? Prisons have to run past capacity to make money. Schools have to be crowded to turn a profit. But here? Hardly anyone is here compared to the other institutions. Have you been to the horse stables? They're magnificent. I mean, I grew up with horses, but I can't even imagine what kind of credit line I would need for stables anywhere near those."

The answer to that question ended up being pretty

obvious. Transitioning from red to yellow, we had to take the next step of commitment and give back to the system. We helped the researchers to gather information about choice making and product identification. After group session, anyone who is in the yellow level has to report to the research facility on the third floor. There, the illusion of this being a ski resort starts to fall apart just a little. The rooms up there feel more like you would find in a very upscale doctor's office; it's not laid out at all like a cabin or a lodge or anything.

You go into a data collection room and sit down in a comfortable chair. A researcher puts little stickers on your head—one on each temple and one on the back of your neck. They put these little clamps on one finger on each hand. They give you a shot of something that's supposed to be relaxing and it doesn't feel unlike the study medication they give you in the seventh grade when academics start to become more challenging and serious. It's like your body feels focused and the room seems smaller, making whatever you're looking at appear brighter and clearer. You can hear yourself breathe, but your mind doesn't wander. It's a nice, familiar feeling, like taking a practice test in school.

The room gets really dark, and a Clear Channel plays in front of you. Sometimes it's just a lot of random images, that I feel like they are a control to get a handle on your brain and where things are firing. Or something like that. We learned a little bit about human data development sophomore year, and this seems to be something like that.

Then, there are scenarios that happen. You're faced with a series of decisions really quickly and you don't even know, really, that you're in control of anything. Just all of a sudden, the picture is of a vending machine with a bunch of buttons, each one with a drink on it. Gatorade, Red Bull, Pepsi, Mt. Dew, Coke. And before you know that you've really made the decision, you see a hand reach out and press the button that you would have reached for.

The picture changes again, and you're in a store, looking at a wall of deodorants. The men's deodorants all go from red packaging to black packaging, covering shelf space of about seven feet long by six feet tall, every few square inches a different product that makes the same claims as the others, but with different languages of manliness, just like in a store. And before you realize you've done it, you've picked the one that speaks to you, the one that says something about who you are, and you see a hand reach out and get it and the picture changes again.

Row after row of cars. The emblems, the logos, all so vivid. The body styles familiar, each one the latest model. Before you've even finished scanning the scene, you see yourself getting into the car you want.

None of the choices really surprise you, but they're made so immediately, sort of faster than you think you could make them in real life. They're immediate and sudden and satisfying. And every time you make a choice, there's the small click that comes from the machine next to you, registering that the decision was made and noted and that something was extracted from that.

This goes on for a while, and when it's over, you're taken to the spa, where you can choose to have a massage or get in the sauna or the hot tub—something relaxing until the concentration drug wears off in your body. It's not a terrible routine, not as relaxing as the first stage of the whole thing was, but not at all terrible. David tells us that providing market research is important for Americorp in staying ahead of European and Chinese rivals and that it's giving back that doesn't cost us anything. It will create a map of who we are as consumers and that will not only help them a lot, but it will also let us learn a little bit more about who we are.

It gets exhausting, all the concentrating. I don't like the whole massage thing, really, so I sit in the hot tub for a while, then I got back to my room to sleep until the drug effects are over with. I usually miss lunch, which is fine with me, really, because breakfast and dinner are so big and usually just about anything I would want.

Within our group, when we talk between sessions and stuff, we don't have the kind of suspicions that we had when we first got here. Instead we feel like we kind of get it better. Like the first stage, in our red shirts, we were really put at ease and given a big chance to rediscover what it is that we're working for in life—all the nice entertainment and relaxation and contentment. But now we're into serious work to repair our credit, being really reflective, giving back, identifying any kind of hangups that we might have that would make our choices be unhealthy ones or ones that would cause damage to ourselves in some way when we get back into the world. I feel like when I finally do leave here, I will have an advantage over everyone else in class. I will have this window into myself and how I interact with society that no one else has, and I'm really, really grateful for the opportunity.

Chapter 15

Darrel was put into our group to lead us by example. He moved on out of our group pretty quickly after that, and I don't see him much at all now. I only saw him in his green shirt once. I almost bumped into him while walking into the foodcourt. He was coming out and we both stopped and did one of those awkward sidesteps, where we're in each other's way again, and then we do the same thing one more time and then laugh about it. Only, he didn't laugh or do a tension-dissipating smile or anything. He just looked at me, nodded, and I walked around him.

His eyes were emptier than before. He had eaten every breakfast with us for the first three weeks we were here, attended every group meeting. He was an uplifting and personal guy and I was really excited to tell him congratulations on his green shirt, but I never got the chance, because he just kind of looked through me and let me walk around him. I thought for a minute that he didn't recognize me, what with the yellow shirt and all, but then I thought that couldn't be it. I finally settled my mind on the idea that he was probably feeling a little bit bittersweet about leaving soon, getting a job, and all of those things that go with Reintegration once it all becomes real and applicable. We've been warned that that's a very tough moment. I'm ready for it because I just have to go back to school, and I've been keeping up with everyone and everything there, so I'm not worried.

David asked me if I would be a leader for a group of redshirts when they come in. I see it as a little bit of an honor, but I also see it as a good sign—that I'm ready to be a leader and help people to reintegrate quickly and healthily. It gets me thinking that, maybe if this is something I'm good at, I could take a new aptitude test and see if being a counselor like David could be in my future. How exciting it would be to live and work here all the time without the threat of Reintegration. And not just the technology and the food and all of the perks that this place carries—which I'm not even sure if you'd have access to if you worked here—but the view outside every single window and watching the sun arch across the sky from up here on top of the hill.

One day I get back to my room to see a couple of researchers busily at work. "What's going on?" I ask them.

They're navigating a tangle of cords and holding the Dreamcatcher next to my bed. I don't use it for dreaming, but I have been plugging it in at night for music and white noise and lectures so that I don't have to sit with my own thoughts too long while I fall asleep.

"We've got a real perk for you," the researcher holding the box says. I've never seen him before, or at least not enough to recognize him. "You're Type O, right?"

"Yeah," I say.

173

"We just got clearance this morning to install a prototype Dreamcatcher 3 in your room. How about that?"

"A DC3? It works with me?"

"That's what they're hoping and this thing isn't going to be on the market for another year or more. You're going to help us pioneer this for everyone else of your blood type. You're a regular hero."

They had a silver case that they opened up to reveal a black Dreamcatcher box inside padded by thick foam. It didn't look very different than the DC2, except that it wasn't covered in all the stickers telling the features that are included when you buy them at the store. They pull it out of the case and start hooking it up to the wires in the wall where the old one was installed.

"Will it work?"

"It's supposed to," the man says. "There may be nuances within each individual that impact the effectiveness, of course, but we won't know until there have been many more trials. What we do know is that giving us research on this is going to help you get that yellow shirt off and get you into something green!"

Even though it's obvious that I'm not going to get to take a nap right now with all this commotion going on, I feel like it's necessary for me to sit around and watch them put it in. I know they're not going to ask for my help, and that they're not going to want to make a bunch of small talk with me, but yet I feel like just walking out right now would be like expecting them to do something for me without making myself available to help or assist or anything. It's like having a plumber in the house or something.

They go about their business as if I'm not there and I'm still pretty exhausted and drained from the market research and from the hot tub afterward. I sit down on the opposite bed and keep watching them work.

"I hear you're getting a roommate soon," the one researcher says when I sit down.

"Is that right? Does anyone have a roommate?"

"Lots," he says. "New bunch coming in. They like to put some of the redshirts with upper yellows, you know."

Upper yellow? I do feel like an upper yellow, I realize. "I didn't room with anyone before," I say.

"This country isn't one-size-fits all. This is research! This is science! We personalize your experience, like a good company would do for any consumer. If our psych eval shows that you'd do well with a roommate, you get one. If it shows you're a loner or a leader, then you don't get one. It's that simple. And, all of that can just remain completely unseen to you, right? Why make the marketing visible?"

I nod in agreement. And I wonder how much this researcher is supposed to talk to me and if he's really supposed to know all of this or tell me all of this before anyone official tells me. And, why does a researcher collecting data on the new DC unit know about my roommate situation or about me being an upper yellow? Then I remember something that we are always taught in school: trust the professionals. Until you're an expert yourself, you don't need to bother thinking very much, just let the experts do that. It makes it all easier.

"There you go, all done," he says. The other researcher, the one who never said anything, doesn't look at me, but just stands up and walks away. Maybe he was just a tech or maybe he's not supposed to talk to anyone or maybe he's having a bad day. "You wanna try her out?"

"No, not till tonight," I say. "I want to have time."

He leaves now, and I feel absolutely wasted. I think that the shots they give us here must be much stronger than the ones they used to give us in school. And I think that they've gotten stronger as we've gone along. It's so tiring to sit and concentrate so hard on everything for so long. It's not at all tiring while you're doing it, but you've just got to relax after. I flip on the Clear Channel and put on the Dreamcatcher headphones for better sound, and watch highlights from the high school War Games matches.

That night, I try the Dreamcatcher and nothing happens.

Well. Almost nothing.

That night is the first night that I have the nightmare.

Everything is black. Pitch black, darker than anything I've experienced. I'm disoriented and hardly have a sense of who I am; I hardly know enough about myself to wonder where I am. I feel intense pressure all over my body. I try to open my eyes to dispel the darkness, but I finally realize that my eyes *are* open. I try to sit up, but I feel pinned down, like I'm experiencing gravity at an intense level. I try to scream, but can't, as if my mouth is full. In my head, I'm yelling, like my internal voice is yelling. Behind this, behind the darkness, I feel like there are voices whispering.

When I wake up, the Dreamcatcher is operating on music mode. There's a small red light blinking that I figure is showing the error. I suppose that the DC3 doesn't do what it intended, or else these dream programs everyone's into really suck.

At breakfast, I tell Sarah and Chevy about my dream experience.

"I guess I never knew a Type O," Chevy says. "Sucks, man. There's some pretty good stuff out there. Not all of it, but a lot. I can't imagine my day without having the DC to look forward to at the end of it."

"I lost my subscription for a while," Sarah said. "I caught a huge hit on my credit and my account was suspended. It was crazy. I haven't slept without one for what, five years?"

"I know it's been at least that long for me," Chevy says.

"I had natural dreams. After a couple nights of hardly being able to sleep at all, I had natural dreams."

"What was it like?" Chevy says. "I don't even remember dreaming before the DC."

"It was terrible. They were unfocussed. They fell apart in strange ways or switched directions altogether. People would switch and change identities. Places weren't right— even my house wasn't the right place. I can honestly say that I hated it. In fact, once I had the room in my credit, I put my subscription back online before I paid for a rail pass. I literally walked to work, no matter what the weather, for two months, just so I wouldn't have to be without my Dreamcatcher at night."

Chevy nods his head. "I remember that. About places not being right. What's up with that? How come we can't get something as simple as a place right without being awake? Do you do the whole natural dream thing?"

This last question was directed at me. I felt like a relic sitting there among them. "Yeah, I dream."

"And stuff changes around and people change and you have no idea that you're having a dream?"

"Um, I guess so," I say. "I mean, I guess I can remember a couple times when I knew it was a dream. But, I guess usually I don't know. I mean, if you're battling Chinese security administrators and indigenous tribes in the rainforest, do you know that you're in a Dreamcatcher program?"

"Huh, I don't think so. But I'm not really doing a lot of thinking, I guess."

"I think we just tend to accept the reality around us," I say. "Reminds me of something my brother said to me before I came here."

They both nod their heads and go back to eating and talking about sports.

After breakfast, it's back to the usual routine. I go to mentor the group meeting with the new redshirts. We share insights that we've experienced over the last week since they arrived and we talk about people back home and we talk about how we got into this situation and about the wisdom of our system and why our faith wavered and how we can get it back and become participants again. It's the sort of normal group-conversation. The leader of this group—Daniel—says a lot of the same things that David did. He even makes some of the same facial expressions and wears the same kind of glasses. There are so many similarities between the two leaders that I start to get a little confused about it. I'm guessing that they have training seminars and standardization policies and stuff that make them fit a certain mold. I'm sure it's a heavily researched mold that they know to be effective for trust building. I mean, you can't blame them because they're trying to help us, but it still feels somewhat insincere.

Comet's voice keeps coming back to me. He was suspicious of all of this, but you know what? He was the one who put me here. I'm taking the hit and I may as well enjoy it.

After group, I leave the redshirts who mingle and read and watch sports to go up to the third floor for market research. I go through the usual, exhausting steps: the shot; the stickers on the head; the videos and decision-making tests. For whatever reason, it feels like it goes very quickly today, which is a welcome change, but I still feel tired and drained by the end of it. From there, I go to the hot tub and then back to my room to watch the Clear Channel. I'm starting to feel like things are getting really redundant, like my outlook and measures aren't getting any better, and like I'm going to be stuck here for an age.

But when I get back to my room, the two researchers are there again.

"We took a look at your Dreamcatcher," the lead guy says to me. "Trying to figure out what it is that went wrong."

"How do you know it went wrong?"

"We collected some really valuable data last night," he says. "You've helped us more than you could know."

"What's he doing?" I ask. The other man—the one who doesn't talk—is busying himself in the closet I don't use. He's hanging up white shirts and red skirts. His back is to me and I remember that I didn't get a good look at his face the day before. I want to see his face for some reason and however I start to angle myself, it's like I can't get a look at him.

"He's stocking your closet for your roommate," the first researcher says. "She's running later than we expected, but she should be here sometime soon."

"A girl roommate?"

"We match up roommates by age, not gender. It's better for demographic integration within our program. We'll be out of here any minute," the researcher says. "I wouldn't expect your roommate until after dinner tonight. And, I think that we've tweaked your DC3 enough to make it work a little better. Let us know!"

The other man leaves with his back still to me. I never did get a look at his face. I sit down on my bed, put on the headphones, and flip through stations on the Clear Channel for a while. I must have fallen asleep, which triggers the Dreamcatcher, because I have another one of those nightmares, wrapped in darkness and unable to move or even scream. I forgot how vivid it was the first time and how horrifying.

When I wake up, it's dark. I don't remember dinner and I don't remember going to bed. Maybe I was here the whole time, and slept through everything, but everything seems hazy and it could be that I've just forgotten everything. I decide that I'm not going to try the Dreamcatcher again because it's just too disturbing. Like the fear and panic from the nightmare are still echoing in my bones, and I have a vague but powerful feeling of unease.

I wonder if the foodcourt is still open. I take off my headphones and stand up. I'm still in my clothes, so I figure that I probably slept the entire afternoon and evening.

Then, I hear snoring.

On the other bed I see a body. She's facing away from me, but I can see through the glow of light coming through the window, a head of short-cropped dark hair. She's not wearing her Dreamcatcher, but has the headphones looped over her bedframe. I think about walking closer and trying to get a look at her face, but that seems creepy. I stand there for a second, looking at the back of her head, and finally realize that I feel just too tired and weak to think about going to check out the foodcourt. I finally sit back down on my bed, set the Dreamcatcher to music, and lie back down to go to sleep.

"So how did you get here?" I hear a girl's voice say. "Hey, you awake? It's light. We might as well get up. How'd you get here?" I sit up and look over at the other bed. "What? Why are you looking at me like that?" the girl says.

I rub my eyes. "My God, you look exactly like someone I used to know," I say.

"You do know me," she says. "You're Scott, right? Mick's friend? A year younger than me at school."

"Porsche? That's not possible," I say, a little louder than I meant to. Suddenly, I'm feeling lightheaded again. But, the more I look at her, the more I realize that it's her. She looks exactly the same as the day she died.

Chapter 16

"I'm not dead, clearly, Scott," Porsche says. "I'm sitting right here. I'm in Reintegration, just like you."

"Porsche, I was there that night. I was there for the disaster and I saw you get taken away. You're dead."

She laughs. Her short, messy hair shakes with her head. God, she looks exactly like I remember her. "Scott, I'm not dead. I'm right here and I understand your concerns and everything, and I thank you, but look at me. Totally not dead."

"I don't understand," I say. I am staring right at her, and I'm absolutely positive of who I'm looking at. It's Porsche Fairview, the first girl to make varsity on the War Games team from our school. The girl I watched die on the playing field during the Reagan-Cable disaster. And yet here she is, talking to me, just as bouncy as she ever was.

"But I do, so trust me, the one who understands, I'm not dead. I'm starving. Is the breakfast reasonable at this one?"

"It's good," I say. "Probably my favorite meal around here. We've got a Taco Cabana in the foodcourt and their breakfast is pretty wise."

"Good, that'll do," she says. "I could have some breakfast flautas right now. Let's go." She hops up out of bed wearing her red flannel pajamas that all redshirts are issued. She pulls a white shirt and red skirt out of her closet.

Then, she grabs a pair of panties, socks, and cloth slippers out of the dresser. "You mind, bro," she says, "or are you just going to gawk?"

I turn around and face my side of the room. I'm still wearing my clothes from yesterday and I'm just too nervous to think about the two of us being undressed at the same time in the same room. "So what's the deal?" I ask. "How did you end up here?"

"Kicked out of the last one," she says. "This is my fourth attempt at Reintegration. You get five."

"Then what?" I ask.

"I don't know," she says. "They just keep saying you get five chances. I don't know if you just live outside of credit after that or if you get exiled or if they kill you or whatever."

"What are the other facilities like?"

"They all operate on different philosophies," she says. "Hey, where the hell are the bras? They're not in the dresser."

I almost turn around, but don't.

"Why in the world would the bras be in the closet?" she says. "I'm guessing they've packed up more girls rooms than just mine. Where would you put bras?"

"I don't guess I'd put them anywhere," I say.

"You'd put them somewhere, dork. You're probably not likely to put bras in the closet though, right? Is that like the last detail they thought of? I mean, anyone who would have the bras put in the closet must have thought about that at the very end, like they don't deal with girls much and just barely remembered that they even wear bras, not because they don't think about boobs, but because they don't wear bras themselves, so why would they think of them? Ta-da! What do you think?"

I turn around and she's dressed in the standard redshirts outfit for girls. "Looks great. Like a living girl who is dedicated to Reintegration," I say. "So you faked your death or what?"

"I'm not going to have to have to fake it if I don't eat a breakfast flauta, like, right now," she says. "If there's any way for us to have any privacy at breakfast, I can tell you a little bit, but I'm afraid that it's boring and pointless and not what I want to talk about."

We walk down the stairs and it's still a little early, so the place is really quiet. I have my alarm set for 7:00, and Porsche must have woken me up at 6:15 or so. "When I got in last night," she says in a mock-whisper, "everyone was asleep. You were like, dead, man. I tried to wake you up, but you were seriously, seriously out. I'm guessing that you were totally wrapped up in that Dreamcatcher. Is that your bag? Like *West Charles* or something?"

"No," I say. "Not really. I mean, it doesn't really work for me."

"Well let me tell you, you're not missing out on much. Propaganda, conformity, and aspiration prescriptions. That's all they give you, those shows. But, you probably watch all that crap on the Clear Channel, so you're not missing much, still, yeah? I mean, you get it, right?"

"I hear you," I say, as noncommittal as I can.

"What do you mean, you 'hear' me? Like you hear, or you're listening, or you totally believe me and you're on board? Because if you just hear me, maybe you don't understand and then I'm just wasting my time talking to you. So, which is it?"

"I don't know," I say. "You seem really angry and bitter and I don't really remember you that way."

"Maybe I wasn't then. Do you think a thing or two could have changed for me? Has anything changed for you since you've been in the system? Or are you exactly like you were in school, just hopping around being buddies with everyone and updating your Lifebook every time there's a great play in War Games?"

"I don't know which question of yours you want me to answer."

"None," she says. "I just want a breakfast flauta and then I can listen to whatever it is you have to say. And I can decide if we're cool or at odds or whatever.

At the end of the hall, lined with door after door leading to the small living spaces, there is a little grouping of elevators. I double-time my last few steps so that I can press the down button before she gets there. She just keeps walking and goes through the exit door that leads to the staircase. I follow her down the stairs.

"What," she says. "I thought you were taking the elevator."

"I thought we were walking together."

"We were. But then you were going to take the elevator. I don't like to take the elevator for just one floor. Or two, really. I get so little activity every day, why not just take the stairs, you know?"

The stairwell looks exactly like the stairwell at the school. And I mean, exactly. Like they're made from the same plans or the same builder or something. The door at the bottom of the staircase opens up into the main lobby right next to the foodcourt. We walk in and order from the Taco Cabana. When our food comes, we go sit down at a table in the far corner, way out of the way. There's only one other table with anyone sitting down, and they're a couple of redshirts I don't know. They don't even look up when we walk by.

"Mute your mobile," she says. "I don't want anything

posting on accident."

"That's much harder to do after they tweak your mobile for this environment."

"Dude, mute your mobile." It's only now that I look at her wrist and realize that she doesn't have a mobile on her.

"Where's yours?" I ask.

"My what?"

"Your mobile?"

"Is yours muted?"

"Yeah."

"I don't have one," she says. "I manage fine without it. I mean, just like being here, having a mobile is totally optional. Did you really think that every single person had a mobile?"

"They're so cheap," I say. "As long as you log in every day and post a few updates an hour, they don't touch your credit at all. I mean, I don't know if I know anyone who doesn't have one. It's hard to imagine."

"You don't even have to imagine it," she says, with her mouth full of flauta. "I'm sitting right here without one. I haven't had one for a year. You're afraid you'd be anxious without it, right? Disconnected? You're afraid that 'You Will Hardly be You Without It'?"

"That's their motto, right? 'You're Hardly Yourself Without Your Mobile.'"

"Maybe you're not ready for all of this. You think that slogans and labels matter."

"Ready for what?" I ask. "For Reintegration? I've done very well, thank you, and I think that I'm nearly ready to go back home. Isn't that the goal here?"

"That's their goal," she points at the two redshirts eating across the room with her chin. "Those two can't wait to repair their credit, get new jobs, and return to society. I'd bet you that the man over there tried to slip something by the reporting agencies. He took goods or services without reporting it to credit because he had the access codes and thought he could get away with it. Only he wasn't powerful enough to bend the rules. If you're powerful enough, it doesn't matter if you even break them, but you have to be in the club first, am I right? And the girl? She probably stopped releasing credit for something she owed. She tried to get a free ride.

"There's no way out but back for those two," she says. "They want their jobs back, they want their earning potential back, they come here and they repair their credit and they provide wonderful research data for Americorp, and then they go back as new soldiers in the army, believing in their purpose within society even more than they ever did. That's them. You see them over there? In the red shirts?"

"Of course I see them over there."

"If their reason for being here is the same as yours, you should go sit down with them and talk things over for a while. Pump each other up. Heal and strengthen together." She sits unblinking, looking me in the eye. "For real," she says, "my feelings won't be hurt, my ego won't be damaged. I've got my breakfast flauta, I've got a book in my reader, so right there I have two things better to do than to talk about healing and strengthening and getting better. If getting better is your thing, I'm not going to stop you. If looking into this a little deeper is why you're here, then we can talk."

I don't really know what to say to this. I do want to go home, I do want my credit repaired, but I also want what she said—to look deeper in.

"You can't do both," she says, as if reading my mind. "You can't get better and look deeper. They're not compatible. That's why I'll never get better. And I could leave—no one would stop me—but that's just checking out for no reason. At least here I can watch people, eat good food, and bide my time. So I stay."

"Can you," I say, moving my voice to a whisper, "just *fake* it? I mean, can't you just tell them what they want to know and what they want to hear and leave with your credit intact?"

She laughs. "You gotta keep playing after that. If that's what you want, I don't have a problem with that. But you should go talk to them or something. I'm here to talk to you about something else. If you're worried that you'll be thrown off and you won't get better, then please, don't let me get in the way. I don't want to be in your way."

The foodcourt starts filling up with more people. It's 7:00 now, and that's when most people get up and around.

"Look," I say, "you have got to answer some questions for me."

"I'm much better at asking questions. That makes me much more fun to be around."

"Look, that's cool, inquiry is awesome and all of that, but you have to tell me about *how you are alive*. Do you understand that I went to your funeral? That the entire high school had a giant memorial for you at the stadium and people have your name written all over their Lifelines with the dates of your birth and death?"

"Scott, there's nothing more pathetic than when someone dies and everyone tries to own their death. I think it's just great that my demise went to inspire so many people in so many interesting ways. Being memorialized on a thousand Lifelines doesn't do a lot for me. Like I said, I've got a flauta and a book and that's really all I need right now. I don't need anyone's pity or anyone's memorial or anyone spilling tears over me. I don't care if people think I'm alive or if people think I'm dead. I don't care how prepared my friends are for their tests. I don't care what people are having for lunch. I don't care what fashion is in for the day or what shows are on or who kissed who or whose mom is being a bitch or where the party is and what kind of beer is there and how the hell I look in a bikini. Look, right here, look. Flauta. Book. There's my day, right there."

"Normally," I say, "you can't get a flauta or a book without credit."

"Sometimes, Scott, a flauta is just a flauta. A priority doesn't have to be reflective of society. What I want, how I want to enjoy myself, doesn't have to be catalogued and compiled and bought and sold and made to paint a picture of our people's beliefs and behaviors. I don't have to participate to show that burgers sell better on Wednesdays or cakes sell better when it's raining or girls spend more on haircuts than boys and all that. I don't want to commit myself to data at every move I make. I don't want my friends to feel like they're hanging out with me all day but it turns out I've just been logging activity on my mobile."

"I guess it can get to be a drag."

"I don't want there to be some computer simulation of me somewhere, built on my likes and dislikes, that can behave like me and act like me and look like me because every possible angle of my face has been taken and catalogued and liked on Instagram 100,000 times. I want to be one person—a singular event—that comes along when she's born and goes away when she dies."

Here, and I guess she doesn't know it, she's talking about Dad. Maybe her dad had a deployment. Maybe she understands me better than I thought. Maybe she's been reading my Lifeline or maybe something. I nod my head.

"You want to sit and talk with me anymore or do you want to move over to that table or that table and work on yourself and get better and fit in with our world just that much more? My feelings won't be hurt."

"I'm not likely to hurt your feelings," I say. "I don't see any way that I could. What would your feelings even be like?"

"You *get* me?"

"I think it's you that gets me," I say. "But I still want to get out of here. I still want to make things better for Mom and my brother. And, I still want to know how it is that you're here."

"Just smile a minute," she says. "We can talk later. Trust me, it's not exciting anyway." A few red shirts from the group I'm mentoring come and sit down at our table. They introduce themselves to Porsche. She smiles and laughs and acts like everything is just fine.

It's almost impossible to concentrate on anything in group today. The entire time that Daniel is talking to the redshirts in our group about today's theme, Values and Valuables, I'm spacing out. I keep looking at the window at the towering trees and imagining what it would be like to just leave for a while to go for a walk in the woods. That's the first time that it strikes me about how strange the location of this facility is. There's this peaceful and amazing natural space, like people used to vacation in, and we sit inside the entire time just talking about how great society is. I've heard there are horses and a stable of some kind, so maybe some groups go outside for some reason or another, but besides a couple of times out in the courtyard, I don't think I've been outside since I got here. Maybe it is just to make it harder to leave, or maybe the restfulness is supposed to reflect the life-ambition of success and help us invest in our future-farming, as David calls it.

"Scott?" I hear Daniel call out at me. "You with us, Scott?"

Everyone in the group laughs as I snap out of it. I'm the only one in the group wearing yellow, but I'm also the youngest, so it makes me an easy target for the rest of the group to make fun of. "Yeah," I say. "Sorry. I was just watching the wind play through the trees."

"The wind play through the trees?" Daniel says, almost mockingly surprised. "Where did you get that? Have you been reading poetry or something?" Everyone laughs at what was, seemingly, a joke.

"No," I say. "What's so funny? I might read poetry if I

want."

"Do you need to focus more, Scott? Should I call pharm and have them send up a shot of Focusor?"

"No, I'm good. Really. It's just, I have this roommate now. It's new. I think she kept me up last night."

"Well," Daniel says. "I think we can all understand that. And there's another place to link values with valuables: if you work hard in life and can pay your own rent you don't need a roommate." Everyone laughs, and I actually appreciate the way that he sort of pivoted that into a relative thing, and a joke. It really showed how experienced he is as a group leader to be able to divert attention like that.

After groups, I decide to skip the market research today. "Suit yourself," the researcher said. "This is for you, too, you know. You wanna get that credit repaired, we've got to study your cognitive process. This is strictly voluntary, but the more you do, the sooner the credit is repaired."

I didn't spend any extra time on the third floor. I skipped my usual hot tub and instead went out on the back deck with my reader.

The back deck spans the length of the building and is covered by an overhang and filled with wooden rocking chairs. In all the time I've spent here—nearly two months—I haven't seen a single person come out and sit on these chairs. The view of the rolling hills is wonderful and relaxing. I look down the row of chairs and halfway down I see someone sitting there, wearing a white top and a red skirt. I walk down and say hi.

"Dude, I hope you're not following me," Porsche says. "Because there's something I didn't tell you."

I sit down and put my feet up on the bench that she has her feet on. "I'm not following you. I guess that great minds think alike."

"Huh," she says. "Alike minds think alike, Scott. They can be great or crappy."

"So what brings you out here?"

"Finished with the flauta, I guess. Still have the book. What does a girl do for fun around here? These people are total drones, if you know what I mean."

"I know," I say, "but they're nice. And they're sincere. There's something about getting a bunch of people together from all over that feels cool. We all have a pretty big problem in common so everyone's willing to talk about it so openly."

"Yeah," she says. Then she settles back into her book. I pick up my book, but just as I do, she interrupts the effort. "It's just that everyone's problems are bullshit."

"Look, you're just a redshirt, so I understand how you might feel that way," I say. "You'll find out the way that our aspirations and responsibilities really speak to who we are, in time. I mean, the link between your values and your valuables is really inherent, even in the nature of our language."

"Dude, come on," she says. "You think credit is a problem? Think of all the moms out there who lost a baby or a kid this last year. Think of all the kids who are homeless in the streets, starving to death. Jeez, think of the children who are sexually abused day after day after day on this planet. Do any of those people have some resort-getaway like this to recover and repair? Do you think that someone who has their leg amputated or has cancer can just file for bankruptcy and be done with their problems?"

"Why don't they teach the value of human relationships in school? Why don't they take you out and let you see orchestral music playing or take you to the mountains to ooo and ahhh about giant, ancient trees? Why don't they let middle schoolers explore art and music and acting? Why does it have to be family building, credit ratings, job training, and all that? You think about that?"

"I don't think I have," I say.

"That's right, you haven't. Not on the surface, anyway. Maybe deep down inside you feel some kind of discontent, some kind of conflict, some kind of anger. But, then your surface-self just tells you to smother that feeling with something to eat or some new app or just some Clear

Channel time. But deep down inside, you feel it. And here—here they want you to relearn how to smother that feeling. How to think you're content all the time so you can keep the machine running."

She picks up her book quickly and almost snaps back into it. I sit there a second feeling a bit like I've just been kicked in the teeth. Her aggression just kind of came out of nowhere.

Suddenly, I realize something. Maybe she was put here to challenge me. Maybe that's the reason for the whole roommate thing. She's testing me, seeing how much I've learned. I'm sure I disappointed everyone with my choice not to cooperate with research after talking to her. It probably looks like she's influencing me, and that's just what they're testing.

"I'm sorry," she says, at last, not looking at me. "I'm sorry to go off on you. I don't mean to be so brutal or anything. It's just that I feel like I know you since, you know, and I feel like I expected to find you of similar mind."

"Great minds," I say.

"Right, well, whatever. I'm just saying that if you're actually *trying* to be like them, maybe you don't have to be. I know I sound like a nut job, but it's like we don't have that much time. Something inside of me tells me we don't have much time."

"It's okay," I say. "A lot of what you're saying is actually similar to what my brother was saying before I came here. He's actually the reason I'm here."

"How so?"

"He did something. Something," I shake my head, "terribly wrong. And it was for the right reason, you know? And I guess that they told me that he had been in contact with some kind of subversive group. And I took the fall for him."

"Paradigm?" she says. I nod. "Don't talk about it. Not here. Not another word. We can talk about a lot of things but promise me one thing, Scotty, promise me that you will not mention them again, don't get in conversations about them, don't talk about them any time someone wants to talk to you about them. It's just another feeling I have. Don't talk about them with anyone, not even me."

"Okay," I say.

"Not 'okay'. Promise."

"I promise," I say.

"That's better," she says. "Now do you want to read for a while or do you want to go back up and offer some market research to the good people?" She smiles ironically, and I can't tell if she is testing me, or knows that I know that she's testing me, or what. There're a lot of signals going on and I can't unweave them.

"I don't know what I want to do," I say. I pick up my book, but for some reason it just looks like gibberish on the page. I try turning it off and on again, but when it comes back up, it's still just a bunch of symbols, not letters. "There must be something wrong with my reader," I say to her. "I can't read a word of this book."

"Don't hurt yourself, Scotty."

I put my reader down and just look at the hills for a while. Porsche keeps reading to herself and I hesitate to interrupt her, but I'm at loose ends. I've been trying not to look at my mobile all day and I know that if I start to glance at it now, Porsche will jump on me for it. I finally get antsy enough that I decide to talk to her again, to interrupt her reading.

"So what's the deal, Porsche," I say. "Why are you here? How is it that we all thought—think, rather—that you are dead? You still haven't explained that."

"There's a bunch I can say about it, Scotty, but I don't know if I can explain it. To actually explain something means not just telling all the facts, but putting all those facts together as some kind of a logical solution to a problem. I would have to show you how one thing led to another and another and everything would fall into place just peachy. I don't feel like I can do that."

"But you can relate the facts, right?"

"Facts," Porsche says. "Facts are extinct. How can we all share a belief in the same thing? And it's the people who don't share that belief that are crazy, right?"

"I'm kind of surprised you haven't been sent in for a psych eval," I say. "I don't mean to be a jerk or anything, but you are speaking the kind of stuff that they warn us about."

"I'm the girl your mother warned you about," Porsche quips. "What was that an ad for?"

"Shampoo, I think. Or cookware. I can't remember. But don't change the subject."

"Fine," she says. "The subject is that I'm crazy, right?"

"That's not what I mean. I mean, how are you still alive?"

Chapter 17

"First of all, I want to answer one thing that you have to be worried about right now," Porsche says. "I'm not a hologram. Don't act like that thought hasn't crossed your mind. I'd let you touch me to prove it to you but I don't want you touching me because that's kind of gross right now, okay? But I'm not a hologram."

"I did die on that field, though. And I hardly remember it, so don't ask me what it was like or what the afterlife is like or any of that. I was running my play, and everything was fine, then an explosion and I was afraid I was out. You know how many games I had gone without being a casualty? I was pissed, believe me. But I knew something was wrong and everything was white, then black. Just black. So, I don't have any reports to tell you about the afterlife. Doesn't matter, does it? What does matter is that they got me back. It took hours, but they got me back. Not all the way, though."

"I was in a coma. And by the time that I pulled out of the coma, I was in a medically-induced coma. They knew that I couldn't be awake without suffering too much, so they kept me out. You didn't hear about this because my family wanted it quiet. Life insurance had already paid my family. My family has a Science Clause on our life insurance, so my body wasn't going to be buried anyway, and since they already paid, it didn't belong to my parents anymore. They ran the funeral while I was still in a life/death gray state, my parents couldn't stop it and it increased the insurance company's claim to my body. No one really expected me to pull through, but the legal battle over custody of my half-living body was underway, so my parents *had* to keep quiet to not interfere with the courts. I've seen tapes of the disaster, as they call it, and I'm sure you can imagine how little confidence there was in my survival, but they had good lawyers."

"The weeks in the coma were the worst of my life. At one point, I woke up because the drugs in the IV line crystallized and it got blocked up. I felt like I was being torn to shreds, literally ripped to pieces. Of course, what I was feeling was skin grafts and stitches and digital reattachments. But, it felt like I was being torn apart in a black hell. And I guess that's what I really thought was happening, that I was in Hell and that there was no way out.

"But I got better. It was expensive. Really, really expensive. My dad, as you probably know, was a Peacekeeper for Gerber. He was in South America when it happened and he flew up here to be with the family. Only, he never made it out of the country. He was killed in transit to the civilian airport. And since it wasn't part of his mission, we were dropped. And all that debt fell onto my mom's shoulders."

"We have a lot in common," I say.

"Great minds," she says.

"My mom and I had no credit left and I was still in a coma and the lawyers were ready to pack their bags and let the insurance company sell my remains; legally, my body would be 'remains' if the suit was dropped. But then, one day, the drugs crystalized again and I woke up fully. My blood felt like it was burning and my skin had been torn off. But, once I was awake, my body went back to my mom, life insurance took back payment, and we couldn't afford to keep me in the hospital.

"You ask me why I haven't had a negative psych eval? I could be on my way there, but I guess someone needs to have decent credit to pay for those places they send the crazies. Because my mom is the one with a negative psych eval. I don't even know if she's still alive. I haven't heard from her at all in months. I haven't seen her with my own eyes since that night that I took the field. I've been shuffled off in every possible place to be reintegrated. My coming back to life has been a waste. An actual waste. But the people in charge want to do everything they can to get one of us reintegrated, otherwise, where does the money come for our care?"

"I can't tell you that those are facts, you understand. And as far as telling you an explanation, those are created by our own minds to make sense out of something overwhelming. It's not overwhelming that there are hot dogs for dinner at the Noon Burger, so you don't ask for an explanation, right? But if you're overwhelmed to see me here, well, I guess your brain goes searching for an explanation. Do you feel like you have an explanation now?"

I nod my head.

"Well, then, that's that. And we don't need to talk about it anymore. But, there is one more thing that we do have to talk about, the thing I said I had to say to you when you sat down and I was afraid you followed me out here. And, I hate to act like I know everything going on inside that little head of yours, but I have to tell you this and you have to listen and not be all offended when I tell you this."

"That's a good way to start out a conversation, tell me not to be offended by it."

"Whatever you do, don't fall for me. Okay? You cannot have those kinds of feelings for me. You hear what I'm saying and you processing all of that?"

"Jeez, Porsche," I say. "That's kind of blunt and uncomfortable."

"It is what it is."

"And let me ask you something, Porsche, what is it about you that's so diehard attractive and amazing that I would fall in love with you so hopelessly? You're actually kind of blunt—bordering on rude—and you make a lot of assumptions about everyone around you, like you have absolutely no social filter at all. I mean, I'm sorry for your trauma and all, really and truly, I am, but that doesn't excuse just doing and saying exactly what you feel like."

"That," she says, "is exactly why I'm afraid that you'll fall for me. I'm like one of those girls from the movies that the guys adore so damn much. Beats me why the guys can't resist them. Aren't you supposed to like some cheerleader type who's pretty and sexy and has absolutely no self-confidence so she needs to sleep with you to be reassured?"

"I don't know," I say. "I don't know what I'm supposed to be attracted to and I don't guess that I can help whoever it is, if it's you or a loose cheerleader or whatever."

"Control this, lover boy," Porsche says. "Don't fall in love with me. You got that? I can spell it out for you or write it on your Lifeline or whatever it takes to get it through to you. I can mark it on your calendar every morning so when your Wake-Up App goes off, you're reminded that today, you don't fall in love with Porsche Fairview. We can room together, we can talk about whatever and be honest, but if you start feeling things, not only will things get creepy, but you'll be distracted. And the openness to distraction that is built into our minds is something that I think is taken advantage of all the time. Just keep it in your head."

"As hot and attractive as that lecture was, I'm pretty sure that I can tap into my vast reserves of self-control and keep it in my head."

Chapter 18

Porsche and I decide to go back to our room at different times so as to not look too chummy. She leaves before I do and I decide that I'll try to do some reading, but my reader still doesn't work right, and all the letters are mixed up and flashing in and out when I look at it. So, I sit out on the porch and catch up on Lifebook through my earpiece, and listen to a story about the upcoming War Games match that someone posted, and about how well Mick had been doing this season. He's really starting to be one of the favorites from our state for the draft and I'm just so excited for his family when I let myself think about it.

When I get back to my room, Porsche isn't there yet. But, sitting at my desk is that same researcher. His partner is nowhere to be seen.

"I've taken a look at your Dreamcatcher and I really think that we're getting some of the bugs out now. Wouldn't it be great if we got this going for everyone of your blood type? If we can get this working, then I think we can have a DC3 in your house, free of charge, way before they hit the shelves for this holiday season. What do you think of that?"

"Sounds great," I say. "I hope that you're getting some kind of help from me."

"Oh yes, yes, we are. But there is something else that you could do for us. You see, and this might sound strange, but I feel as if there's some kind of a mental block that isn't letting you go into the program very far. And I think, from analyzing the data, that we've finally isolated what it is that is blocking you. A simple conversation with me or with my team—or even one of the group leaders—we believe, can undo this mess."

I sit down on the bed and try to look like I'm taking this very seriously, but I'm mostly just wondering where Porsche is. "And what is this conversation about?"

"The New Paradigm. You said in your entrance interview that you were in contact with members of the New Paradigm and that you haven't let us know about the nature of those contacts. We believe that you're holding back this information, to protect people, no doubt, with the best of intentions, and that this is really blocking your ability to enter this program fully. Since the Dreamcatcher is meant to ride in on your brainwaves, your placing barriers up around you isn't letting this in. I'm afraid that you can't progress very much toward your end-goal here without interviewing about this."

He looks at me expectantly, like now's the time that I should ask about what to do to unburden myself. But, honestly, I don't know what to say about it. The New Paradigm means nothing to me, even if they do mean something to Porsche and my brother. I'm not protecting anyone except my brother, and if I let them know the nature of *that* connection, then everything I've done here will be in serious jeopardy.

"I don't know how to go about talking about this stuff," I say.

"Well, you can speak with me—right now, even, we can start right now—or you can speak with any member of the staff. If you wish to remain anonymous, or go off record, that's fine. We don't need it for our data here. We are not the credit bureau, remember, we are health professionals. You can speak with David or Daniel, if you're comfortable with that, and they don't even need to write it down. But, we feel it will be like a weight off of your unconscious mind.

"Remember that health science is not like mechanical engineering or computer science. It's all problem solving, to be sure, but problems of the mind are intricate and confusing. We are not logical beings, but emotional ones. But, as far as we can tell, this would be a big help for us. A big help for you. So let me ask you, Scott, would you like to tell me about the New Paradigm right now? Any information you have would be really helpful."

I think about this a second and I try and think of what I could tell him that could get him to back off on this. I remember that Porsche said not to talk about them with anyone, but did lying count as talking about it?

"Well, I can tell you what I remember. But I'm afraid you will find it rather anti-climactic."

"That's okay," the researcher laughs. "I'm not looking for drama and I'm not looking for any big discoveries here. I just noticed that you didn't do your market research today and I feel like this might be the big block that you're facing. So please, Scott, fire away."

"Well," I said. "I got the fake ID for the middle school library reader because I wanted to download some books that my parents didn't want me reading, if you catch my drift."

"Of course," the researcher says. "I suppose we've all wanted access to things with some expectation of privacy, once in a while."

I think about his statement and it really doesn't make a lot of sense. Privacy? Like in a bathroom? I don't think I've ever read a book privately or gone to a store privately or bought anything privately. The notion paints the picture of doing all of these things behind closed doors. But, he said that we *all* have that expectation once in a while. And I just find that a little striking and broad.

"Well," I say, "the thing is, this ID that I had already had access to a bunch of reading materials in the archives under Recent Reads. There was a lot there about this New Paradigm group, and I built a fake Lifeline so that I could contact them and learn a little more. And, basically, I really wanted to turn off that hologram that I felt so invaded by and they helped me to do that. But the instant I turned it off, I felt terrible and I went and confessed everything I knew."

As I tell him this, the light in the room gets darker. Out

the windows, clouds gather at a nearly alarming pace. Not regular clouds, but dark, heavy, frightening clouds. And the look on the researcher's face almost mirrors the clouds exactly. His stern brow sits there, unwavering, and he doesn't blink a single time during my whole explanation. He's staring at me, but it's like he's staring at the wall behind me. I almost turn around to see what has his attention so, but his gaze keeps me locked here.

I sit there looking at him for a few seconds, and he still doesn't blink. A flash of lightning outside the window seems to break the trance that we shared.

"You, sir, are lying to me." A clap of thunder punctuates his very quiet statement. "You've been *lying* to me from the day you got here. What you are saying about your encounter with this rebel faction is untrue." He stares at me again, through me again.

"It's all I know," I say, weakly. "I don't know what else you want me to say."

"You know exactly what I want to hear," he says, very quietly, still no blinks, just the intense stare. "And you are going to stay here with us until we hear it. If you won't tell us, there are other ways to access that information. We can pull it from your little hard drive and you'd better just hope that we don't melt the blasted thing in doing so."

In all the time that I've been here, since day one on the train, I've never felt threatened. But here was this researcher in my personal space and delivering nothing but a very frightening threat, not veiled in any sort of kindness.

"You don't have long, little man, before we run out of patience. I don't want to hear of you missing another day in market research. And I don't want you stealing away with this little roommate of yours again. We can't take her out of here—not now, we're working on that, but not now—but let me promise you that she isn't any good for your decision making. Avoiding discourse with her will be your best move at this point."

I feel powerless to get up or to take my eyes away from his. The intensity is deeply unnerving and not at all subtle. Rain is pounding on the window now, and flashes of lightning and thick, rolling thunder echo through the halls. "I will take that under consideration," I finally say. "And I will behave myself," I add like an apologetic child.

"You will," the researcher says. And all of a sudden, the room changes color, it's so strange. He is no longer this intense and frightening monster, but a slim, slightly dorky scientist again. "You will do exactly that, I'm very sure. Your record is impeccable and I see you getting out of here with a full line of healthy credit very soon. Doesn't that sound great?"

"Great," I say.

"And I hope that your Dreamcatcher works a little better tonight, don't you? It sure would be something to get that working for all the O's out there. Sure would be something." He stands up and walks out the door. I don't move a muscle until I hear the falls of his feet echo off into nothing in the hallways.

I skip going to dinner and just stay in my room watching the Clear Channel, trying my very hardest not to think about anything. When Porsche comes in, it's already way past dinner and she looks very tired.

"Rough day," she says. "I feel like I've been so pumped with chemicals that I haven't been able to speak all day. Do they do that to you here? Shove you full of chemicals to get your brain to stop working?"

"Who needs that?" I say. "They have a Clear Channel with 700 stations. You could go months without thinking."

"Still," she says, "I feel like you have to fight hard to think critically. It feels like chemicals." I look and see that she is still in her red skirt, so I know she hasn't started market research. I really don't know where she's getting this chemical stuff. "I've got to go to sleep," she says. "I'm sure you have exciting things you want to talk about, but I've got to go to sleep. Maybe if I get some rest, then I'll be worth something to you in the morning."

She lies down on the bed and the thunder and lightning keep raging outside. I don't know if I remember ever seeing a storm this intense go on for this long, including the hurricane.

"Hey," she says. "You putting that Dreamcatcher on tonight?"

"I don't know," I say. "I've been considering it for a while. You don't use yours?"

"Naw," she says. "They don't work for me. They don't reach me."

"Yeah, me neither. But this is a DC3. It's supposed to work with my type. Maybe they'll give you one."

"They don't reach me," she says again. "And I've just got to go to sleep. G'night."

I don't end up using the Dreamcatcher after all, but I still have the nightmare. Wrapped in darkness, struggling to move, unable to yell. It's a terrible, terrible dream. Every time I'm confused as to who I am and what I'm doing there, and it seems to go on for hours, the way a dream can feel longer than the time it actually takes. When I get up, I'm all tangled in my bed and I can't tell if I was wearing my Dreamcatcher or not. I figure that someone might have come in and put it on me, which would explain the dream, but I don't have any kind of proof, and I guess it doesn't matter. It's just a dream.

The storm is still raging outside. When Porsche and I get down to breakfast, we notice a sign posted next to the entrance of the foodcourt stating that all sessions—group, research, marketing, everything—have been canceled for the day.

"What do you think is up with that?" I ask.

"I don't care," she says. "I'm just glad. I feel like there's some kind of hope for us having a decent day without sessions, you know?"

"I guess. But still, I wonder."

Porsche and I sit in the main hall most of the day, looking out at the forest behind the facility. She's got her book and seems to be really into it. I picked up a new reader from the library, and this one doesn't work either, showing me just blinking scratches of text. It's getting pretty frustrating. So, I just turn the reader to paper mode and just draw for a while. I draw a picture of the forest that's pretty lame, and I end up trashing it so that I can try again. I throw that picture away halfway through and start to draw Porsche reading her book.

"You notice something," she says to me. "The storm stopped, but it's darker than ever out there."

"No kidding," I say.

"I don't think I've ever seen it this dark at noon. Have you?"

"No."

The clouds are thick and dark, like smoke. They move quickly and hang low, just over the trees. The thought occurs to me that I can't believe that I haven't wondered if this really was a forest fire that we were watching. But it doesn't seem like a fire, as smoke-like as the clouds look, it just doesn't feel like a fire.

"You think everything's alright?" Porsche says. "It's ominous. I haven't seen a single person who works here today, outside of the foodcourt. And there aren't even that many patients or sufferers, or whatever we're called, wandering around, either. It's just kind of quiet."

"Yeah," I say. "I don't know what the deal is, but you're right; it does feel ominous. Kind of creepy, honestly."

We stay where we are for most of the afternoon, and I finish my picture of her. I think about showing it to her, but I don't want to get lectured about how I shouldn't fall in love with her again. And that's exactly what it looks like, me drawing her and all. And I start to think how unfair it is for someone to tell you how you shouldn't have feelings for them. After all, what do you think happens the instant you say that to someone?

Besides. It's not like I haven't had a crush on her since I started high school. Even though she was only a year older, she seemed so much more experienced. She had that charm and self-confidence and, mixed with how popular she was for her skills in the field on the War Games, and I found her impossible to resist. I knew dudes who snubbed the thought of liking her because they thought of her as some kind of tomboy. But, what did that really mean? She was, and is, a gorgeous girl. So what if she has short hair and is athletic? God, what do they want from a girl?

When we go to dinner, the atmosphere feels like a funeral. Everyone is quiet, subdued. And still, after the whole day is nearly passed, we haven't seen a single group leader, researcher, tech, secretary, assistant, or anything. The fact that rumors aren't flying around about what's going on is even scarier than a rumor could be. More than the darkness outside, the canceled activities, and the absence of anyone working here, it just *feels* wrong. Porsche and I don't finish our dinners before deciding that we should head back to our room.

"Look," she says when we get there, "I don't like the look of this stuff."

"What do you think is going on?"

"I don't know, but I'm hoping that we're going to have some business as usual type junk tomorrow. Have you tried calling anyone?"

"No," I say. "Let me look." I check out my mobile and see that the voice carrier is down. "I don't know. When it's very cloudy outside I don't get a good voice signal in our room, for whatever reason."

"What about somewhere else? Run back down to the foodcourt or the hall or something. I'll stay right here."

I walk around the facility for a while with my eyes on my mobile. There's no place where it gets any better at all, like the entire voice system is down. That's not unheard of, of course, but it's not at all reassuring. I go back to our room and tell Porsche the news. While I was gone, she changed into her pajamas and I feel a little guilty that I wish I had been there for it; even though I always look away, I like being in the room while she undresses. And now I feel like scum.

"Man," she says. "What about Lifebook? Anything strange going on there?"

"So far, there's no chatter on Lifebook about anything like we're dealing with," I say. "I've been listening in on and off all day. Nothing about darkness or the weather or anything. Everyone is just talking about the big War Games match tonight. We're going up against Walter High, who's having a pretty good season. We can watch it on the Clear Channel, if you want."

"Jesus, Scotty," Porsche says. "Maybe you could just try to imagine how much I don't want to do that."

"I didn't realize," I say.

"You just didn't think, is all. If you had thought, you would have reasoned that I have some pretty heaving baggage when it comes to that sport. I haven't watched a single match since the incident and I really don't plan to."

"Is that when you stopped carrying a mobile, too?"

"Yeah," she says. "I guess it's like this huge dividing point in my life. I mean, it obviously is. I died and was resurrected months later. I was dead longer than Jesus. And I bet Jesus didn't go to any crucifixions after he arose."

"So watching games isn't an option."

"Right. What do you want to do? Go to sleep? Read for a while?"

"Can't read," I say, "I got another bum reader."

"Huh," she says. "I don't want to be some kind of conspiracy spin doctor or anything, but I'd guess that maybe someone doesn't want you reading. Right?"

"Makes more sense than getting two bum readers in a row."

"Here, let me see yours," she grabs my reader from my desk and opens it up. "So what's wrong with it?"

"Same as the last one," I say. "No letters, just a bunch of blinking, mixed-up characters."

"You're reading Steinbeck?"

"I've been working my way through *East of Eden* since before I got here. How can you tell?"

"Because, it's right here."

I jump over on her bed and look over her shoulder. It's like I can almost make out the words, but the minute I look closely at one word, it changes or dissipates or dissolves into something confusing. It's hard to look at for much longer than a second at a time, even when I try intently.

"I can't read it," I say. "You're telling me that this looks perfectly normal to you?"

"Yeah," she says. "Here, take mine. I'm embarrassed to let you know what I'm reading, honestly, now that I see you're sitting around reading Steinbeck, but let's see. Try to read it."

I take her reader and flip it on. Again, it's the identical problem. And I can't read a single word.

"This makes sense to you?" I ask. "You can read this, like, perfectly normal?"

"Yeah," she says, staring at me. "This is trippy. Here, read this." She flips her reader to paper mode and writes a big number 4 on it. "What's this?"

"The number 4."

"And what's this?" She scribbles out a drawing of a person with a Mohawk, smiling.

"It's a really lame picture of a happy face," I say.

"And this?" She makes a bunch of marks and scratches across the screen. I can't make out what it is—shapes that dissolve and change into each other. Her reader is definitely not acting like it's in a typical paper mode.

"I can't figure out how you did that, but I can't tell what the hell it's supposed to be."

"You can't read," she said. "You can't see the letters and words and make sense of them. But you can see, right? I mean, can you spell your name?"

"S-C-O-T-T," I say. "Not bad for a sixteen-year-old, right?"

"Right," she says. "I don't know what this means. It might mean that I'm rooming with a nut job. Or, it might mean that something or someone is really screwing with you. How long has this been going on?"

"A few days, I guess. I wish I were keeping better track. But I feel crazy, Porsche. Like crazy. I feel like getting out of here."

"After we sleep," she says. "This is voluntary, they keep telling us, and after this day, I'm really ready to un-volunteer myself. We can take the rail back to the main station. From there, you can go back to the suburb and I'll head on into the city. And we'll keep in touch. I'll have my mobile on me and everything, like a real human girl."

I have second thoughts about this plan when I

imagine leaving her. And what do I tell Comet and Mom? That I failed? That we have to downgrade to the projects because our credit can't carry a house like ours anymore and that it's all my fault? "I don't know," I say. "What if we're freaking out for no reason?"

"Then we'll be so happy to be in our groups tomorrow."

In the morning, when the Clear Channel wakes us up, it's still dark outside. Pitch dark, like the middle of the night. You can't make out any shapes of clouds in the sky, but I feel like if you shined a huge light up there, you'd see the thick black smoke crawling along like a stormy ocean. We get dressed to head down to breakfast when we make a really alarming discovery.

"Did you lock this door last night?" Porsche says.

"The doors have no locks," I say. "That's one of the things they push in orientation, remember? That there are no locks and no need to lock your door? You're not pushing it right." I step forward and discover that, sure enough, the door is not going to budge at all.

When I push my hardest, and find that it's exactly like pushing against a brick wall, our room lights up from the Clear Channel.

"Good morning," a voice calls. We walk out of the small

hallway and both sit down on my bed. "This is a recording, so please do not feel the need to respond." On the screen in the same researcher who installed my Dreamcatcher. "We here at the Reintegration Institute have an important message for all participants. There has been a singular event outside these walls that is calling our attention elsewhere today. You may have noticed that things weren't running smoothly yesterday and I'm afraid that it's not getting better any time in the near future.

"There is no need to be alarmed. We are suggesting that you all stay where you are for the time being and until further notice. Don't worry, we have staff working feverishly to make sure that you are all fed and taken care of. Think of today as a sort of day off for all of you. You can continue your readings and your studies via Clear Channel, and you can take a few moments to call your loved ones and check in at home. We've even set up Clear Channel Conferencing so that your groups can meet together virtually after breakfast, if you so choose, though there will be no leaders present.

"We're proud of the work that you've all done so far and we're proud of the work that our professionals are taking on as we speak. I need to impress upon you that this is nothing to worry about and that information will come to you as timelines are illuminated and facts are gathered. Thank you, and God Bless the Dollar."

The screen goes back to being a wall.

"That door lock," Porsche says. "is a very strong suggestion."

"Right," I say. "I'm guessing that they know that it's futile to try and call our families, right? Like what he means is that they're busy getting the system to work, right?"

"Surely," she says. "And I'm guessing that the video conferencing will be just peachy, don't you think? No one will be freaking out and spreading rumors." We both know the truth, that there will be no conferencing.

We do get food delivered to our room, and they've either been keeping track of our orders or checking out our Liflines and Instagrams, because they know exactly what we want for breakfast. I have a staunchly manly eggs and bacon, while she has biscuits and gravy and a pecan roll. The food is delivered to our door by a servant who smiles but doesn't say anything. There are two armed guards standing behind him when the door is opened, and we drop any notion that we had of rushing the open door. The sight of them makes the hair on my arm stand up.

Porsche got sick of doing reading experiments with me and finally she recedes to her bed to sit and read. She agrees to let me watch the Clear Channel, since there really is nothing else to do, so long as I have my headphones on and she doesn't have to "listen to the damn, devilish thing" while she's reading.

I start watching a wrestling match between a couple of

pretty popular wrestlers, but when it gets pretty obvious that this was from last week, I turn it to the music channel. They're not playing music, of course, but instead talking about the new styles that this season's musicians are wearing, and it's not really interesting to me. There's an old movie on another channel that I've seen one too many times, and nothing on the news at all about this strange weather phenomenon, much less anything that would clue us in to what's going on with the staff at the facility, why we've been seemingly abandoned. I page through the rest of the channels and find nothing interesting, so I start back at the wrestling match, which is still going on. I watch for a while before I fall to sleep.

And I have that nightmare again. I can't move and I can't see and I can't scream. In the darkness, I feel like I can hear people moving around and talking, but it's like my ears are stuffed with cotton because I can't make out what they're saying. I struggle and struggle and struggle, just like every time I have this dream.

Suddenly, I'm pulled out of it. "You okay, man?" Porsche has taken my headphones off and is straddling my chest and shaking me. "You look like you're having a seizure," she says.

It takes me a minute of looking around the room, and then up at Porsche, before I'm acclimated to where I am, who I am again.

"Do you have seizures? Is this something I should know about?"

"No," I say. "I don't have seizures. Not that I know of, anyway. I have nightmares."

"One hell of a nightmare," she says. "What was going on?" She gets off of me and heads back over to her bed. "Sorry, didn't mean to be on top of you. I was just afraid you were going to fall off and hurt yourself. It's like you were trying to scream and your whole body was kicking around, but you weren't really moving, like you were stiff as a board."

"That's pretty much the dream," I say. "Just darkness and fear, pretty much."

"Huh," she says. "Freaky."

"I think it's the Dreamcatcher," I say. "It's tweaked to work for my blood type and every time I've slept with it, I just have this nightmare. Like I'm just completely pinned down or cramped and I can't really see or hear or move. And I try and I struggle and eventually it just ends. If this is how Dreamcatchers work for the rest of the world, I can't imagine how they ever got to be so damn popular."

"Pretty sure that's not how they work," she says. "I can't imagine why you'd still sleep with the damn thing on!"

"I fell asleep this time," I say. "It triggers the programs when we fall asleep. I usually just set it to music or something, so my mind doesn't wander too much. And the sleep cycle hemi-sync stuff works fine for me. It's just the dreaming programs. I don't know how to shut them off here."

"Don't wear it, that'd shut it off."

"The other night I went to sleep without it, but it didn't work. I had the dream and woke up with it on. I guess they came in and put it on me. Or else I put it on out of habit at some point when I was half-asleep. I mean, I'm so used to sleeping with it on, I don't know if I can sleep without it."

"I hope you're not hopeless," Porsche says at last. "Here we are in this really bizarre, really strange situation and I'm stuck with the dork who can't read or sleep. You think you're maybe not as okay as you think you are?"

I unravel the syntax of what she said and come to the conclusion that she could be right. I came here thinking myself perfectly normal, taking the fall for my brother, figuring that I'd be out of here in no time. Now, I'm questioning my sanity or my ability to survive through a really strange reality that I've been thrust into. "I don't know," I say to her. "Let's check and see if group conferences are really going on, huh?"

We flip through the channels on the Clear Channel and we check every possible input, but there's no place to even have some kind of internal conference system. We figured that they'd just be on, automatically, like some kind of override, but there's nothing like that happening here.

Lunch is never delivered to us either, and we're just stuck in our room, with her reading and me mostly looking out the window at a world that looks like it's swallowed in darkness. "How long," I say at last, "until I finally give up and have to eat you?"

"Um, good luck with that one," she says, "because I'm totally outliving you and you look way tastier than I do. I'll just wait till your guard is down, like when you're trying to read or when you're flipping out in your sleep, and I'll just open a vein of yours and watch you turn pale."

"Jesus," I say, "I was joking. That was dark."

"Whatever," she says and goes back to reading. "You're the one who brought it up. I just thought you might want to know who you're messing with before you start planning your Thanksgiving."

"What good's Thanksgiving without a sale?" I say.

"You bored?" She says. "You can watch the Clear Channel without the phones, if you want. I don't mind."

"Naw," I say. "I'm good."

"I can read to you."

"No thanks."

"Here," she passes me my reader that's next to her bed.

"Just draw or something. I don't like just having you sulk there. Do something. Draw."

She goes back to reading and I start drawing her. I look hard at her facial expression as she reads, a mixture of concentration and surprise. Her hair is messy, but like actual messy instead of the forced messiness that she puts on it when she fixes it in the morning and covers it in gel. Her eyes are pale green and I match the color on the tablet by weaving two greens together. "You staring at me?" she asks.

"I'm drawing you."

"Cool," she says.

I draw her long fingers holding the reader and her silver bracelet that hangs on her wrist. She bites her bottom lip as she starts reading a new passage, and I go back to her face to catch the change. Her ears have little holes where she must have used to wear earrings, on her lobes and up on the top of her ears. I try to match the darkness of her hair and still get the texture visible and I do an okay job of this.

In the middle of my concentration, I sort of lose track of time, and I end up being startled when there's a knock on the door. I stand up to answer it and there's the server guy standing there with two meals. Sashimi for me and some kind of a burrito for her.

"Can you tell us what's going on?" I ask.

This time there are no guards with him, just him and a

pushcart. He leans in and whispers to me, "it's been a little strange, to be honest. But we have word that things will be back to normal tomorrow. There's a lot of apologies going on, and whatever this weather thing is seems to have contributed."

"Is everyone okay? Like all the other people here?"

"Fine," he says. "They're all fine."

"So why aren't we allowed to get out of here and mingle?" Porsche says.

"Oh, it's not that you aren't allowed," he says. "It's that everyone's working hard to reboot everything and they just don't want everyone standing around watching and getting in the way, potentially. You understand. There's a lot of work to be done and they just can't have it gummed up. This inconvenience should be really minimal from this point on."

He leaves and closes the door behind him. We hear the magnetic lock click back into place.

"Tomorrow," Porsche says. "Tomorrow we'll do things a little differently. We don't hang out in our pajamas all day. We get up, take a shower, and get dressed. We carry ourselves with some kind of self-respect. This has been miserable."

"I know. Terrible day," I say. "But I don't guess that we really have to worry much about tomorrow, if what he said is true. It should be back to normal." I don't really believe what it is that I'm saying. But it helps. Her smile seems to acknowledge that she knows I don't believe it. I don't bother to finish my drawing. I just eat and go to bed.

Chapter 19

Morning comes and things are not normal. The room is nearly completely dark, only a little light coming in from the window. The Clear Channel does not wake me up, and the ambient noise of the whole facility functioning is no longer there. It's dead quiet.

"Any idea what time it is?" Porsche asks before I say anything. I take a look at my mobile and can't get it to turn on. I try and flip on the lights and there's nothing. The Clear Channel doesn't light up when I try.

"Nope," I say. "Feels like morning, but it doesn't look like it."

"No, it doesn't. Let's try the door, shall we?"

We both walk over to the door and find that we can't budge it. "Doesn't seem right," I say. "This is some kind of electric lock, right? I mean, like an electric controlled magnet or something?"

"Yeah," she says. "But if they're not turned off by electricity, maybe they just stay on? Beats me. But we're stuck until someone comes to get us."

"When's that going to be?" I can feel myself kind of freaking out here, but I try hard to keep it under control.

"Don't know," she says. "Guards or no guards, this time we rush them when breakfast comes."

We spend a long time—seeming much longer than it is, no doubt—listening. We sit by the door, looking into each other's faces, almost able to make them out in the dark, with our ears against the door. We never hear one sound. Porsche gets the idea to try and tap on the pipes in the bathroom.

"Good idea," I say. "Do you know Morse code?"

"No," she says. "But do you think the guys next door know it? I just want to know if anyone is alive or if it's just you and me who've been left here."

We grab her reader and use it to hit against the bathtub facet. We do three hard taps and then wait for a reply. Nothing. We do three more. We wait. Nothing.

From there, we spend some time banging on the walls as hard as we can. We pound and pound without any result, nothing to hear.

By now, breakfast time has certainly passed. We try breaking the windows, which we think Porsche might be able to fit through, but we can't break the glass anyway. If we could just see, I feel like we could figure something out. Like, maybe there are screws we can undo somehow, or maybe a ventilation system in the ceiling that we can go up through and find our way to the outside, like in a movie. But there's hardly any light at all. And we're getting hungry and the walls are closing in on us.

Sometime in the afternoon, we notice that it looks like it

could be snowing outside. We spend some time debating if this is true or not before it becomes obvious that it is snowing, since there is so much coming down that they start catching what little light there is. We sit there for a while looking out at it, wishing that we could get out there, no matter how cold it is. We work a while longer at breaking the window, using a chair to take turns mashing away. Not so much as a crack appears.

"What would they have done if there was a fire?" I say. "Isn't it a complete hazard to have only one entrance and exit? I thought that this wasn't a prison."

"They probably had some electrical system to get the windows to all burst open or something."

"No, that'd let too much oxygen in at once, wouldn't it?"

"I don't know, since when did you become a fire expert?"

We wait. We occasionally check our readers to see if they're working. I check my mobile over and over again. It's one of those stupid things that I know it's not working, and yet every few seconds I have this new and totally original idea. We'll be sitting there and all of a sudden it just comes to me, "oh, I should check my mobile and see what everyone's up to", or "oh, I should check my mobile and notify the police that we're here!" Over and over. It's like my body will never be used to the idea that it's not there anymore.

"You want to play 20 questions?" I ask.

"No," she says. "Do you?"

"Would you play if I do?"

"No, I'm just curious as to whether or not you want to play. It's a pretty lame idea right now and I just can't imagine sitting there across the room from me and you trying to think up stuff for us to do."

"Fine," I say. "I'm just trying to not let it get to us. I'm just trying to try and have some kind of conversation."

"You're being a dork," she says, flatly.

"That's what I mean," I say. "You're letting it all get to you. I'm trying to save us from that."

"That's fine, Scotty. But look around you. If the rest of your life is miserable because I wouldn't play 20 questions with you, at least you know that wasn't a very large part of your life."

"How do you figure?"

"Scotty, it has to be past dinner," she says. "No food, again. How many days of this do you think we can take?"

"I've got an ace in the hole," I say. "I'm going to overpower and eat you."

We laugh a minute. A sort of pathetic laugh. "We won't last long enough for you to eat me if we don't have water," she says.

"Have you checked the water?"

We both stand up and feel our way to the bathroom. She holds my forearm with her hand and it feels nice. She grabs my arm tight, but I notice that she's not shaking and she's not squeezing. I kind of thought she would be more scared than this. I feel like a little bit of a wuss because I realize that it could be that I'm more scared than she is.

We take a while to find our way there and I don't go too fast because I'm enjoying the contact with her. We get to the bathroom to turn on the faucet, and it works.

"Oh thank God," I say. "What a relief."

"Does it taste right?" she says.

I fill my palms with water and drink it. "Totally normal," I say. "What a miracle. I mean, it could be laced with poison and we could die, but at least we won't die of thirst. That seems like the worst."

"Poison, I'm so sure." she says. "It might be better if it were. Get it over with."

"Are you kidding? This will help us to last *days* longer. The longer we can last, the better chance we have of figuring something out."

"That's almost cute," she says. "Almost."

We move back to our beds and lie down. I search the room with my eyes and just can't see anything. I imagine how my eyes must look— huge, black pupils opening in the darkness. I search my head the same way I search the room but it's kind of dark, too. Nothing to say, very little to think.

"I guess this is goodnight," she says.

"I guess so." I put the headphones on out of habit. I'm just not sure if I can sleep without the feel of them on.

That night, I have the nightmare again. There is no electricity, no Dreamcatcher. But I still have the nightmare.

I wake up from the dream in a sweat. "You must have been dreaming," I hear her voice say. "You woke me up."

"Sorry," I say. "Same damn dream."

"I figured."

"Is it morning yet?"

"How the hell would I know?"

"I don't know," I say. "I just mean, does it feel like morning? I hate going to sleep after the dream."

"Well, Dodge," Porsche says in a mocking tone, "there is a lot to get done today, so I don't want to see you sleep in for too awful long, you hear me young man?"

I laugh at this and stand up. I look out the window and can make out the outline of some trees against the dark sky. "Morning," I say. "There's actually a little bit of light out there. Almost."

"It'd be brighter if the window would open," she says. "I think that should probably be our project for the day."

Without losing a moment, I grab the chair from my desk and start to pound on the window with it. I work up a rhythm with the hitting and my breath. Pound, two, three, Pound, two, three, Pound, two, three. After a while I'm tired and make my way to the bathroom for a drink of water. Then I come back in and sit down. There's enough light coming in that I can see the outlines of everything, including Porsche.

"Hey," Porsche says out of the blue. "You want something to eat?"

"Sure," I say. "Anything I want?"

"No, well, yeah, just so long as what you want is a Powerbar."

"No way," I say. "I totally call bullshit on you."

"No, really. I have a few. Like six or seven. I squirreled them away those first days before this happened."

"Why?"

"Beats me," she says. "Sometimes a girl gets a feeling. And they had this big pile of them down there and people were grabbing them and liking them on Lifebook. So I grabbed a few and shoved them in my bag."

"And you're opening them up now?" I say. "Why not yesterday?"

"I was saving them for an emergency."

"Bull."

She gropes around for my hand and puts a wrapped Powerbar in it. "How's that for bullshit?"

I start to eat and then think that I'd better slow it down. It's the best thing I've ever eaten, though, and I just keep going.

"You might want to make it last," she says. "I think I only have three for you. We'd better have one a day."

"It's gone," I say. "Gone already. I can't even wait for tomorrow. I hardly know what to do with myself without another one."

I stand up and start taking whacks at the window again. Pound, two, three. Pound, two, three. "Do you think I'm doing any good?"

"It's fun, isn't it? What do you care if it's doing any good?" she says, her mouth full of Powerbar. "We may as well enjoy ourselves."

"Oh, I know," I say. "I think this should be a

videogame or a Dreamcatcher program—Hitting Windows with Chairs in Near Total Darkness. It'll be a huge success." Pound, two, three.

After a few more hits, I put the chair back down and rub my hand along the window. I'm pretty sure that I feel a crack.

"That's encouraging," Porsche says. "For real. Want me to take a turn?"

"Have at it," I say and I sit down. I see Porsche's dark form as she stands up and lifts the chair. She bounces it in her hands a little to get the balance and feel for it. Then she pulls it back and yells out loud as she sends the chair crashing against the window. She lets go of it and lets it fly. It smacks into the glass and comes flying back at me.

"You okay?" she asks.

"I'm fine."

She sits down on the bed next to me, out of breath. "That's hard," she says. "Trying to break that window takes a lot out of you."

"You did one hit."

"I'm exhausted."

We sit in the dark, next to each other on my bunk. I am hungrier than I've ever been; eating the Powerbar just made things worse, I realize. It dawns on me that we are going to die here. I can't imagine why or what could possibly be going on outside, but this little room is the last place I will ever see, and I can hardly see it in the increasing darkness.

Then, we see something.

Floating in the air in front of us is a large, fluttering leaf. It's almost luminously green and its direction jerks back and forth, up and down. I realize that it's not a leaf, but a butterfly.

"It's a moth!" Porsche yells.

The moth lands on the chair that had fallen on the ground at our feet. It splays out its wings, as if to give us a better look at it. It's the largest moth I've ever seen. It glows green, a small eye-shaped spot on each quarter of its wingspan. I've seen pictures of moths like this, but I have never seen one in person before.

"It's a luna moth," I say. "Where did it come from?"

As if on cue, we feel a cold breeze.

"I think it broke," Porsche exclaims, stupefied. "Look, it broke!" The window that the chair had bounced off of is entirely absent of glass. I get up and look closely and see that the pane didn't shatter, but popped out of the frame and is lying on the ground outside. How did we not see this before? Why did it take the moth for us to see it?

"How about that, Scotty?" she gloats. "You try it like 500 times and get a little bitty crack. One go at it and the damn thing pops out for me."

"Don't worry," I say. "I feel thoroughly emasculated."

"Damn right. And I think I can fit through there."

The whole room becomes much colder and snow starts to find its way through the window. With the coldness, comes fear, for maybe the first time since we've been in here. There was some kind of calm acceptance about our space in the darkness, but the world outside seems so unwelcoming and aggressive. It doesn't feel supernaturally cold, or anything, but considering it's October, even at this elevation it would be pretty unthinkable for snow to be falling. I guess that while we were just locked in, it was like we were watching the world go through this change, and even if we were stuck and if we were never getting out alive, we weren't a part of what was going on. Whatever it was. And now, I feel wrapped up in it.

"What then?" I say. "You get out and then everything is fine?"

"I doubt that. But what are we going to do? Just stay?"

She climbs up on the desk and crawls through the small opening. Her slippers fall off and land on the ground in front of me. As I pick them up to hand them back, I look at the thin cloth of the slippers and I try and imagine what these are going to do against the snowy ground. I can almost feel her feet freezing inside them.

"Here," I say, putting my hands out. "You have to come back in. This isn't safe."

"Scott, don't worry. I'll try to find some way to get back in and find some supplies and food. We're going to be fine, you and me. There're only like four Powerbars left and that's not going to last us long. Hand me my shoes. I think I see a way down."

"Where?"

"There's a tree out here nearly touching. Looks like a good climber. How lucky is that?"

I hand the shoes up and then I gather the blanket from her bed and hand that up, too. "Wrap yourself in this," I say. "It's freezing. See if you can find more blankets or jackets or something." She smiles down at me while she wraps the blanket around herself. She disappears into the darkness, hugging the side of building. The minute I can't see her, things feel even colder inside. I wrap myself in my blanket and try to imagine what she's doing, wishing I could have bent myself down and fit myself into the small space to go after her.

I feel singularly alone now without her. Alone in a way that I've never known before. All I can try and do is shut down my brain and wait.

Chapter 20

I struggle hard to keep a single conscious thought in my head without Porsche here. The hunger and the loneliness are at least as overbearing as the cold and the darkness. I feel consumed by emptiness as every aspect of by being is uncomfortable. I've already eaten my bar for the day and I'm doing everything I can not to eat Porsches. Part of me feels like she'll find vast stores of food, so it will be fine for me to eat all of them, and the other part of me just fears that she won't find anything or, worse, won't come back at all.

I eventually abandon the top of my bed and climb under the blanket as the darkness deepens and the room grows colder. I try harder to shut everything out, but my mind keeps rushing to Mom and Comet. I figure that whatever is going on, it's some kind of worldwide disaster. Only now do I truly realize that Porsche and I have hardly discussed what it could be and how the world is dealing with it. We've been so lost in our sense of personal doom that I didn't let my mind stir enough to go out to my own family. And, now that I think about it, I mostly feel like dirt for not having thought about it before. I just lie under my mattress, somewhere between awake and asleep, trying to compose rational thoughts about my family without having it hurt like hell, thinking about what a terrible person I am. I don't even know at which points I'm fully awake and at which points I start sleeping, until I have the nightmare.

The nightmare comes this time and I could almost swear

that I am awake when it first hits. I'm just lying there, trying to stay warm, when all of a sudden it gets even darker. I can't move, though I struggle. I can't yell, though I try. I hear murmuring voices and this time—for the very first time—I feel something; a hand grasping my upper arm. But when I wake up from the nightmare, I'm back in the reallife nightmare. Darkness, the cold coming in, the mattress on top of me.

It's morning now, I can see, or at least daytime, since there is some light coming in through the window. My stomach is in pain and I think about the Powerbars. Then I think, maybe I shouldn't eat them. Maybe I shouldn't eat or even drink anything and just get this over with.

"Hey, Scotty, you in there?" I hear Porsche yell.

I stick my head up from the mattress and see her silhouetted in the window.

"Oh, hey, I can see you. Sorry I didn't get back here last night," she says. "I finally got a window open to get into the complex and by then it was nighttime. I couldn't find any way to get up to the second floor. I couldn't find anything."

"Anything?"

"There is no one here, Scotty. No one."

"Have you looked in the other windows? Maybe you can just see if the other residents are trapped and waiting or what."

"They're tinted," she says. "No way to see in at all. I knocked on a few, but didn't hear anything. I didn't get much further inside, either." She's just sticking her face inside, not making any move to get back inside. "I got into the lobby, and all the doors were locked from there. It was useless. I yelled and hollered and was only answered by darkness. It started getting cold, so I wrapped up as best I could and slept behind the reception desk."

"Did you get anything that can help us? Anything at all?"

"No, sorry. No food, no clothing, no weapons."

"Weapons?"

"Hey, you've got to be thinking, Scotty. We don't know what's happening next. I think we're going to need weapons if we're going to get much further. Don't you?"

On the one hand, I'm totally encouraged to hear her think that there is a "next." But, her painting of what that next is disturbs me. I was thinking that either this was the end, or things would go back to normal from here. "Come on back in," I say to her. "If you can't get anything done in the compound, you might as well stay here. We've still got a little food."

"Keep it," she says. "It's early, I figure, since the light just started. So I'm going to set off."

"What in the hell are you talking about?"

"I'm sorry, Scott. I'll come back, I swear. If there is any way for me to come back, I will. I will bring food or I will bring help, or I will die trying."

I reach out to take her hand, but she pulls it away, afraid I'll try to pull her in. "Take the food," I say. "And don't come back. I'm fine to stay here. If you find help, help yourself."

"Look, Scotty, I'm not going to get all sentimental and I'm not going to make promises for you to hold onto or look forward to. The reality of the situation is that we have no idea what the reality is, so that's what you can hold on to. Everything is lost or it's not. But you can't lose me or shake me by being all noble about coming back for you. I have no reason to abandon you and nothing in the world is more meaningful to live for than to come back. So will you see me again? Probably not. But if I'm alive in a week, it will be because I found something or someone that helped me live. And I'll come back and get you out of here or I'll come back and visit your body." Her voice doesn't shake, doesn't waver. It doesn't sound determined or excited or brave. It sounds resigned. I can't quite make out her face in the darkness.

"Well, I'm glad you didn't get sentimental," I say. We both choke out a half laugh that's more recognition of lightheartedness than actual lightheartedness. "Good luck to you. If it's more than a week, don't come back. There's no reason to visit my corpse."

"Okay then," she says. "Good luck to you, too. If things go back to normal, don't take any more shit around here. I'm going to follow the rails. I guess I'll head toward the city, since I think it might be closer. But who knows. Catch ya."

She turns and edges away from the window, climbs on to the tree, and then is lost to the darkness.

Chapter 21

I have no idea how long she has been gone. None. The compulsion strikes me to try and keep track of time, but it's something I just can't do. Without my mobile, without a clock, without a calendar, time doesn't make sense to me. I don't know how long I made the food last, but I know that it wasn't long enough. I try to keep track of how many light periods there are, but I lose track almost instantly. I occupy myself by taking a button off of my collar and throwing it across the room, counting to 30, and trying to find it.

Until one time when I don't find it. Then I just stop playing.

The sink still works, which is a minor miracle, but the kind of a miracle that I feel like mocks me. I literally feel like I'm being made fun of every time I go and get a drink. I start collecting snow so I can at least feel like drinking that makes me a survivor instead of just some idiot stuck in a room. But the snow, somehow, makes me feel thirstier when I shovel it into my mouth.

At some point I managed to rip open the mattress so that I could crawl inside of it. It felt warmer in there at first, but the cold always seems to make its way in. That's when I get out, feel how bad the cold really is, get a drink, and then crawl back in to the mattress.

I try not to imagine what the other rooms are like. Filled, I assume, with dead residents. People just like me, trying to make things better for their families, slowly suffering until they die with no one around to know about it. Maybe tucked into their mattresses. Maybe with roommates. But, unless they squirreled away their food, I can't imagine that any of them are still alive.

And that gets me thinking.

How did she know to hide food? And not just any food, but something really dense with calories. And what was this she was saying about weapons? Does she know something I don't? The window seemed to be just big enough for her and just too small for me. How did she get it open when I couldn't?

It's just to keep my mind busy, I tell myself. I'm not becoming paranoid, because that wouldn't be helpful. I'm not losing my mind, because that doesn't make any sense at this point, either. I'm just trying to stay busy by taking a look at her and what she had done for me and recognizing the small little conveniences.

What would the point be in not trusting her? When I verbalize this thought to myself, I start laughing. I laugh and laugh. Like, what if she checked the door and said that it was locked and it wasn't? And this is just some kind of setup. I laugh at this and then I go and check the door. I remember, once I'm standing there with the handle in my hands, that I had already checked it. And then I laugh a little more.

I crawl back into my mattress and wait.

I have a dream at one point that I wake up and the world is new again. There's sunshine in the window, but I hardly notice it because the glorious Clear Channel is on. I watch *West Charles* and all the characters look so beautiful and so wonderful and vivid. Their voices sound like music and their problems seem so petty. Billy won't sleep with Sue. Sue is in love with Billy but settles for Charles. Big. Fucking. Deal. The whole show, with all of the over the top drama that you can imagine and it doesn't hold a candle to my life.

At some point in the dream, I notice that I'm eating pizza from Wasabi. And it's like the best thing in the whole world. It's brought to my door by Mom. And it's only then that I realize that now I'm in my bedroom.

"Everything is fine now, dear," she says. "It's all cleared up. Things were scary there for a while, but it's better now. Eat up."

I start eating and I'm watching the War Games on Clear Channel and our school is playing Reagan again and I see that Porsche is taking lead instead of Mick. I start to tell Mom about Porsche, about how she's alive and how I met her at the credit Reintegration facility. She just stares at me while I tell her.

I see my dad walk by in the hall behind her. And I don't know which dad of mine it is and it doesn't matter because it's all so glorious. And I tell this to Mom and her face kind of shifts.

"If only," she says. "If only you could get out of that damned room."

And there it is, the dream ends and I'm tucked into my mattress again and the coldness is nearly unbearable. I wonder which will take me first, freezing or starving. But before I can wonder that for long, I just go back to thinking about the dream I just had. How wonderful it would be if it would all just stop. If all these problems could just go away and all my real-life problems would come back. Economics tests, party evites, cutting carbs, acne, aftershave, baked potato chips, high volume eggs, brand hunting at the back-to-school sale at the mall, the sinking feeling you get when you wake up and realize that you've run out of deodorant, all these normal, human problems. I just want them back. I just want to be human again.

I catch myself yelling it out the window. But it's almost like I'm watching myself yell and what I'm yelling doesn't really even make any sense. The sentiment is there, the passion for what I want and I feel the need to vocalize it. I picture the world as a big wheel turning and I picture it crushing me and I want so badly to yell and yell until it just gets off of me and lets me climb up on it while it keeps turning and brings me to the top.

When I'm through yelling, I instinctively check the Clear Channel to see if there's a signal or power. I just want to fucking see the pretty people on *West Charles* get bent out of shape over nothing. I just want it all back so badly.

I don't know how long it's been. How long anything has been. But I am tucked into my mattress, and I am still. I am not awake, I am not asleep. And this is how I've been since the beginning of time, as far as I can tell. And I hear my voice mumble something, the same little prayer I've been saying over and over whenever I think of it since the surface of the Earth cooled and hardened and vegetation grew and oxygen took hold of the atmosphere. "Please," I mumble. "Please." It's the sigh of the trees outside, the breath of the wind, it's just as constant as the darkness around me: "Please."

"You here?"

"Please."

"Scotty! Are you here?"

I'd heard her voice on and off for days. I learned to stop paying attention to it. But there was something compelling about the tired desperation in her voice. For days when I heard her, she was healthy and strong and vibrant—like when we met. But this voice was tired and tested, worn.

"Scotty! Dodge! I can't see you if you're in here and I don't want to just visit your corpse, remember?

I shoved my head out from in between the mattress and looked upon the black form in front of me.

"Oh, thank God," she says. "He's here," she yells out the window. "He's here and he's alive." She turns back to me, "now we just have to get you out."

"How're we gonna do that?" I say. "Can you get inside?"

"Hey!" she screams down behind her. "Can you guys work on getting inside? Find some way to get up to the second floor? Room 248."

I hear replies but can't make out the words. "Who's with you?" I say.

"Here," Porsche reaches into her pocket and throws a package at me. "Fruit pie. Lemon. We've got all the junk food in the world. It's pretty wise."

"You look better," I say. "How long has it been?"

"I think it's been four days. Four really long ones. I met up with them yesterday at the rail depot just down the hill. Luck, just amazing luck."

I rip open the package and the fruit pie is the best thing I've ever eaten. Far better than any turkey dinner I've had at Thanksgiving and 1,000 times better than the best sashimi I've ever had on my birthday. The richness and sweetness of the lemon and the flaky, processed crust marry perfectly together. For a few seconds, the sensation of having food in my mouth blinds my vision and smothers my hearing. All I can do is taste it. It's the only input open for my sensations.

"But you've got to know something, Scotty," Porsche whispers low to me through the window. "I don't trust them. I know they're your friends, but I'm telling you that I smell a rat. They're way too eager and they, well, don't seem themselves."

"My friends?"

"Just listen to me, Scotty. I know you're not feeling well (and you look like shit, BTW) and I know you're going to be excited to see Mick—"

"Mick?"

"Just listen to me," she holds out her hand in a stopping motion. "I'm not going to lie to you, I'm not going to lead you wrong. When it comes down to it, I'm the only one that you can trust."

Just as she says this, there's a pounding on the door. "Yo, Dodge!" And unbelievably, it's Mick's voice. "Is that really you?"

"Yes!" I call out. "In here! Get this door open!"

I see light creeping in through the crack under the door. It's the first real light I've seen since the blackout started. "Hold on, bro. We'll bust this thing wide open!" A repetitive pounding starts on the door, getting louder and louder. It stops for a second and then I hear voices, and it starts again, even harder and louder. Porsche and I sit and listen to the noise, her perched above me and me halfway out of my mattress.

"Goddamn," Mick says from the other side. "This door is made out of iron or something. I swear. We've got seven guys here taking whacks here. But don't worry, we'll get you out!"

"Listen, Scott," she whispers. "I can't go into this all now. I think they want something from us."

"You're paranoid," I say. "But we can talk later, okay, I promise."

"Scotty, I think you should come out through the window. I can't tell you why, I really can't, but I think it matters."

I laugh for the first time in days. "Porsche? You know I can't fit through there. You were lucky to get through."

"You haven't seen yourself, Scotty. You're thin. Thinner than you think. I can see your outline and I have to say that even through it's only been a few days, I hardly recognize you. Come on. Give me your hand. Let's just try. I mean, that door isn't coming down right now anyway, is it?"

I get fully out of the mattress and stand on top of the desk. I reach my hand out and feel Porsche's. I can feel the strength in her grip and I can feel how weak mine has become. She grabs my other hand, too and pulls as I scramble up towards the window. I can see that I'm going to get stuck; it's clearly too small for me. But somehow, amazingly, I feel myself be pulled through the window, hardly touching it on any side. In a blur, I'm standing on a ledge, outside for the very first time in I don't have any idea how long. The snow is falling slowly, but somehow it seems brighter out here. I look out at the dark trees against the dim sky and feel absolutely light and free.

"This is amazing," I say to myself. "Just amazing."

And just as I say that, the door in the room comes bursting open and Mick is standing there with half of the War Games team. A couple of them are carrying flashlights and the light seems blinding. "Thanks," he bellows, "for making us do that while you could have just gone out the window!"

"I had no idea I could," I say. "I've shrunken."

"Well, c'mon, you two. Let's get downstairs."

"No way," I say. "No way I'm coming back into that room. Never. Not if my life depended on it. I'll see you down below." I follow Porsche's lead and grab onto the pine tree that takes us down. She makes it look easier than it really is because I have trouble finding the footing, especially in the dark. We hit the ground and start walking towards the front of the building.

"I'm not trying to harsh your buzz here or anything," she says. "Really, be excited. Be very excited. We're out and we're safe at the moment. I came across them in the rail station, like I said, and they're headed toward the city on some kind of expedition. They were eager to hear about you and know you were here. They feel like you can help them."

"Help them? With what?"

"Mick wouldn't tell me," she says. "He seems really suspicious of me, and who can blame him, right? I mean he was there when I died, as far as he knows. Not that he wasn't stoked to see me. But anyway. I just don't know what kind of fool's mission they're on and what they think we can do for them. It seemed less sentimental or affectionate, you know, and more like they were excited because you can help."

I struggle to act like I'm really listening to her. I just nod my head and decide I'll figure things out as we go along. For now, it's enough for me to just hear my feet on the ground and to feel my aching legs stretch.

"Just keep your guard up and stay close to me. Really. Promise?"

I nod.

"Promise me, now!"

"I promise," I say. "How about another fruit pie?"

She pulls one out and hands it to me. Again, I'm awestruck with the sensation of food.

"OMG, Dodge! It's you!" A girl runs out of the front door and wraps me with her arms. It takes me a moment to realize who it is.

"Lily? Is it really you?" I grab her and pick her up and swing her around. "I can't believe it! I feel like I'm dreaming!"

"It's me," she says. "And it's you. Mick is here, and Tay, and the Martin brothers. A few others, too. God, I'm so glad to see you! Here, take this." She hands me a jacket, some kind of military jacket that feels amazing on my shoulders.

I think as I try and soak in as much of Lily as I can, that maybe they were acting weird to Porsche because they didn't really believe I was there. Or that it wasn't going to be real to them until they actually saw me. But I am overwhelmed with the comfortable feeling that everything is going to be okay.

Mick and the others come out a few seconds later, guided by those blinding flashlights. I don't think I've ever hugged Mick before, but I feel like I'm never going to quit squeezing him when I do. He feels strong and powerful in my frail arms. Every person who I come into contact with act like a mirror for me, showing me how thin and weak I've become in my time locked in the room.

Once the greeting and the shoulder slapping is all over, we sit down and dig into their food stores. We sit in a circle on the deck where the chairs all sit like nothing ever happened. Someone piles wood into the middle and starts a raging fire. The warmth is unreal and even blots out the sensation of eating. The flashlights are turned off and one of the Martins produces a lantern. It's the most civilized moment in my life, it feels like and such a far cry from my previous life. We feast on Twinkies, and pies, and salt and vinegar chips, and chocolate covered pretzels. I can't eat half as much as I want to because my stomach starts to really seize up, like it's made out of stone.

They all tell the story of how they ran into Porsche, how she snuck up on them at night, not knowing who they were, and how surprised they all were when it all came clear. Mick talks about how surprised he is to see Porsche still alive, and the story he alludes to about her survival seems a little different than the one I remembered. I figure he remembers it wrong.

"So what's the story?" I finally say once the last few days have been covered a few times. "What the hell is going on?"

The smiles all drop and everyone gets silent. Finally, Mick speaks. "There are rumors," he says. "The one I heard the most is that the corn is gone. All of it. That there was some kind of group that took it upon themselves to just try and eliminate humanity. But I don't know if that's true."

"Some kind of war," Taylor says. "The power grid was either shut down by Americorp to freeze things up and stop the approach of the rebels, or else the rebels shut it off to arrest the strength of the corporation. It depends on who you listen to."

"But what about the sky?" I say. "Why has it gone dark?"

They all shake their heads. "Nuclear winter?" one of the Martins asks. "Is that what it could be? Maybe the city bombed to hell and this is the fallout?"

"Or a meteorite, or a super volcano, or an electromagnetic pulse. Everyone has a different idea. But we've been chosen to go and find out what's going on. There's enough reason to believe that the New Paradigm group is behind some aspect of it. And if we can find them or hook up with some kind of peacekeeping forces, we can help out. We just can't sit by. And with all of our Peacekeepers on deployment, we're the only ones qualified enough to fight."

It's only then, really, that I let myself notice it. Every one of them is armed to the teeth. Rifles stick up from every pack. Knives and handguns strapped to every leg. I've joined a war party of some kind, a children's crusade, all these athletes who are playing at being heroes. And I just want to go home.

"Good luck with that," I say. "I'm headed home. I've got

to check in on Comet and Mom and make sure that everything is going to be okay if the sun ever comes back."

Mick swallows a mouth full of dried teriyaki birria. "They're fine, Dodge," he says. "The last thing I did before leaving town was check in on them. Your whole complex has sort of joined together and it's kind of like a block party. They have plenty to eat, there was no violence in the area, everything was fine when we left them."

"That's good," I say. "But I've got to be there. They've got to know that I'm okay."

"I'll take you there myself," Mick says. "After we get what we're looking for."

"Really, Scott," Lily says, "there's nothing to worry about. As frightening as this has been for you, they are actually almost having fun."

I nod my head, but Porsche's eyes catch mine and she's staring knives at me. And she's right. Something doesn't feel good about this. Their attitudes are too cohesive. Like, maybe that's something you learn on a team that I just wouldn't understand, but it seems like with all the lingering questions, there would be a lot more disagreement, a lot more trepidation about what should be done. But they just sit there, the seven of them, looking down and eating contentedly.

"The problem is," Mick says, as if the decision has been

settled and I'm coming with them, "we travel so slowly. I don't think there are a lot of places to refuel on food between here and the city. And we're pretty sure that's where the New Paradigm is running operations, right, Dodge? I wish there were some quicker way to travel."

"Has anyone checked the stables?" I say.

Part III

Chapter 22

I can't get my goddamn horse to behave to save my life. I'm astounded at the nimbleness that every other person has with their horses while mine wants to run back to the barn every time I let my guard down. It's gotten bad enough that no one laughs anymore when I yell or fall or get way off track from everyone else. They're just annoyed with me. No one has offered to trade me horses, because I think they think it's me and not the horse at all.

Of all the luck and coincidence and wondrous things I've ever seen, walking into a stable full of living and contented horses during this apocalyptic nightmare has been the most amazing. The door didn't need to be broken down, just unlatched. And when we walked in, it was warm and cozy and lit by several soft electric lanterns. I couldn't figure out for the life of me why these lights were working.

"It works off of a different generator system," Lily said. "It was the same way at my mom's hospital, where they had both kinds of generator. Either the stables are an older part of the facility, or they figure that they're more exposed to the elements, so they don't run on the same lithium backups that everything else runs on. They burn old-fashioned fossil fuels to keep the lights on. And it worked, too. They've been fed and mucked and everything, just like they should have. We probably saved their lives though, because they're going to run out of fossil if no one refills it sooner or later."

Whatever the explanation, we just lingered in there for a while, soaking up the warmth and looking at the animals. The Martins grew up with horses and were able to saddle them all and give us a talk about how to ride them. None of us are sure what the weather will do to them or if we'll be able to find enough to eat once we run out of the oats that we tied to their sides, but we all agreed that we all had a better chance of surviving together.

How someone could run out on these animals, much less Porsche and me and whoever else, is really beyond me.

"They could have been run-off," Mick says while we ride along the tracks. "Attacked. You might not have even heard it from upstairs."

"But they would have left us alone? Not killed us, not taken us with them? It doesn't add up," I say. "And we never did check the other rooms." It was something that none of us could agree on, checking the other rooms. We reasoned that there was no way that anyone else was alive. And we finally reasoned that there was no call to do a search of the bodies, as it would take too long and exert too much effort on our little party's part. Porsche thought we should check just one room to see if there were bodies, but since the place was operating at low capacity and since we weren't sure which rooms were occupied when the blackout started, we overruled her. She sulked for a while and threatened to stay behind, but we knew she was bluffing.

We raided the building for food, but found nothing except a vending machine in the workers' lounge. We shattered the glass and filled our packs with more packaged food. The fact that the kitchen was cleared out was further evidence that there was plenty of time for all of the workers to leave.

"Could be," Mick said, "that they evacuated and just missed you guys. In all the confusion and panic, that could easily have happened. Or, maybe they hated you guys and left you behind altogether. Or maybe," and here he looked at me closely, "they felt like you knew something they didn't want to get out or risk losing. They thought they'd come back, help you out later, figure out whatever it is that makes you so valuable. But things didn't go as planned."

"Maybe," I had said. "Maybe they wanted me for my extreme horse riding skills." This sent Mick into a huge belly laugh, like the kind he used to do when we would be out at lunch together, joking around. How nice the world used to be.

Everywhere I go, Porsche stays right by my side. She seems to be regarded by the rest of the group as a little bit crazy. The whole bunch of them seem to be laboring under the notion that the both of us were being held in some kind of mental institution or that Reintegration is somehow synonymous with insanity or something. But even Mick and

Lily, who were both on Porsche's varsity team last year, keep their distance from her, never smile, and rarely ask her opinion about anything. I start to worry about her myself, especially when I talk to Mick alone—for once—and he brings up how fishy her story is.

"Look, I like her and I'm as glad as anyone that she's still alive. But frankly, I don't know how far we can trust someone who has come back from the dead like that," he said in hushed tones. "Really, Dodge, you keep mentioning how well she came through for you, how she saved your life, and that's all fine, but maybe she was left there with you in order to do just that. You ever think about that? That there's something off about her whole presence? Like things are a little too easy when the rubber meets the road?"

And it is exactly what I think, a good deal of the time, that things are too easy with Porsche. But I don't say anything, because I don't want it getting back to her that I doubt her—if the doubt is legitimate or not, it does me no good. So I generally just shrug my shoulders or nod whenever the conversation goes this way.

"I get it," Mick says, "you've got a thing for her. And that's totally fine with me. But don't let that blind you, okay buddy?"

"It's not exactly like that," I say.

"So you don't have a thing for her?"

"Well, that's probably the case. Can you think of a female friend I've had since high school started that I didn't have a thing for?"

"Of course not."

"But it's more than that. We've been through a lot together. And it's been intense. And I feel like we have a real connection."

Mick stops his horse and I follow his lead, with a little effort. He looks me in the eye. "Dodge," he says, "things aren't what they seem anymore. She's not what she seems. You can't trust her. I get it, she has to tag along, but I'm telling you not to trust her. Let her talk, nod your head, but don't listen."

"And I can trust you, right, Mick? Things aren't what they seem, right?" I eye the rifle he has slung over his shoulder nervously.

He pulls something out of his backpack. "Here," he says, handing me a large leather case with a handgun inside. "I've been meaning to give this to you. You need to be armed. We all do. There are reports of fire fights all over. A real life insurgence right here in our homeland. Rebels, outliers, nonconformists, unintegrateds. They have lots of names and it's easy to see where they're coming from. When you're not part of the system like we are, you have limited opportunities. It can make you crazy. We can see that, right? But what's the answer? Takeover? Restructuring? Or should they just join up, integrate with the rest of us? This is what we're facing."

"Mick, you just broke me out of a Reintegration facility. How can you trust me?"

"Because," he says, "you're one of the most reasonable people I know. I've known you for so long, we're part of each other, right? We need to hold the lines and dig out this insurgence group, the New Paradigm. And I think you have information on how to do that."

As he says this last part, Lily and Porsche ride back to where we are. "What's the holdup?" Porsche says.

"You boys going AWOL?" Lily asks.

We laugh a little. "Sorry," Mick says. "We have a lot to catch up on. And I'm starting to wonder how reliable Dodge's horse is. You think you can manage now, Dodge?"

"Yeah," I say. "I think I've got her under control for a while. Thanks for the pointers."

"You want to just trade him horses?" Porsche says. "You could just trade him if you're such a great rider, Mick."

"We should get moving," I say. "I'm fine. Thanks for all the concern. I'll be fine."

We ride until the dim light in the sky starts to dim even more. The snow is falling gently, and when the wind starts to blow, it cuts through my jacket and reminds me of my room a little too vividly. We start scanning the horizon for somewhere to bed down before it gets too cold. They have brought a collection of tents, but Mick says that they haven't had to use them yet and that they don't really trust them much anyway. They've been finding abandoned houses, stores, or rail stations to sleep in and that's what we're hoping to find soon.

When we finally start lighting the lanterns, we spot a dirt road leading away from the rails. Without any other real option, we ride down the road looking for anywhere that would be warmer than the outside air.

"So, no one here really knows the landscape?" I ask Mick. "I mean, surely between the nine of us, someone has gone to the city enough times to be able to pick out where a reststop is or something."

"Not from the rail. It goes too fast and you never need to stop," Mick says. "I've been to the city a dozen times to catch the other rail line to get to War Games matches around the state. You never stop. And I don't know about you, but I can't think of the last time I looked out a window during a commute. Probably before I got my new Mobile2, ten years ago."

We ride along for about ten minutes before it starts to get really cold and dark. It's then that Taylor comes riding back toward us from the darkness. "There's a barn," he says, "abandoned or at least unused. No house in sight. Sound good?"

"Perfect," Mick says. "Everyone, follow Tay."

Everyone aims their horse at Taylor, who turns the light on his lantern up and hooks it to the back of the saddle. I'm a little blown away that Mick is so engrossed in his role that his orders are basic common sense to the rest of us. Follow Tay? Didn't everyone just hear Taylor say that he found somewhere to stay, and don't we all presumably want to live? Mick announces this as if this is his decision, as if he just delegated survival instincts to all of us.

"So, who made you leader?" I ask him.

"Coach," he says. "I mean, obviously when I made Second Lieutenant at the end of last season. But Coach also sent us on our errand."

"Why didn't he come? Doesn't he have real combat experience?"

"Sure, he does. He has a family, too. Has to stay back and take care of them. None of the violence has hit home yet, but we feel like we have a way to make sure it doesn't. Finding you, well, that's part of it."

"Look, Mick, I don't know what you think I can do for you guys. If I had any confidence in my ability to take this animal back home to Mom and Comet, I would."

"They're fine, Dodge. They're fine. You want them to stay fine, you'll stick with us."

"Just let me know, right now, before anything else, Mick. What the hell do you think I know?"

"How to save us all," he says, without a trace of irony.

It's not a barn, at least not in the way that he meant it. What he thought was a barn was actually one of those chain field trip destinations, History Now! It's a huge complex with different ages of American and Americorp history represented. One section is Colonial, where you can take part in the tea and tobacco trades. The second is a Western expansion area, inspired by the Manifest Destiny period, where Native Americans were brought into our trading practices. You study that in the 5th grade. Then there's a smaller section that you study in the 7th grade called The Depression, which shows the failures of social programs. And there's one section depicting the Food Revolution of the 21st Century, showing how primitive farms were changed to the multi-level farming structures that they use now. Our barn, the one that Taylor found, is in the outskirts of the Food Revolution. So, in many ways, we are now taking part in a recreation of the past.

There is plenty of room for us to sleep in the loft and plenty of room for the animals. Food for them, too. When we get up into the hayloft and roll out our sleeping bags, everyone keeps talking about how lucky it is. And I just think, it's another ridiculous coincidence, as hard to believe as any of the others. I'm thankful for it, just as thankful as any of the others, but if every single day my survival depends on this kind of absurd luck, how long do I really think I'm going to live? All it's going to take is a single misstep and I'm done for. All of us are.

To stay warm, Mick instructs us to strip down to our underwear. If we sweat when our body temperature rises as we fall asleep, our clothes won't wick away the moisture, but the bags will. There are nine of us, and he advises that we get into pairs, all except the person on watch, and that we zip our bags together to share body heat better. Everyone has to take a one hour watch, except Porsche and me, since we're not part of the team. We insist that they let us help out, too, but Mick lays it down that they're just not ready to have someone not on the team take a watch. It raises too many questions. I feel like they can't trust Porsche and they think I'm incompetent. Whatever the case, it means that Porsche and I are climbing into a sleeping bag in our underwear together.

"Don't get too excited," she says to me. "Remember our rules."

I nod my head, thinking that her rule is total shit. We set up as far away from the others as we could without trying to seem suspicious. They didn't seem to mind, as they all kind of have their own rhythm going with this watch thing. After all, I can't imagine how they know how long an hour is right now with nothing electrical working. Once inside the bag, pressed up against Porsche, I feel again how bony my own body has become. I also feel warmer than I've felt since we broke that window in our room, however long ago that really was. I had forgotten what warmth was like, and now it glows through me, and I take pleasure in settling down into it. The pleasure I get from the physical warmth is far beyond any sexual feeling I was afraid I'd have in this situation.

"I have an idea for you," she whispers when things settle down and get quiet. "I think that I know what you should do about your dream."

"You do?"

"You struggle and can't move, you yell and can't make a sound? Don't struggle. Don't move. Don't yell. When you find yourself in this dream, try and remember to just sit there, get calm, be quiet."

"You don't understand. It's like pure fear. You ever been claustrophobic? It's like that times a million."

"You don't have to whine about it to me," she says. "I've seen what you go through with the dream and I'm not looking forward to being right next to you when it happens. So I get it, it's tough and it sucks. But if there's any way, I think that it would be a good idea to not fight it next time. Don't fight it, just go with it and accept your disarmament. See what happens. You always wake up, right?"

"I guess so."

"Do you have the dream every night? Or every time you fall asleep, or whatever?"

"No," I say. "Just every so often. And once I could have sworn I wasn't even asleep. Like this nightmare pulled me out of waking consciousness. I'm afraid of it trickling into my day."

"Well, Scotty, that's a whole new can of worms, isn't it? How sure are you that you were awake?"

"Not sure," I say. "Not sure at all."

"Let's go ahead and assume that you were asleep for now. Let's not push too hard on this thing."

"What thing, Porsche? What are you getting at?"

"Look, Scotty, there's a lot going on here. For whatever reason, it seems like there's a lot going on about *you*. What is this info that they think you have? I mean, I'm sure you're a smart guy or whatever, but this is kind of stupid, don't you think? I mean, you have any ideas?"

"Porsche," I say, "I feel helpless. I feel like I'm sitting here and watching all of this happen to me. I don't know anything. I haven't been to the city since the eighth grade and, to be honest, I have no idea what this New Paradigm is. I'm in over my head. I want to stay alive and I want to see my family. I don't care about Reintegration, I don't care about integration at all. And somehow I feel like I'm in the middle of all of this."

In the dark I can see that she is nodding her head. "I get it," she says. "I get it. See, I'm more on the other side. I hate Reintegration. I hate the idea of Americorp for everything they've done to me. All my life, not just to my family. I've been their puppet. We've been their puppet. Our lives have been colonized, compromised, and our earning potential has been harvested on the illusion of seeking happiness. That's what I think."

"Be quiet with that around here," I say. "In case you haven't noticed, your old teammates are out here questing to get things back to normal. I'm fine with that. Normal is good."

"Normal is not normal, Scotty. But don't worry, I'll shut up. I just want you to understand that when push comes to shove, I'm not helping these people out. If we ever figure out what they're after from you, I just want you to think twice. I understand that I might not be as convincing as they are. It may not be as easy to imagine changing things for what you actually believe—it's always easier to adopt the beliefs of someone else."

"So I should just adopt *your* beliefs?"

"If you examine yourself, Scotty, you might see that our beliefs aren't really that far apart. Great minds, Scotty, great minds."

The room is quiet now, and pitch dark. The only sounds come from the shuffling of the horses down below. I don't know who took first watch, and I don't really care because I think it's overly cautious. I figure these guys are all too excited to use their sports skills and try and put it to some kind of practical application. Like the time when Derek Munro knocked some kid out using a karate chop in middle school because he started taking karate and the kid mouthed off to him. I didn't ask where they got the weapons, which would be a totally valid question, considering they're really hard to get a hold of and you need like three operating licenses just to own one. But if their coach was involved— and why the hell would he be—that would at least explain it.

All I know is this: to stay alive and make it back home I have to stay with these guys— at least for now.

Sure enough, I have the dream. It comes on in such a familiar tone now that on some strange level, I feel like I never left the dream, but have been here all along. The fear and panic spread quickly through my body, just like usual, and I feel all my muscles start to spasm and flex against the invisible restraints. But just as I draw a breath to scream, I am reminded of Porsche's words. I try and relax. I try and let my muscles go limp, let my breathing slow down. I imagine my heart pumping more softly. It takes all of my strength to smother the fear and ignore the panic. I relax. I turn into water.

Somehow, it works. I am calm and still and suspended in absolute darkness, held in place by some kind of gravity, solid and unmoving. I slow down my breathing and I can hear my breath. There's something calming about hearing my breath. Now I'm calm and still lost in this total darkness. Without the panic to guide me, I try to think about what I should do. It's then that I realize that I really don't remember reality at all. I don't know where I am or who I am, really. There are images and thoughts that, once I approach them in my mind, disappear like mist.

Now I'm just someone nameless and formless, lost in the void. Without the fear and without the panic, I'm really not anything at all. I float there and realize that I am not calm any longer, but not panicked either. I am not relaxed. I am not even floating. Maybe, I think, maybe I am the darkness or part of it. It's clear that it's part of me.

Chapter 23

Commotion snaps me awake.

"See?" I hear whispered in the dark. "See? Just on the horizon."

Straw or hay, or whatever this stuff is, shuffles and dark figures move around in the near total darkness.

"Here, take these. Look. See?"

"What's going on?" I whisper to Porsche.

"They're watching someone on the move, out near the rails."

"Who is it?"

"Beats me."

All seven of them are gathered at the single window that they have opened. I watch their shadows for a while, hardly moving in the dark. I can feel the tension in the air, and I know that something really frightening is going on, but they move around with such little urgency and I can't wrap my mind around what it is. Finally, I slip out of my sleeping bag and crawl over to the others in my boxers.

"What's going on, Lily?"

"We're watching a huge group of people on the move."

"How?" I look out in the direction everyone is looking,

and I see nothing but a thousand shades of darkness.

"Hey, can I get those binoculars?" Lily reaches out and takes an object from one of the guys near the window and hands it to me. "Take a look through this."

I look through the binoculars and I see orange and red splotches moving along in the darkness. "What the hell is this? Something headed back home?"

"They're thermal binoculars," Lily says. "They don't use batteries, it's the hybrid lenses that let you see the body heat."

"How did you guys get these? Aren't they like, majorly expensive?"

"All this stuff is like majorly expensive," Lily says. "We're lucky to have any of it."

"What do you think this is?"

"They don't move like Peacekeepers," Mick says. "They're coming from the city and I would guess that they're armed."

"You don't know that," Dwight Martin says. "You have no idea if they're armed or not."

"Taylor says he saw something, and I think I did, too. But if they're not armed, why in the world would that many people be moving this late at night in the dark and cold without any lights?" Mick says.

"There were lights," Dwight says, "at the beginning. But they shut them off."

"That's what's got me worried," Mick says. "If they've got hybrids like ours, they could know we're here. I mean, we're in the barn, but don't you think that nine horses give off a pretty big heat signature?"

"True, but this is good, thick wood. And it's got to be cold on the outside," Dwight says. "But, the fact is that we won't have any idea what's going on from here. If we feel like this is anything to be worried about, we've got to check this out in person."

Mick stands up and starts shuffling through his pack. "Who's coming with me? I'd like one more person."

Dwight stands up. Mick hands him some kind of clothing that is rolled up into a ball. Grabbing the edges of the balls, they shake them out revealing some kind of military windbreaker. They shake them out and put them on over their jackets.

"What's with that?" I ask Lily.

"They hide heat signatures. In this darkness, they'll be totally invisible."

The windbreakers stretch up over their heads and then pull down over their faces like some kind of ski masks. As I look closer at them, I notice that the fabric on the windbreakers isn't just black, but there are different shades of darkness woven in, almost like they reflect the darkness all around us.

"Those can't be standard War Games gear," I say. "Those clothes and binoculars? Are those really useful in the stadiums?"

"You never know," Mick says. "We're a well-funded team. What was the last budget? 90 percent of the school's funding goes through the War Games program, one way or another. Everything else is much cheaper since we moved to the national curriculum."

"If we're going to be competitive," Dwight says, "we have to have the budget. We were looking at going to state this year for sure. You know they've been running our highlight reels on the Sports Network? Have you gotten to see that from inside that...wherever you were?"

"A little," I say. "I know you're having a great season. I know that. I just, I mean, you think you'll finish?"

They all look at me as if this is the first time that it's occurred to them that things might not go back to normal. "Yeah, of course, right?" Dwight says.

"Of course," Mick says. "This is just a sidetrack. We'll get things back. You buy that, right, Dodge?"

I nod my head. "I think it would help if we knew what the hell was going on."

"You got that right," Mick says. "We'll talk, okay, bro? Sometime after I get back?"

"Sure," I say. "Just take care out there. It's not a game, right?"

"You got that right," Mick says, blending into the dark so well that I can hardly see him. He and Dwight slip down the ladder to where the horses are, and I can clearly see that the horses are spooked by them; they jerk away and whinny softly. They go out the barn door, and from there, we cannot see them at all. We take turns with the binoculars and watch as the procession continues. At one point, Phil claims to see them, but we doubt him. He doesn't really say that he sees them, but that he can see their affect on the brush as they sneak by.

"It's them," Phil says. "They're there. I know because that's exactly the route I'd take if I were out there." I catch a few of the others roll their eyes at this statement.

Eventually, the procession passes by. We try to guess how many their numbers are, but they end up totaling somewhere between 50 and 200, so we know that we really have little concept of their magnitude. Everyone seems nervous until they pass, and then they all relax. We all sit and hold vigil for 20 or 30 minutes before they come back, clearly in one piece.

"It's clear," we hear Mick say in his authoritative voice. "They passed."

"But what did you find out?" Lily says.

"They're headed back to town," Dwight says. "I'd say there were about 75 of them altogether. Not Peacekeepers, but security of some kind."

"Americorp security," Mick adds, as if that were necessary. "Probably going to town to back up the locals and make sure things don't get out of hand. Make sure rations are holding out. Maybe just to check on things and report back."

Everyone agrees with this.

"Why didn't you talk to them?" I ask. "If they were Americorp, why not talk? Aren't you on the same side? You afraid they'll put a stop to our little cowboys and indians game here?" In my mind, I can't help but wish that I were quick enough to slip away and join the security administrators and get back to town. I can't stop thinking about Mom and Comet.

"Dodge, we're handling this, okay?" Mick says. "We have a mandate here to follow through with. It might be a small part, but it's a part. We don't want to spend all night explaining ourselves." Everyone nods. "Speaking of the night, we need to get some rest. I think that with them passing by like that, we can probably skip watch. What do you guys think?" Everyone agrees with him and we all start crawling back into bed. When I get back into my sleeping bag, pressed up against Porsche, I realize just how cold I feel.

"I think, if we're going to say it's all clear, maybe we can snap a couple of Sterno sticks and warm up a little?" Lily asks.

All heads turn toward Mick. "It's probably not the best idea," he starts. But then his tone changes, like a man letting a puppy climb up on the couch after all, "okay. Someone have a pot to drop them in?"

Lily grabs a small pot from her pack and either Dwight or Phil grabs two Sterno sticks and snaps them to life. They start glowing and he drops them into the pot. We all move our bags closer to the glowing pot, and the warmth feels like heaven.

"Anyone else keep imagining what this would look like on Lifebook?" someone says. We all laugh.

"Mick Poland and eight others have checked in at the old barn," Mick says. We laugh again.

"Phil and Dwight Martin and seven other friendships like Sterno sticks!" I say. "Mention Sterno sticks four more times for free heat!"

"Dodge Goode dislikes riding horses. Bookmark this activity for future consideration?" Lily says, and we all laugh harder. "Perhaps searching for riding lessons on 'VideoPages' would help your enjoyment!" Lily's tone of voice perfectly mimics the Lifebook female voice, and for whatever reason, we all find this hysterical.

"Porsche Fairview likes resurrection!" Taylor says, monkeying the male Lifebook voice. We laugh and laugh at this one. The mood is so light; it's as if we're all having an elaborate campout. Even Porsche laughs a little, and it's the lightest I've seen her act since we joined up with the War Games guys.

I have the nightmare again, and I instantly remember Porsche's advice. I breathe deeply and relax. I hear some kind of bubbling, some kind of gurgling, like white noise that is gravitating together, forming new sounds, falling in line, falling out, over and over. I concentrate on hearing and I think I can make out voices. I start to wonder if I'm hearing the War Games team talking in the barn, watching me in my sleep. But then I realize that, since I'm not struggling in the dream, I'm probably not struggling in real life, either. I try to hear what the voices are saying, but when I try to focus on them, they just disappear. I relax deeply, listen to the sounds and decide that I am making sounds out of ambient noise— my mind panicking to make sense of things.

Now what? I think. I start feeling myself, trying to make sense out of myself. Do I have a form in this nightmare? Am I solid? Or am I not just wrapped in darkness, but part of it? And now I realize that I don't know who I am anymore, and that I don't know what I am. I can't remember what I was thinking about. It's like once I'm here in this nightmare long enough, I disperse and lose not just my mind, but my body.

Then I remember; I was trying to make sense out of myself. I start with toes, and I feel like I'm wiggling them. I think of my arms, and I try to move them. For just a moment, for the smallest instant, I feel my arm budge. I know it's there. I know my toes are there. I know my arm is there.

I will try, now, to open my eyes, I think. I struggle to think of my eyes, to imagine the lids opening, and finally, they do.

I'm looking at Porsche's face. "You okay?"

"I think so," I say. "Where are we?"

"The barn," she says. "You dreaming again?"

I nod.

"I could tell. I couldn't wake you. I was shaking your arm. Did you feel that?"

"I might have," I say. "Can we go back to sleep?"

"We're trying to get going. Ready to ride?"

"No. Never."

The packs are all packed in half the time I could imagine it being done. They work like soldiers with a clearly defined goal, a pilgrimage, a destination. But I can't help thinking how this hasn't been articulated. They are serious and they are on their way, but I don't think they know where they're going or why. There's a blind devotion to the idea that if they just get there, everything will be okay. And where is the goal? Over there somewhere. That's all.

I would be just as happy, I think, to sit inside the barn for the day and eat a lot of dried barria, which we seem to have plenty of.

But we must move. Mick says so. No one asks anything. It's time to go, so it's time to go, and the goal is the goal, and everything will be fine when we get there. I can feel that Porsche feels the same sourness to the expedition. There doesn't seem to be any room for other ideas, though. So we pack our pack, too.

We head down the ladder and each claim our horses. I look at my horse, standing snow white in the dark, like the opposite of a shadow. I can't believe it, but no one will trade with me. It's clear that any one of them is better than me on horseback, and it would only make sense that we should take turns on the horse that demands to be an asshole. But no one trades with me. He backs away from me slowly as I approach him, but I grab his halter and I look the horse in the eye and I beg of him, "let's have a better day, buddy." His look does not fill me with confidence; I feel like he half-closes his eye in skepticism. *It's on*, he thinks. I nod in agreement.

The barn doors are thrown open and I'm taken aback by how bright it is. It's not bright in any normal sense, but there is an almost reddish glow from the horizon that gives us the hint that a sun is lurking out there somewhere. I remember a day when there was a dust storm when I was little, and I remember seeing the pictures on Mom and Dad's Lifelines, and the skies looked kind of like this; I mean, they are reminiscent, but it's not quite right. I remember fires and I remember storms, but none of them really look like this. I'm continually struck by the newness of the experience, ever since the sky went black.

Everyone mounts their horses and begins to file out of the door. My horse kicks away from me and keeps a distance between us. Every time I think I have it, my left foot planted in the stirrup, he jerks away, walks a few steps, and stops. He stands still, like he's the most well-behaved soldier in the world. We go through this farce over and over, drawing the collective eye rolling of the entire group. "You guys want to just go on without us?" I say, and everyone chuckles politely. Finally, Porsche rides forward on her black mare, grabs my horse's halter, and jerks it toward her.

"Get on. Now," she says.

I get my left foot into the stirrup, swing my right leg over, and settle myself in the saddle. The whole group erupts into applause. I take a bow that more resembles a curtsey, and we finally get the hell out of the barn.

We ride down the dirt road, and rejoin the rail and ride slowly, watching the reddening sky. Everyone is quiet, a few whispers between a few riders, but not a lot of group talking or anything. Porsche rides next to me, and just like last night, she's really quiet.

"This is foolish, you know," she says at last.

"Should we ditch them? Ride back to town?"

She shakes her head. "We need to see this through. You'll understand before long."

"Do you understand?"

"I'm beginning to," she says. "You don't have to stay close to me. You can hang with your friends. We'll have time to talk soon enough."

"You're being mysterious," I say. "I'm not a big fan of that right now."

"Get over it." She rides up ahead of me, toward the front of the pack, knowing that I don't have enough control of my animal to catch up.

I see something square up on the horizon, breaking the consistency of trees and hills poking up into the distance. At first I think it's some kind of building, but as we get closer, I see that it's a billboard. We all pause at it for just a second, looking at the first evidence that a city is up over the curve of the Earth. The billboard shows Guy Mann, The

Mattress Outlaw—a guy who's on all kinds of cheesy Clear Channel ads and billboards, constantly acting like the police are after him for selling beds for so little. Only, this ad isn't for his furniture chain, it's an ad for Clear Channel billboards. "Advertising with Clear Channel is the best thing I've ever done," it says. "Besides stealing all those mattresses!" And there's a little logo for his company down there. So it's like one or two ads embedded in each other. And I can't help but imagine, if there were another ad, an ad telling about the advantages of advertising your firm in an ad about the advantages advertising your firm with a company. Like setting up two mirrors in front of each other.

We see more ads as we come in to town. An ad for Monsanto, "Happiness is a bite away!" An ad for MasterCredit, showing a family relaxing on a beach, "A thousand travel points for every qualifying purchase!" An ad for a strip club, "All that stands between you and Paradise, is your decency." On this one there's a "Click Now for Mobile Discounts" icon, and all the guys start clicking the dead mobiles on their wrists and laughing. An ad for Noon Burger, "The Tokyo Triple Trouble Barria Burger, Now with Bacon, Eggs, and Wasabi!" The picture, illuminated by the lanterns we carry, makes my mouth water. I realize I'm maybe as hungry now as I was back in the facility.

"Wouldn't be so bad, would it," Mick says, "a Tokyo Triple Trouble?"

"God, no," I say. "Sounds like a million credit points right now."

"I can't wait until things are back to normal. I can't wait until we graduate and can start living our lives for ourselves. Building our careers, just like we've trained to. Well, I guess you will want to go to college, right? Get some kind of exec job? You're set up for that, right?"

"I'm set up," I say. "If next year goes well, you know. Then I'll be able to go. Well, if they accept my Reintegration."

"I'm sure we can get that fixed," he says. "Help us out and all of us will vouch for you."

"What is it, Mick? What do you think you can get out of me? You know that I'll do whatever I can to help you. Hell, if you were on the run from the law like Outlaw Guy Mann, I'd help you out. But I have to know what you want me to do."

"The thing is," Mick says, "I just have to know that you're on my side."

"I don't even know what sides there are."

"I don't really know what you were into," he says. "What got you into the whole mess. I mean, obviously you've been keeping it from me. And when all of this went down, I had started wondering if I really knew you at all. I mean, I know that you've been dealing with some pretty deep junk ever since your dad died. And I don't envy you. But you've been hiding things ever since then. I just keep wondering if you're going to come clean to me or what."

We ride past a billboard for butter, "Spread a Smile on your Wholegrain!"

"Mick, there's probably a lot you don't know about why I was there. Or maybe you know more than I think, since you went by and saw my folks. I don't know what they told you."

"Did you read your dad's Lifeline?"

"What?"

"Since he died? Have you read his Line?"

"No."

"I did," he says. "Everything was there. Pictures from his childhood. Birthday parties, school trips, TV shows he liked. You see when his family moved here from Winwood, when he met your mom, how he dated other women when he was too shy to approach her, his War Game matches, his first jobs and his credit building. You wouldn't believe how much he wrote when you were born. And twice as much when Comet was born."

"I know," I say, "he read us what he wrote every birthday."

"I'm just saying. His life story is there. And it's so sad

that he died, man, so sad. But you can see the meaning of it all. You can see the way that he built his credit to provide for you guys. You can read so much about his tours in South America, how strongly he felt about the forests. It's all so *meaningful*. You see? I'm telling you this because I understand that sometimes it can feel pointless, but when you realize that we all have the right to work and buy happiness, and you can see the ways that your dad bought happiness for himself and for you guys, you really start to *understand*."

I shake my head. I'm unable to think about my dad right now.

"It's a damn shame he died. But don't blame the system. Don't blame the corporation. Why you were in touch with those Paradigm jokers is beyond me. But you have no loyalty to them."

I hear these words and I see that he wasn't just trying to make me feel better about my dad or give me some kind of completion that my family might have come to while I was gone, he was trying to get through to me.

"They don't put just anyone in those Reintegration places," he says. "Plenty of people fall through the cracks. Plenty of people have to move or downgrade jobs or work for free without any upgrades. You were cut a deal for two reasons. One, your dad did a great service. Did us all a great service. But the other reason. That's the one you're holding back."

I just look at him.

"I pulled your file. I knew there was a deeper reason. Something they wanted you to volunteer. Now's the time, bro. Tell me where they are, who their boss is. You owned up to reading about them, right?"

"Right," I say. "The reader I checked out. I thought I could keep it anonymous."

"But you've met with them. You had mobile conversations and two weeks ago, you met with them. They have the records, so you might as well tell me."

We pass a billboard for the Mercury Line, the line that crosses the whole continent. It says, "We put a price on seeing the world because you couldn't." And there's this totally happy family, with a little kid asleep on the dad's shoulder. The mom's hand is around the dad and her smile is so contented.

"That where we're going?"

"You'll lead us there," he says. "We'll take care of them."

"They're causing the world to end?"

"The world as we know it."

"And everything will go back to normal?"

"With cooperation."

Suddenly, there's a loud pop in the distance, followed by more of them. Bullets bite the air around us. Mick whistles and leads the others to take shelter behind the billboard. My horse, though, makes a break for it, running right towards the gunfire.

Chapter 24

I fall out of the saddle, but my left foot slips through the stirrup and gets stuck on the other side. I am being dragged, and I struggle desperately to cover my face with my jacketed arms. The feeling is similar to what I would think of as falling down a mountain, the rocks and pebbles and grooves hitting me like gunfire. The next thing I know, my yelling and screaming is suddenly smothered, and I'm in the dark, the pitch black nightmare starting right now, and I wonder if I'm not dead. I struggle harder, and yell louder than I have in the previous nightmares, my body feeling like I *must* get up, I *must* get away. But I can't. I'm stuck, like normal.

The nightmare ends just as suddenly as it began, and I'm lying on the ground in the near darkness, my left shoe off, my horse dropped on the ground maybe 20 feet away from me. The bullets are still ripping through the air. My face is torn to pieces, if I'm to believe how it feels, and my fingers are numb with pain. I turn onto my stomach and scramble, pressed against the dirt, to the shelter of a tree, far down from where the rail is. I hear gunfire answered from behind me, from where my group is, and I just try and make myself flat against the ground.

At times, there are breaks in the sounds, but just as soon as I am sure it's over, it starts again. Eventually, I hear shuffling footfalls, as my group advances up to where I am. Taylor gets to me first.

"Holy shit, you okay?"

"No."

"You don't look okay. Porsche! Get up here. I'll cover." He stands and fires a wide spray of gunfire and I hear Porsche run up from behind another grouping of trees.

"Oh god," she says when she sees me. "Hold still."

"I'm not going anywhere," I say. But then I think of the nightmare and hope that I'm telling the truth.

"Stay with him," Taylor says. "You have a stimpack?"

"Yeah," she says. "No one gave me a gun, but I do have a stimpack."

"There aren't many of them left," Taylor says. "They'll either leave or they'll be dead in just a few minutes. Just stay here. Give him a shot and get some of that Pfizercream on his face."

"I know what to do, Tay, thanks a lot. Go shoot the assholes or something, okay?"

Porsche puts her hands on my shoulders and presses me into the ground. She opens her pack and starts rubbing my face with some kind of gel that is soothing and numbing and smells like alcohol. "Just sit here. He's right; it will be over soon."

More footsteps approach, hurried and shuffled. A hand

touches my shoulder. "He gonna be okay?" It's Mick's voice. He holds my shoulder firmly, and Porsche is pushing down on me, too.

"Why are you guys holding me down?" I try and say, but I feel like my mouth is full of rocks.

"Hold still," Mick says at me. "Calm down."

Everything goes black again. The nightmare starts again. I'm trapped in the darkness, struggling to get up. I can feel the hands on my shoulders, holding me down back in the real world. I can feel the fingers on me and I'm trying to yell, trying to talk, and I can't. And I hear, "hold still" over and over, and "calm down."

Then, I feel an electric shock run through my body. The nightmare disappears and I'm lying in the snow under a tree with Porsche holding me down. The gunfire is farther away from me than it was before. Porsche—if I can see right—is smiling at me. "You've passed through," she says. "You'll be okay. I'm glad. It was too soon. We've got a lot more to talk about. Let's see if you can stand."

She pulls me to my feet and I'm surprised to find that I don't feel so bad. I'm wiped and I'm tired, but I'm okay. The gunfire in the distance is gone, and I hear a series of whistles, like bird calls, where the pops used to be.

"What did you give me?" I ask.

"A lot," she said. "Don't worry. You should be feeling

better." We walk together, me leaning on her heavily, back to the billboard where they originally took shelter. On this side, the billboard is for Cialis. And it's my dad. Looking all happy, his arm around a girl half his age who is definitely not Mom.

Behind the billboard, on the butter ad side, are the horses. All of them except mine. "Good riddance," I say.

"Aw, don't say that," she says. "You can't blame him. Making a horse carry you under these strange conditions. It's not his fault. And it's not yours either."

"I was making light," I say.

We sit down on our packs on the snow-dusted ground. I bite into some jerky and drink some Aquafina and start feeling a little better still. It's a solid 25 minutes before the guys come back. They seem light and relaxed. Tired, but at ease.

"They weren't so tough," Dwight says.

"It's just the periphery," Mick says. "Scouting, maybe. And we don't know if anyone got away and let the rest of them know. At least there are no radios. So, that's working for us. But we need to probably ditch the rails. Find another way in to town."

Everyone nods. They start climbing up on their horses. "Here," Porsche says, handing her pack to Mick. "When we get up there, someone needs to grab his pack, too." She turns to me. "Come on up." Porsche has a sweater from her pack spread on the animal's skin. She pulls me up and I sit on it. All of the soldiers—that's how I see them now—all look at Mick, searching for some kind of approval.

"Yeah," Mick says, taking Porsche's pack, "this is probably the only way. Hold on tight, eh, bro?"

I nod.

"I know the way from here," Mick says. "Pretty sure, anyhow. I think we can make it through the woods until we hit a road of some kind. We can't risk the rail anymore."

"Where, exactly, are we headed, Mick?" Lily asks, clutching an arm that Phil is tying into a sling. "The city is big. And if it's really controlled by the NP, how do we expect to get through?"

"We gotta find their headquarters," Mick says. "I'm fairly certain we can take down operations from there. At least gather enough intel for the Peacekeepers when we get back."

"Are we going to get back in one piece?" Lily says. "This is dangerous. I'm not that excited anymore. Was that group we saw last night leaving to get away from these asshole insurgents?"

Everyone's quiet for a minute. We all stare at Mick, waiting for some kind of answer.

"Do we even know if this is 'the other side' that we just fought?"

"You didn't look at the bodies with us," Mick says. "NP written all over their gear." He lifts up some kind of badge that one of them would have been wearing on his shoulder. They all look at it meaningfully, but I can't make out what it means at all. I forgot that I can't read anymore. "They're New Paradigm, alright. I don't think any of us knew that they were so militarized. I think we gotta sneak in, identify the headquarters, bring the intel back home to the Peacekeepers. We can do this, fellas. We do this every single week."

The quietness falls over us again. Everyone's staring at Mick for some kind of answer. The high that any of them might have felt from the victory is gone and trepidation is falling over us. No one died, not on our side, but now they're feeling lucky about this. It's feeling serious.

"If we knew where the headquarters was, this could end," Mick says, looking at me. "You've met with them. You logged into their computers with that ID that you bought. Dodge, please, end this right now."

The eyes switch over to me. They all know. Or think they know. Porsche sighs.

"Listen, guys," I say, "I know that you're all thinking that I'm just being weak or that I'm being obtuse. But I really don't know how to help you. I don't have any idea what any of this is really about, what you guys are talking about, or why you could possibly think that I could safely lead you anywhere, especially the headquarters of a group that's trying to kill us."

"You're our only chance, Dodge," Mick pleads. "We can't go back to town. The other Peacekeepers have abandoned the city. Where's your sense of adventure? Where's your sense of cause? Don't you want the world to go back to normal?"

"Please," Lily says, holding her arm. "If you can end this, Dodge, please do. Help us bring the world back. If you just lead us, I know that this can all end. We all know that."

"I need to be honest with you guys. I don't even know if I *do* want things to go back to normal." Once I say it, I know that it's true. Just then, another crack echoes in the distance. Everyone hits the ground except for Lily, who falls off of her horse with a new wound. We stare at her as she scrambles to get behind the billboard again, and shot after shot rings out. Soon, the billboard is being torn to shreds with bullet holes.

"There's more already," Mick says. "You should have helped us, Dodge. I don't know how we'll survive this."

"How in the world can I help?"

"You *know* how!" he yells at me.

The base of the billboard is some kind of steel, and we

can hear the gunfire thump against it hard. One of the twins crawls over to the side and starts returning fire blindly. As this is happening, the sky is getting darker and the air is getting colder. The gunfire is so constant and overbearing that it feels like it's part of the weather phenomena, like a machine gun of thunder striking focused at us.

It gets colder. A frost begins to settle on us from out of nowhere. It gets so dark that the last thing I see is everyone's face looking up, as if for some kind of redemption. But the gunfire doesn't stop.

"You know what I wish?" I hear Mick's voice say, amidst the chaos. "I wish we had a Red Bull right about now."

And something clicks inside of me, but I can't put it together yet. "Scotty," Porsche says. "You get it? Tell them you'll help. Tell them."

I call out to everyone, "fine, okay, I'll take you there!" And the gunfire ceases. The world gets just a little lighter, as if an instant sunrise has been activated, like the alarm that Mom uses to wake up in the morning. As the light comes out, I see that all faces are not looking up any longer, but pointed at me.

"You mean it?" Mick says. "You'll take us?"

I nod. Everyone takes this as some kind of sign and, against all logic, they get back up on their horses without any kind of concern for the gunfire that just moments ago was raining down on us like hail. They look at me intensely, their eyes pulling me to my feet.

"Come up, Scotty," Porsche says, reaching out her arm to pull me up on her mare again, "we'll lead the way." She takes our horse out from behind the billboard and positions it right inside the tracks. No gunfire reaches out for us. It is dramatically silent. "Well? Is everyone coming?"

"On the tracks?" Dwight asks. "Is that fine, Mick?"

"Look, guys. If Scotty here is going to take us, willingly and fully, there's no violence, right?"

They all look at each other again. Then at me. "Is that how it's going to be, Dodge?" Mick says. "You don't want to tell us, you want to take us?"

"I don't know where to say," I say, which is true. But I also don't understand what's going on. "But I'll take you wherever you want to go."

"Mick," Porsche says. "Tell them it's okay. Tell them that if Scotty takes us without a fight, there's no fight. We can call it off and end this stress, right?"

"You want it that way, Porsche?" Mick says.

"Scotty wants it that way. We want it that way. Hell, they can all go home if they want to."

"What's she talking about, Mick?" Phil says. "This is

sounding crazy."

"How do we know that's how it's going to be?" Mick says. "How do we know that we have cooperation?"

Porsche sighs again. She turns and spurs the horse just a little, and it walks, bearing both of our weight. As soon as the horse starts moving, the sky gets a little lighter. After a few feet of walking, the brightness increases. It's not fully bright, but the sun is up, and you can see where it is behind the clouds. The redness is gone and it feels like early morning. An overcast morning, but the oppression of the darkness is scattered, retreating to the shadows of the trees.

The soldiers form up behind Mick, and their horses climb up the tracks and get behind us. Down the tracks, 100 yards or so, is a pile of white. As we get closer, I see that it's not a remaining snow drift, but it is my horse, lying in a heap. I look away as we pass by it. Further on, I see the bodies of the opposing soldiers. Two of them, anyway. Gathered around them are the soldiers that were just firing at us. They are looking down at their comrades, and don't even twitch when we walk by. I can't see a single one of their faces. The first body is contorted onto his stomach, his face hidden from me. The second is a woman, splayed out on her back. It's bright enough that I can see the details of her face. This time, I can't look away.

She looks familiar. She's an older lady, sort of heavy-set, older than you'd think a soldier would be. Way out of high school, anyway. I look back at my friends and think how ridiculous it is, them killing her, actually killing her. And I start to get panicked a little as this really sinks in. The clouds gather thicker, and the sky gets darker. I'm afraid that it's coming back, and that makes me even more frightened.

"Calm down," Porsche says. "If you freak out too much, you'll slip into the nightmare. We don't need that right now, okay?"

"What?" I ask. "None of this makes sense to me, Porsche. None of it. I feel like I'm hanging on by a thread."

"It's not the time for that. Everything should be clear soon. I know this because it's clear to me, finally. Now I can guide us through this, up to a point. You just can't lose it. You have to hold on. If you freak out, you start to leave into the darkness. We don't need that right now, you follow? We're in control now. Not them."

I look behind me, and there are my friends riding behind us. Their faces are stoic, and they look straight ahead, deadly serious. Lily is the only one showing any kind of emotion. Slightly afraid, clearly in pain, holding her arm. I look at her for a minute and try to get her to make eye contact for me.

"You're so cliché, Scotty," she says. "The girl is the scared one. The girl is the hurt one. Is she really the only one in the group that you find yourself having sympathy for?"

"What are you talking about?"

"These people all mean something different to you. That's why they're here. That's why Lily getting hurt was the final straw. You see?"

"No."

"You trust Mick, right?"

"Yeah. I mean, I always have."

"You look up to Phil and Dwight. You think they're cool?"

"Yeah, I guess."

"But Lily, she's the little, scared one you want to take care of. Taylor's brave. And Mick is brave."

"Lily's brave," I say.

"Sure she is. But that makes you want to take care of her more. Makes you want to baby her?"

"Just what the hell are you getting at?" I ask, a little angry.

"Hold on," she says. "We're going deeper. Okay? Don't freak out."

She pauses our horse at the bridge that leads into the city. Below us is a river, dark and quickly flowing. The bridge arches up over the tracks and splays out. Steel wires hold the bridge up to the arches. Whenever you see the logo for the Comet line, this bridge is there.

"We're crossing into the city now," Porsche says. "This is what you want, right?"

Mick nods his head.

"We're crossing in and Dodge is going to get the lay of the land. He's going to take us to where they meet and where he had his conversations. But the rest is for us, okay?"

Mick nods again.

Porsche spurs the horse and it begins to cross the bridge. The sun comes out a little more, and in front of us the city is illuminated. It's brilliant and beautiful. I haven't been here in so long, yet it looks exactly the same. In fact, the way it comes into view, the way the light hits it, is exactly like I remember it from when I was young, when the city really made an impression on me. Only, we're approaching it at the pace of a horse at a calm canter.

"It looks so familiar," I say. "This is just how the city looked when I was little. When I visited."

"No," Porsche laughs, "you've got it all mixed up." She can't stop herself from laughing. "This is exactly what the city looks like at the introduction of *The Clearkids Morning Show*. You know? 'Good morning children, how happy are you?'" She starts to sing off-key, and I feel like she may have lost it. "'Good morning, Scott, so glad to see you!'

See? It looks just like that! Then there's a picture of you and a picture of Comet when they say your names. Remember? Or, whatever kid is watching the show sees their picture and hears their name. This is the shot of the city from the show. Don't you see it? Imagine a huge rainbow over the city and the sun catches the Airtrans Tower."

Just as she says that, a bright, ridiculous rainbow appears over the city and the sun pokes out of the clouds enough to reflect obnoxiously from the tallest tower. "'Good morning, Scott Goode, how happy are you?' Can't you just see it?"

It's so obvious and so familiar that I start to feel a little sick.

"Stop clowning around up there," Mick says. "Maybe get going a little faster, don't you think?"

"Sure thing, Captain," Porsche calls back. "They can't help it now," she says quietly to me. "They've let us be in control and I've told them that it really relies on your memory. So it's really going to be painted with your memory right now. Are you getting it yet?"

"Who is letting us be in control? Mick?"

"I told you," she says, seriously, all the mirth gone from her voice, "that's not Mick. And those aren't the twins and that's not Tay and you haven't seen Lily since you took the Economics and Integration test."

I turn and look at the riders behind me, all stoic and serious. The trees are lit green behind them, the bridge runs up over their heads in a firework display of chrome and shine. The river down below, still dark, still rushing. I wave at them, but they don't wave back.

"Now the trick is," Porsche says so quietly I can barely hear her, "to find some place to go here. Some place that you might know of, but some place suspicious. Then we can get away for a while. Know anywhere around here?"

We're nearing the other end of the bridge and the outskirts of the city. "Not really. I mean, nowhere suspicious. There's a tattoo shop inside the Walmart, I'm sure. They always get a bad wrap."

"Nothing like that," she snaps. "Something personal. But something that's here. Either you can think of it, or I have to."

I shake my head, too weirded out to think straight. "I have no idea what you mean, Porsche. No idea at all."

"Okay, fine. Remember when your dad took you here and you went to that comic book store? The one where he used to go as a kid?"

"Okay, yeah."

"Next to it was a bar. And outside the bar was—"

"Okay, outside the bar was a bunch of tables, people

sitting around and smoking greens. There was a guy playing piano with an ugly face that I couldn't look at," I say. "His nose was all deformed and he had marks on his face."

"Right," Porsche says. "Your dad went up and scanned his card, gave him a credit boost. Remember? But you still couldn't look at him."

"Dad said that he was from a Peacekeeping deployment. He didn't know him, but he knew guys like him. Probably didn't get medical because he was deemed off-mission when he was injured."

"Bingo," she says quietly. "That's where we're going. I want you to think about that evening. Think about it hard."

"I have no idea how to get there."

"That's what I'm here for," she says.

We're surrounded by towering buildings. When I was here before, cars were running, and light rails and rickshaws were carrying people everywhere. People were walking or riding Segways all over the sidewalks. That's all gone now, with just the few of us riding through the street on horseback. The clop-clop of the hooves is rhythmic and pleasing as it echoes off of the building. But there is a sound in the distance that gets louder and clearer. The sound of activity. Voices and glasses and piano music. We turn a corner and there, just a block away, is the bar overflowing with customers, next door to the comic book shop where I spent my birthday money in the fifth grade. I remember it so well, and this is exactly what it looked like.

"Check it out," Porsche says. She points with her chin at the piano player, and he's the same deformed Peacekeeper that I saw when I was young. His face is still revolting to me, and I can feel it in my stomach.

"This is the place?" Mick says when we stop in front of it. "Are you sure?"

"This is where we met them," Porsche says.

"I need to hear him say that."

Porsche looks at me. Her eyes are soft. They're not pleading, but understanding. She's not straining to communicate through them to me.

"This is it," I say. "I can't tell you if this is the headquarters or not."

"A name," Mick says. "A name and we can end this thing."

"We need to go inside," Porsche says. "To get the name."

"Bullshit," Mick says. "You've got access to the name, Porsche. Don't tell me you don't."

She shakes her head. "I do, but I don't. We go inside, I will find it. That's how it works. It's not nearly close enough to the surface. You guys really need to understand, this wasn't that important to us. We were thinking about his dad. We weren't thinking about all these politics. Just family. It's all deeper than you imagined—your part, that is. So we have to go deeper to find it."

I try not to look at her strangely.

Mick looks at us both with deeply accusatory eyes. "Going deeper is dangerous," he says. "For him," he nods at me, "get the name and get out."

"We have every intention of helping out."

"Hurry," he says.

Porsche and I get off the horse and head into the bar. Inside, everything changes again.

"You mind telling me," I say, "just what the hell is going on?"

Chapter 25

The inside of the bar is dark and candlelit. It's wooden with low ceilings and longboard tables with bend seats. It's filled with people sitting and talking in low voices. Off in the corner, some drinkers are holding glasses in the air and singing. There is a fire raging at the far end of the building in a stone hearth and something is strung over the fire, drying or cooking, I can't tell. The smells are dusty and ancient. Out the door, which is askew, I can see a dark night, with white snow falling slowly. When Porsche had opened the door for me, it was dark, tinted glass. Now it is a heavy, wooden door. The way people are dressed varies from modern clothes to some kind of animal skins, like from a movie.

I get the distinct feeling that the world is falling apart, breaking into pieces, and that what is left are the little scraps of existence that clouded my mind on every level the instant that the Earth lost its ability to hold together. I would fall down onto the floor, dizzy, if I didn't already feel like I was falling through space or floating in the clouds.

"Everything you see," Porsche begins, "is inside of you."

I look at her, lit by firelight, inside a strange hall of some sort. I feel like I'm dying.

"That's always the case," she says quietly. "But it's more so now. Everything you see is a sensation in your brain. It's an interpretation. A metaphor. Only now, we're deep inside. We're in your genetic memory now, and the deeper we go, the stranger things can get."

"What are we doing here?"

"Getting away, for one," she says. "Getting guidance and closure, for another. When you're ready to go deeper, let me know."

I look around myself. I hear the singing and smell the cooking, and everyone looks familiar and alien at the same time. "How will I know when I'm ready?" I ask.

"You will ask that very question," she says. "And now, Scotty, our relationship is about to change." She moves close to me, very close. I start to back up, but she grabs my arms and presses up against me. "You're a bright boy," she says, "and I told you not to get feelings for me."

"Right," I say.

"But you have feelings, right?"

I nod.

"Like I said on the way, we all represent something. Everyone that was traveling with you, everyone you've seen since things started falling apart. They couldn't get rid of me though, see? So what do I represent?"

"I don't know."

"In a story—a love story—what does the girl represent?"

"What are you talking about?"

"A conversation that you had with your brother. In a love story, who does the man fall in love with? Some girl full of flaws and goals and life and independence? Is he attracted to her determination or her work ethic or her frustrations?"

"No," I say, starting to remember.

"No," she says. "What does he fall in love with?"

"Himself," I say, understanding now. "He falls in love with his own psyche. The part of him that is confident, knowing, free. He falls in love with how he wishes he could see himself."

"Right," she says. She steps closer to me and wraps her arms around me. She presses into me, and just like a rubber film on packaging, I feel my surface tension break. She sinks into me like Jello. I feel myself take a deep breath, and I can feel her deep inside of me. I move my fingers and I can feel her fingers move inside of me. My heart beats both of our blood. It's something that I somehow knew, all along. Something that I couldn't ignore for another moment. She and I are the same. She and I are one. Two expressions, one body.

The room changes again. It gets darker. The sensation is that of falling into an endless pit, without experiencing any of the panic or excitement of the fall. Almost like the whole world did a quick zoom-out, leaving me standing in an endless sea of darkness; far darker than any darkness I have known on this entire journey of mine. Far deeper than even the darkness of my nightmares. Yet, it is not all there—this darkness isn't the blotting out of light, but the absence of being. I am standing there, as if on a blank page of blackness. I can see myself perfectly clearly. I can think more clearly than I ever have in my life, with whom I thought of as Porsche residing deep inside of me.

I look around. In the distance, I see an orange glow. I make my way toward it. My steps are strong and confident, though I would think that if this were a normal reality, I would have fallen over for lack of any stabilizing feature to balance me. I feel comfortable where I am, and for the first time since I left home, I feel absolutely no fear.

The orange glow is a bonfire. Sitting next to it, is Dad.

Chapter 26

"Scott," he says. "I'm proud of you. You've made it this far."

I rush to hug him. I feel him and I smell him and I know him. It's more solidly him than any other time I have touched him in my life. It's not Holodad and it's not a memory. Only at times like this do you truly realize that each person has a smell, has a feel, has a presence that is unique to them. Only after not seeing someone, after have thought the person lost, do you fully understand the place this person had in your life. It's him, and my senses fire with recognition. He's so real that I realize that it can't be.

"You're getting the hang of it," he says. "Your senses remember me well. You can construct my every feature and my voice and my smell and my very presence."

I am lost in his presence, and I fall on the ground near his feet, bowing down as if before a deity, my fingers laid upon his black combat boots. I cry for all I am worth, and I feel the tears emanate as if from every pore of my body. Every tear is me begging for forgiveness and absolution. I have this strange need to melt into Dad the same way that Porsche melted into me. I rub his boots with my fingertips, thinking over and over that I'm not worthy for this moment. That every aspect of my life doesn't add up to this instant in his presence. I want to fall into 1,000,000 pieces and just experience complete atonement. But all I can do is cry.

Dad lifts me into his arms, as if I am a baby. He settles

me and holds me, and I feel like the whole universe is alive with forgiveness and solace. I am torn to pieces by emotion. Only dissolution could be so painful and pleasurable at the same time.

"Scotty, we don't have much time. You won't last long here and we can't waste time."

I raise my tear-stained face to meet his and find it nearly too bright to look at.

"You're deep in. Deeper than they were prepared for. They think you're dying."

"That's okay," I sob.

"You will die if you stay this deep too long. But this is where you need to be for the moment. But we have to talk quickly."

"Where am I?" I say. "Like, for real? I understand that we're in my head. But where am I?"

"You're in a medically-induced coma." His words flood me. "They have put you through a program to extract information from you. Information that you don't have. You understand that? Somewhere inside of you, you know this. That's why I know this. You're talking to the you that knows what's going on back where your body is."

I nod. "But when?"

"They were installing a Dreamcatcher into your room.

Remember? That night, you put it on. You've not had it off since then. They were able to move you up to the third floor and get you down very deep. It's a procedure related to the market research, but more advanced. And because this Dreamcatcher is a prototype for your blood type, everyone in the scenario ended up looking like someone you know. Like the early Dreamcatchers for other people."

The fire next to us starts to die down a little. Other than the fire, we are surrounded by the absence of everything. Absolute and endless absence.

"So the world is not coming to an end."

"They wanted to show you what they feel they're fighting for. The end of the world as they know it. This cult they're so worried about must be onto something. An awakening, of some kind. We should be proud of your brother for recognizing it."

"He doesn't," I say. "He's just angry."

"Emotions are hard to trust these days. We filter our emotions, tame them, and are taught that they mislead us. We are sold a world of pleasure and contentment, and in a world like that, sometimes anger can lead the way to understanding. Or frustration. Any number of intense emotions. But whatever the case, he's on to something. They're on to something."

"But I know nothing," I say. "I can't tell them now, but

they have the wrong guy."

"Only they're so sure they're right, they've let it go too far. And you've been too clever from the beginning. Deep inside, you knew to resist them. The program was meant to wear you down. Diminish you. Isolation, starvation, danger, cold, hopelessness. You knew to put up a fight. They didn't expect it." His hands rub my head, my neck, and my back. I feel so fulfilled.

The fire gets weaker.

"You can't stay past the fire," Dad says. "That's the end of this. The fire. And you're so deep, they don't know how to wake you up. They're scrambling. They can't lose you on something like this. And if you wake up without their help, you stand a better chance of remembering. You're not supposed to remember anything. You're supposed to hand over your information without thinking about it. Just like all of us have done all our lives."

"I want to stay," I say. "I don't want to go back. To face them. To do anything."

"Your mother," he says. "Your brother. They're going to need you. My job is to give you the tools to deal with them. To deal with it all. If you can retain them."

I nod. The fire next to us is still large enough to warm us. There is nothing but Dad, the light, and me. All else is void and I feel like I can understand everything.

"Just like Porsche told you. Like you told yourself. The world is inside your head. Always. What you think you see is a hallucination. What you feel is your brain communicating to you everything around you. The entire universe, all of human understanding, is just a few fires of neurons inside your head. It's folded up in there. And there are those who have decoded it, meddled with it, and turned you and everyone else into little worker bees."

I nod.

"Worker bees, working to build a world for other worker bees to work in. You can feel this. I know this because you know this. Everyone has been implanted with hitchhikers; values, ideals, goals in life that you didn't consciously choose. You make decisions that you never deliberately made. You identify with meaning as brought to you by the highest bidder. All of these values, all of these goals, every last hitchhiker is there for a reason. They all align with the goals of the greater society—moving forward with money and power and peopled by worker bees."

I nod.

"You have to wake up soon. You must. But when you do, your brain will have no more hitchhikers. Do you understand me?"

I nod.

"You will not have any parasites. You will not live your

life through everyone else's definition. Everyone else's interpretation."

I nod.

"This is a new paradigm. A new way of being. And instead of being wired, instead of being logged and instead of being sponsored, it is alive. It will exist only in your neurons. Only in your brain, so long as your heart pumps blood through it. Each pump is precious."

I nod.

"A man's life is short." He looks deep into my eyes, holding my face. "Make yours worth it. For every moment that it lasts. Now," he says slowly, quietly, "open your eyes."

And the nightmare starts, but this time I am fully calm. I cannot move, I cannot talk. I hear panicked voices around me and a long, drawn out buzz. I calmly and slowly open my eyes.

I am in a hospital room of some sort. Lights above me illuminate the masked faces around me. The buzz transforms into a rhythmic beep. The doctors cheer and hug each other. One of them leans over me. "You gave us a scare there, buddy," he says. "We thought we lost you."

My arms are strapped down to the bed. My mouth and

throat are filled with some kind of rubber tube, pumping air into my lungs.

"Not much longer, buddy," the doctor says. He takes the Dreamcatcher headphones off of my ears. "We'll get you back to your room. Just hold on. Stay calm."

I stay calm.

My eyes are open.

www.ingramcontent.com/pod-product-compliance
Lightning Source LLC
Chambersburg PA
CBHW030558180626
46816CB00005B/1599